THE TRIBULATIONS OF ELORIA

BOOK ONE:

The Last Shadar

By

Dan Rendell

immortalise

THE TRIBULATIONS OF ELORIA – BOOK 1: THE LAST SHADAR

Cataloguing-in-Publication entry is available from the National Library of Australia http:/catalogue.nla.gov.au/.

This edition first published in 2023
Hackham South Australia

ISBN paperback   978-0-6457721-9-7 (gloss cover)
      hardcover   978-0-6457720-9-8 (gloss cover)
      ebook   978-0-6457721-1-1
      paperback   978-0-6457720-1-2 (matte cover)
      hardcover   978-0-6457720-0-5 (matte cover)

Typesetting and cover by Ben Morton
Internal art created by S.E. Davidson of www.thesketchdragon.com

Published in Australia by Immortalise via Ingram Spark
www.immortalise.com.au

Acknowledgements

Dr. Mark Worthing: I don't know what you saw in my first draft, but over the past two years you've helped me improve my writing, and most importantly, you've given me the chance to share Eloria with the world—thank you!

Ben Morton: Thank you for taking my manuscript and turning it into a book, which I hope will be enjoyed by many.

Dionne Lister: Thank you for helping me edit my problem chapter. Your passion to see other writers succeed is something I will never forget.

S. E. Davidson (www.thesketchdragon.com): For two years we collaborated on the images and maps for this book. Thank you for your willingness to make adjustments when needed. I look forward to working with you again in the future.

Cheryl Maclean: Thank you for supporting this project and giving me the honest criticism I desperately needed; my writing is the better for it! Your encouragement has played a significant role in this venture, and you'll always be family to me.

Lyn Rendell: You read to me each night when I was a child, you taught me how to spell big words, and with your help, I began to write my first story when I was twelve years old. You planted the seed for my writing and now that seed has grown into a great tree. My only wish is that this tree will bear good fruit for the Kingdom of God. Thank you from the bottom of my heart.

Joanna Dare: There were times when I wanted to quit, but you told me to follow my dream. The world said I couldn't, but you said I could. You have supported, and continue to support my writing, and for that, I can never thank you enough.

Steve Rendell: Thank you for encouraging my writing and for instilling in me the values, morals, and sense of justice that I've carried since childhood.

Will Rendell: Your love for those early drafts convinced me that I wasn't just writing a story, but something more meaningful; and no matter how many people discover the world of Eloria, you'll always be the first Elorian!

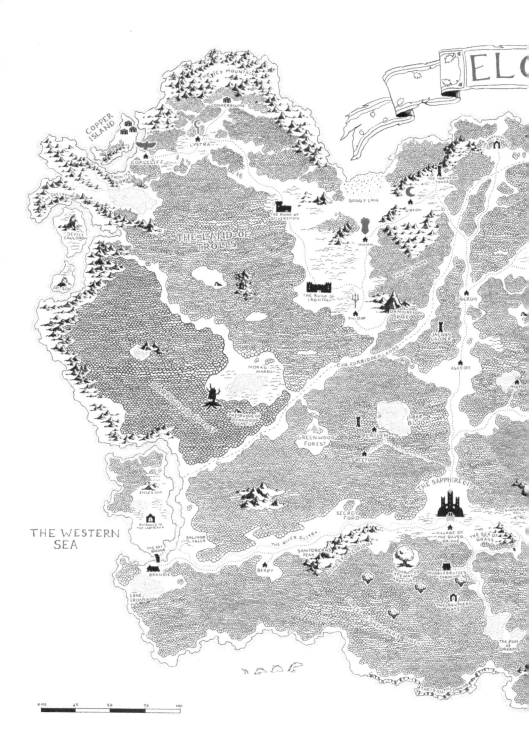

Chapter 1

A Nightmare to Remember

Through a misty forest, Jack Campbell was running for his life. He had no idea where he was going; he just knew something was hunting him. In the darkness, he caught glimpses of moonlight peeking down through the jagged branches of the black trees. He glanced to his side and saw the menacing figure running parallel to him, edging closer as it moved in for the kill. If he didn't think of something quick it would soon be within reach. Unexpectedly, the creature let out a shriek of laughter, as if enjoying the thrill of the hunt. The sound sent a jolt of fear up Jack's spine, causing a sudden burst of adrenaline. *What the hell is this thing?* he thought. *Why does it wanna kill me?*

Up ahead, the trail broke off in several directions. Jack ran to his left, hoping the dark figure would lose sight of him. As the seconds went by, the foliage became more dense and difficult to navigate. The trees were closing in around him. Glancing back, his eyes widened; the dark figure hadn't been fooled by his change of course. It was now only metres away and rapidly gaining!

The creature's silhouette was human-like, except for its burning red eyes and long skinny fingers, which were razor sharp, like the twisted talons of a garden rake! He tried to run faster, but it was useless. No matter how fast he ran, the dark figure wasn't giving up. And with the sound of its high-pitched, cackling laughter getting louder, Jack knew it was barely centimetres away from being within reach.

With his legs burning from strain, he glanced back one last time, only to see the figure spring towards him with its talons outstretched, tearing towards his face like death from above! Its large mouth was agape, revealing a red glow, emanating from behind its jagged black teeth! As the creature was about to wrap its talons around his neck, Jack was suddenly awoken by a piercing tone!

His alarm was sounding at 06:30am. He opened his eyes and sat up in a state of panic! His heart was pounding and his body covered in sweat. Never before had Jack experienced such a realistic nightmare.

He slammed his fist like a hammer onto the *off* switch, then placed his hands on his chest. His heart was drumming like a stampede as he struggled to catch his breath. "What on earth—I haven't dreamt like that since I was a kid!" he coughed, before getting out of bed.

He couldn't dwell on the strange occurrence for long, because he had to get ready for work. Jack had been working in the security industry for over a decade, and the labours of his job—including the pressure to make ends meet—had taken a great toll on him, both physically and mentally. Most people didn't think shopping mall security was that big of a deal, but Jack had experienced many things, things of which the public was unaware, or rarely privy to. And despite the dangers of his job, Jack was very good at it. In fact, he was site supervisor for one of the busiest malls in Sydney.

A veteran of his profession, Jack knew that once inside the mall he would have to deal with customers from all walks of life. Most of them were good, honest people, simply going about their daily routines. A small percentage, however, were unscrupulous characters that most would be glad to avoid.

Yet, despite the stresses of his job, Jack had never been late for work. He had a perfect attendance record; a fact which he was most proud of. He was promoted about four years ago, and was next in line for the coveted security manager position. All he had to do was bide his time until the current manager either retired, or was transferred to a different site. Examining his uniform, Jack reflected on his career and how his colleagues respected him. He felt it was just a matter of time before he was promoted the next security manager. It was his one goal, and Jack had spent the last decade working towards it; and now, at thirty-three years of age, his time to shine was just on the horizon.

Satisfied with the state of his uniform, Jack quickly showered, dried himself off, and proceeded to get dressed. A few minutes later he was wearing a striking, charcoal-black suit, with a matching black shirt and tie. The inside of the jacket was lined with red silk, and as he was doing up the last button he turned towards the mirror, gazing upon his reflection with a sense of purpose. He combed his short dark hair, then placed his security licence and mobile phone in his jacket pocket before heading downstairs. After breakfast, Jack removed a keyset from a wooden rack, affixed to the wall behind the refrigerator, and left the house.

Upon arrival, Jack parked his car and entered the mall by way of the staff entry. Walking past the shop-fronts, he caught the attention of the cleaners and gave them a nod of respect. They were the lifeblood of the shopping mall. Without them, everything would come to a screeching halt. Arriving at the security office, Jack knocked on the plexiglass window beside the door and patiently waited. A moment later, the window opened and Nathan, one of his colleagues, appeared. "Morning, Jack," he said, before closing the window and proceeding to open the door.

Jack shook his hand. "Morning, Nathan." He then approached the control room desk and filled out the sign-on sheet. Removing his security licence, Jack placed the lanyard around his neck, making sure the details of his licence were visible. Then, taking a radio, he switched it on and pressed the button to speak. "Radio check…"

Nathan picked up the control radio. "Reading you loud and clear," he replied.

Jack had been working with the control room operator for many years. Nathan was someone he could rely on in the event of an emergency. But his colleague was also ambitious, and Jack saw him as a potential threat to his dream of becoming the next security manager. Even though Nathan claimed to have no interest in the position, Jack had become paranoid of the other guards. After all, it's a dog eat dog world, and everyone's looking to further themselves by playing the game, aren't they?

Whatever the case, Jack was certain the job would soon be his. Despite the accolades received by the other guards, none of them carried the weight of his decade-long tenure. Jack wasn't just the site supervisor; he was the senior guard, which more or less made him a shoo-in. As he removed a keyset from the rack, he heard Nathan say, "By the way, have you heard the news?"

"Heard what?"

"We've got a new security manager—Roy's left."

"Huh?" Jack turned his head. "What're you talkin' about? Who?"

"Some guy with a degree in management. Apparently, he's never done security work before," Nathan scoffed, as he leaned back in his chair.

"Oh… is that so?"

"I'm sorry, Jack. Everyone knows the job should've been yours."

All the guards were aware of Jack's ambitions, and Nathan's reaction came as no surprise. "Well, I guess it wasn't meant to be," said Jack, placing the keyset in his pocket. "I think I'll go and start the Unlock now."

Leaving the office, Jack managed to maintain his composure. But in his mind he was screaming: *That Job was mine!* All he could do was keep repeating it over and over again as his face turned red. He wanted to believe Nathan was mistaken. Jack wanted to believe that Roy was still the security manager and that he would be his replacement. He tried to remain composed as he unlocked the mall, allowing the first of many customers to enter.

After an hour of unlocking doors and switching on escalators, it was almost 8:00am. He proceeded to open the remaining doors, through which most of the customers would enter. Already, people were waiting outside with impatient looks on their faces.

With the mall open he headed back towards the control room, which was just a fancy name for the security office. When he opened the door, Jack saw that Nathan was still seated at the control desk monitoring the cameras. Nathan sat back in his rotating, swivel chair and turned towards him. "Don't worry, Jack—there's always next time. Who knows, maybe this new guy won't last. I can't see him bein' much good if he doesn't have any experience."

"Look, Nath, I know you're just tryin' to make me feel better, and I really appreciate it. But in all honesty, I don't wanna talk about this."

"No worries," said Nathan, switching his focus back to the cameras.

Making his way to the water cooler, Jack removed one of the plastic, dispensable cups. With a deep sigh, he watched as the cup began to fill, thinking how empty his life was. Staring into the cool liquid, Jack was suddenly distracted by the sound of the office door being opened. He observed as a man entered the room; a man, whom he had never laid eyes on before. The stranger approached the security manager's desk and draped his coat over the back of Roy's old chair. Jack knew who he was.

Unexpectedly, something cold touched his hand. Jack's cup was overflowing, so he pulled it away to avoid spilling more water. He then straightened his posture and took a few sips, sizing-up the man who had taken his job.

The stranger was young-looking; short and stocky, hardly the sort of person you would expect to be a security manager. His brown eyes were set above a hooked nose, and his black hair was slicked back with styling gel. His olive complexion appeared to be rather oily, shining beneath the lights of the office. However, Jack knew better than to judge someone by their physical appearance. As he finished his drink their eyes locked. Approaching the centre of the room, the security manager stopped behind Nathan, who was still seated at the control desk. "Morning, team! I'm James, your new security manager," he declared, puffing out his chest with his hands on his hips.

The guards exchanged a glance. "Good morning, Sir," they replied in unison.

"Call me, Jim," he grinned, as he stepped up to the control desk. The guards continued to watch as he removed a radio from the shelf. "You're *Jack*, and you're *Nathan*, right?" he asked, glancing back and forth.

"Yep, that's right, Jim," Nathan replied.

"Nice to meet you both. If you guys have any problems, just give me a call on the radio. My call sign's M5."

"Okay, Jim," Nathan smiled.

"Sure thing, boss," said Jack, with a hint of sarcasm.

Switching on his radio, Jim clipped it to his belt and proceeded to leave the office. As the door closed behind him, the guards smiled at each other. "I guess he doesn't want a radio check!" Nathan laughed.

"He seems alright," said Jack, tossing his empty cup in the recycling bin.

In truth, Jack wanted to punch Jim in the face for taking his hard-earned job. *It doesn't make any sense,* he thought. *The guy's a joke! It's a bloody disgrace!*

Walking over to Roy's old desk, Jack noticed some documents with Jim's name on them. He discovered that Jim's surname was Cockrane, the same surname as the centre manager. And when he saw the tiny picture frame by the corner of the desk with both of them together, Jack's pale face resembled a red tomato. He remembered the centre manager had a younger brother. "It's not *what* you know—it's *who* you know!" he hissed.

"Huh?" said Nathan.

With his jaw clenched, Jack balled-up his hands into fists. If he didn't leave the office he was going to explode. "That son of a bitch!" he growled. "I oughtta wring his bloody neck!"

As he stormed out of the office Jack glanced at Nathan, who had a look of bewilderment on his face. "What's the matter with you?"

Ignoring his colleague, Jack made his way out into the mall, trying to distance himself from the office. He had risked his own life to protect the customers, retailers, and even the managers on occasion. For ten years Jack had been dealing with drug addicts, drunks, thieves, vandals, corporate politics, and now it was all in vain.

"They've handed him my job on a silver platter," he whispered to himself.

Chapter 2

Human Garbage

After three hours of patrolling Jack finally calmed down. Looking around, he could see many customers doing their Christmas shopping. It was only September, and Jack knew the mall would get busier with each passing day, which meant that every guard would have to deal with the increased crime-rate. Continuing his patrol, it wasn't long until Nathan was calling him on the radio. "Control to S1."

"Go ahead."

"There's a code white in the chemist store on level one."

"Copy, I'm on my way," he answered, before heading down the nearest escalator.

When Jack arrived at the store he saw two female staff members having a heated discussion with a male customer. The customer was pale and thin. He wasn't wearing any shoes, but was wearing dirty socks with holes in them. *Oh great*, he thought, *another junkie!*

Jack surveyed the situation as he cautiously approached, knowing that drug-addicts were highly unpredictable; when one of the staff members noticed his presence, she glared at the irate customer, and said, "Security's here now!"

The oddly-dressed man took one look at Jack and burst into tears. "Please don't call the cops on me!"

Jack turned to one of the staff members. "Alright, what's happened?"

"We caught him opening packets of nasal spray and shoving them down his pants!"

Jack stared at the sobbing customer. "Is that true?" he asked. "Were you stealing nasal spray?"

"Yes," said the sniffling man, "but please don't call the cops on me. I'll never do it again—I swear!"

Jack looked at the staff members. "So you actually saw him stealing the product?"

They awkwardly glanced at each other. "Yes. We both saw him do it."

With a slight nod, Jack removed his notebook from his jacket pocket and looked at the thief. "May I see your drivers' licence, sir?"

The man sniffled as he wiped away tears. Removing his wallet from his pants' pocket, he took out his licence and handed it over. While Jack was recording his details, the alleged offender continued to sob. "Please don't call the cops. I'll never come back. I'm beggin' ya!"

One of the staff members turned to Jack. "Do we have to get the police involved? Can't we just give him a warning?"

Jack was still busy taking down the man's details. Finally, he glanced up at her, and was surprised by her empathy. A man had been caught stealing from her store, and now she wanted to let him go? Jack would never hesitate to ensure that any offender was swiftly dealt with, but it wasn't his decision to make. He glanced at her nametag; Jack could tell by the look in her eyes that she wanted to let him go. "Well, Karen, since I didn't actually see him steal anything—I can't arrest him. But I can assist you in making an arrest, which I'm more than happy to do?"

"*We* have to make the decision?"

"That's the law. But if it were up to me, I certainly would," Jack replied, before giving the man his licence back.

Karen glanced at the thief, who was still sniffling and wiping away tears. She turned to her co-worker, who just shrugged her shoulders. Finally, Karen said, "Um, I think we'll just give him a warning this time."

A big smile spread across the offender's face. "God bless you, Miss! I promise I'll never do it again—thank you so much!"

"See that you don't. Or next time I'll have no choice but to call the police, okay?"

With a smiling nod, the thief proceeded to leave the store, but just as he stepped back into the mall, he flamboyantly spun around and stuck-up his middle fingers. "Gotcha!" he joyously cried.

The retailers looked at each other in disbelief as Jack struggled not to laugh. The offender hurried towards the nearest escalator and flew down like a bat out of hell. Jack knew the thief was long gone, since those particular escalators led to one of the two main exit doors. Jack knew a junkie when he saw one—the thief's actions were no surprise to him. On the other hand, the staff members were embarrassed. "You took down his details," said Karen. "Isn't there something we can do?"

"Not really. You've already let him go. If we arrested him now, he'd probably end up suing us. But if he ever comes back, you have the right to refuse him entry to your store."

"Oh, okay, I guess. Thanks for your help anyway."

"You're welcome," said Jack, putting away his notebook. "If he happens to come back, just give us another call," he added, before leaving the store.

Stepping back into the mall, Jack unclipped his radio. "S1 to Control."

"Control, go ahead."

"It's now *all-clear* at the chemist store. I'm just heading back for an incident report."

"Copy that," Nathan responded.

Retailers are so gullible, Jack thought, making his way back to the control room. *I saw right through that junkie's crocodile tears.*

It then dawned on him that with his aspirations of being the next security manager shattered, he would have to keep dealing with what he referred to as *human garbage.* By the time he arrived back at the control room, Jack's thoughts had rekindled his rage. Standing outside the door, he couldn't help but feel a sense of defeat. "What am I still doing here?" he whispered to himself. "If ten years gets me nowhere—what's the point?"

With a deep breath, he opened the door and went inside, where Nathan was waiting. As he approached his desk to fill-out an incident report, Jack gave his colleague a silent nod. "So, what happened?" Nathan curiously asked.

"Another junkie tryin' to steal nasal spray. The staff didn't even wanna make an arrest—they just gave him a bloody warning," said Jack, sitting down.

"You're kidding?!" Nathan laughed.

"Yep, retailers'll never learn," Jack scoffed, removing a pen from his pocket.

After completing his report, he stood and walked over to the control desk where Nathan was seated. Looking at the sign-on sheet, Jack noticed that three other guards had signed-on and were now patrolling the mall. One was a female guard, Christina, whom he was very fond of, but when he didn't recognise the other two names—a dark suspicion entered his mind.

"Nathan," he said, with a stern voice, "who the hell are Matthew and Carl?"

Turning in his swivel chair, Nathan was reluctant to speak. "They're Jim's guards. Apparently he knows 'em from another site. He used to work in a phone shop or something before he came here. That's how he knows them, or at least that's what Cecelia from customer service reckons. Don't quote me on any of this."

"So, where're Frank and Zoran?"

Nathan swallowed hard. "Jim moved them to another site—please don't do anything you're gonna regret. I'd hate to see you burn your bridges."

Jack wanted the security manager position because it was a stable job with the corporation that owned the shopping mall. They employed his company to provide guards. Even though his colleagues weren't technically fired, they'd been removed from site, which basically amounted to the same thing. His former colleagues would have to start working at another mall, making their chances of advancement more difficult. It was a sad but true fact of life for any security contractor.

"Frank and Zoran had been working here for years!" he angrily said. "How long till it's our turn? Do they like stringin' us along while they dangle our hopes above our heads? Do they want us to believe their bullshit lies about opportunity?"

"There's nothin' we can do—Jim's in charge now. You of all people know how this place works. At the end of the day, we're just contractors," Nathan reminded him. "Just give it some time. We don't know how Jim's gonna fare in this place. You know what the managers are like. He'll be walkin' on eggshells for months."

Chapter 3

A Wasted Life

Jack paced back and forth as Nathan nervously observed from the comfort of his chair. *The bastard takes my job and sacks two of my friends—I ain't gonna stand for it!* he thought. *How long till he sacks me? It's just a matter of time.*

As he continued to pace, a dark cloud was beginning to fog his mind with thoughts of fury and destruction. Jack stopped for a moment and took a deep breath, trying to remain composed. But when he thought about all the years he had spent dealing with criminals, drug addicts, and juvenile delinquents who would curse and spit at him, Jack was about to erupt.

Then he thought about all the good he had done. Like the time he saved a man's life who had gone into cardiac arrest. He remembered the lost children he had recovered, including a five-year old girl who had been abducted by a convicted sex-offender—released on bail. Jack had tackled him in the car park and held him down until the police arrived. He had never forgotten the girl's face, or the image of her parents crying as they held her tight. His efforts had been praised by all that day.

But now he felt that his loyal service meant nothing to the corporation. Jack began to feel that he was having a nervous breakdown. "Ten years of this shit. It's all been for nothin'!"

"Calm down, Jack. I told you not to burn your bridges," Nathan warned.

They heard someone opening the door to the security office. Jack stood firm, preparing to have it out with Jim, but it was only Christina. As she stepped inside, she immediately noticed the expression on his face. "Hey, Jack, how's it goin'?" she asked.

"Hey, Christina," said Jack, as she approached.

"I know what you're thinking; I feel bad for Frank and Zoran, too, but there's nothing we can do. They're good guards; I'm sure they'll do fine at their new site."

Jack shook his head. "It's not just them. I feel like I've wasted ten years of my life in this place. I feel betrayed..."

"No, you haven't wasted your time here. You're the best supervisor I've ever worked with. And no matter where we end up, we'll always keep in touch," Christina smiled, before stepping closer to give him a friendly hug.

"Damn straight!" Nathan added. "No one deserved the job more than you."

"Thanks guys—that means a lot, but honestly, I don't think I can do this anymore," said Jack, having run out of patience.

The guards glanced at each other, but anything they were about to say would be in vain, because Jack had already made his decision. He was going to resign—effective immediately. "Look, guys, I've decided to—"

Before he could break it to them the door opened again. This time it was Jim! Walking towards them, his expression was one of confusion. He stopped behind Nathan and placed his hands on his hips. "What's goin' on? Why're you all in 'ere?" he barked. "The two of you should be outside patrolling—not socialising."

Christina looked at Jack to see a big smile on his face. "We were just talking about the changes to the roster, that's all," she answered. "We weren't socialising."

Jim glanced at the back of Nathan's head, who had since returned to monitoring the cameras. He then glared at Jack, struggling to understand why his senior guard was grinning at him. "So, what's your excuse for being in the control room? Were you really discussing the changes to the roster, like Christina says?"

"Well, to be perfectly honest, we were discussing the fact that two of our colleagues have been removed from site—by you! Perhaps you'd be so kind as to tell us why? After all, it doesn't seem fair to sack people who haven't done anything wrong!" Jack scowled.

Jim looked like someone had just hit him in the face with a wet mop! The last thing he was expecting was for someone to question his actions. He coughed to clear his throat. "I don't have to justify my decisions to you. I have my reasons, and they're none of your business. *I'm* the security manager—not you!"

"You know, I expected such an answer from an inexperienced security manager, Jim. We all know you've been handed this job by your big brother. Isn't that right?" said Jack, with a devilish grin.

Nathan turned in his swivel chair. Jack's colleagues were now struggling to contain their amusement. Nathan, in particular, was doing his best not to laugh. No security contractor had ever spoken to one of the managers in such an insubordinate way. Grinding his teeth, Jim's body was shaking all over. "Who the hell do you think you are? You think being site supervisor gives you the right to speak to me like that?! I oughtta sack you on the spot!"

Jack smiled at his friends. Their presence emboldened him, giving him a boost of confidence. "How dare... *I*? Did you really just ask me that?"

"Yes! I most certainly did!"

Jim's bottom lip was quivering; Jack boldly stepped towards him. "I've spent the last decade of my life in this place and I've dealt with all the politics and human garbage I can handle! So if you think I'm gonna stand here and be belittled by a scumbag like you, then you've picked the wrong guard on the wrong damn day!"

Jim was lost for words. Jack continued, "You know what, I'm done with you. And I'm definitely done with this place. To hell with it—I quit!" he said, slamming his keyset down.

He removed his radio and tossed it to Nathan, causing Jim to flinch as the object flew past his head. Jack's career was over; it was time to go home. "Goodbye, Nathan. Farewell, Christina. I wish you both the best of luck."

"Bye, Jack. Don't forget to keep in touch," Christina replied.

He smiled back at her, then approached Nathan at the control desk. "It's been a privilege working with you, my friend," he said, shaking the guard's hand.

"Same here," Nathan replied. "I don't think I'll ever forget this day."

He was about to leave, but Jack returned to the security manager's desk as Jim stood there in silence. Tapping his fingers on the desktop, he said, "Do you know who sat here for the past ten years?"

Jim gazed up at the ceiling. He then looked down at the floor as Jack sighed in disappointment. "Roy, who used to sit at this desk, was both respected and admired by his colleagues. He was a man of integrity and honesty; he treated everyone with respect and dignity. And I'll tell you this: not once did he remove a guard from this site without giving the rest of us a good reason for doing so."

After a brief pause, Jack slowly walked up to him. "Maybe when you've got some experience under your belt you'll earn the respect of your staff. But respect is a precious thing; it must be earned—never demanded."

Jim's gaze didn't leave the floor. Jack knew that upon his departure, Jim would call the head-office and have him blacklisted from working in another mall. Still, it made no difference; his career was over, so he strolled out of the office with his head held high.

Making his way back to the parking area, Jack experienced a surge of emotions—including a sense of freedom. It was like being released from prison after serving a ten-year sentence. He wasn't sure what it meant; all he could think about was going home. As he stepped into the car park, the sun shone brightly upon his face. He savoured the fresh air, then got in his car and drove home.

Security work had been his life, and the repercussions of his actions had yet to sink in. Jack had not considered that until he gained new employment, he could be in store for some rough times ahead. His feelings of freedom and joy were a moment of bliss, but it wasn't going to last...

Chapter 4

A WALK IN THE FOREST

Jack felt peaceful when he arrived home. He grabbed a six-pack of beer from the fridge, went to the lounge room, and took a seat in his favourite chair. He placed the beers on the coffee table and cracked one open. As the golden nectar touched his tongue he couldn't help but think: *What am I gonna do? I can't start all over again...*

While consuming the beverage, Jack could feel his mobile phone vibrating inside his pocket. He was too caught up in the moment, however, and didn't feel like answering. When he finally examined his missed calls, Jack realised that Nathan had been trying to contact him. *I guess he wanted to discuss todays' historic events*, he thought.

He tried to relax, but was overwhelmed at the prospect of having to go job-hunting, especially after being employed for so long. His moment of bliss was starting to wear off. Like an approaching wave, the repercussions of his actions became clear. Jack was a creature of habit, and his bridges had been burnt to smouldering ash. "How could this happen?" he sighed. "The good guys can't win. Work hard they say —it'll all be worth it—what a pile of shit!" Jack knew that unless he went somewhere to clear his head, his thoughts were going to consume him. "I've gotta get outta here."

He knew there was a national park across the railway tracks, just a five minute walk from home. After finishing his beer, he put the rest back in the fridge before heading upstairs. He carefully removed his uniform, then grabbed a pair of brown cargo pants, a pair of light-brown boots; a white shirt, and a black jacket.

The Australian bush was not to be trifled with. Jack wanted to make sure his arms and legs were covered, in case of poisonous snakes or spiders. Once prepared, he picked up his phone and house keys, and noticed his phone was displaying more missed calls from Nathan. Despite his former-colleague's loyalty, Jack stubbornly refused to call him back. All he wanted to do was forget about work. Jack switched off his phone and put it in the side pocket of his cargo pants. "Just one day of peace—that's all I want," he whispered to himself.

After making his way downstairs he stepped outside and locked the door behind him. With the sun shining and magpies warbling, Jack made his way along the concrete path. The warm breeze was beginning to ease his troubled mind. When he arrived at the railway tracks he carefully looked both ways to see if a train was coming. These tracks were infamous; and despite the recent death of a local drunk, the council still hadn't erected safety barriers. They hadn't even replaced the old warning sign, which was barely visible, due to the overgrowth of gumtrees. Once he was safely across, the forest stood before him. However, upon seeing it, Jack sighed in disappointment.

The close proximity to civilisation had taken a great toll on this once beautiful landscape. The rough, dry Australian bush was home to many native species, but the forest appeared to have been recently ablaze. Stepping towards the burnt scrub, Jack could see broken bottles of spirits, lowering his expectations. As he headed into the blackened trees he could only hope the interior was untouched.

Jack had been to the forest a few times, and there were plenty of native birds, wombats, echidnas, possums, and small creeks containing freshwater fish, yabbies, and eels. Heading further, the trees were gradually becoming greener. Jack heard the sound of laughter and glanced up to see a kookaburra sitting on a branch. He might have thought the bird was mocking him but took it as a welcoming sign.

Making his way through the bush, Jack came upon several game trails and knew there were invasive species nearby, including deer and wild boar. *I've never seen a stag*, he thought. *Maybe if I follow one of these trails I'll be lucky enough to see one?*

As quietly as possible, Jack began to follow one of the trails. He was trying his best not to alert the animals, but with each step, he could hear the crunching of leaves beneath the weight of his boot. The forest was full of gum trees, thick shrubs, and thousands of dead leaves and sticks. It was difficult to see further than twenty metres. Each time he glanced down at the trail Jack's heart would sink at the sight of a cigarette butt or broken beer bottle. He wasn't a tree-hugging hippie by any means, but he firmly believed in respect for all life, regardless of how small or unimportant it may seem. After walking about three kilometres, Jack heard something unusual. "Wait a sec, I've never heard running water in this place before..." he said to himself.

To Jack's knowledge, the only water in the forest was stagnant, which had been formed over time, by natural processes, like excessive rain. And since most of Australia was in the grip of a drought he was naturally curious. The water didn't sound too far away, so he moved closer, trying to home-in on its location. After walking a few more metres, he stopped abruptly. Jack realised there were no more dead leaves beneath his feet, or shrubs by his legs. When he glanced up and saw the forest had changed, the hair on the back of his neck stood up. Everything was lush and green, featuring moss-covered rocks, towering oaks, yews, willows, beeches, and green grass. It was like he had stepped into an English wood!

Turning around, Jack could see nothing but the same surroundings —the whole forest had changed! He tried to retrace his steps, but nothing was familiar; just as he was starting to panic, he heard a familiar sound. "The water!" he gasped.

The sound of running water was the only thing connecting him to his previous surroundings, so he decided to follow it. As he was making his way through the green forest, Jack could sense it was alive. The air was cool and fresh. The patches of soil were rich and dark, and the grass was covered in morning dew, despite the fact it was mid-afternoon.

As he breathed the forest air, his mind became clearer; giving him a sense of peace. Jack couldn't see any signs of human encroachment. Everything was pristine; not a single piece of broken glass or cigarette butt. In fact, he couldn't find a single track. There were no signs of life. There were no insects buzzing about, or tiny animals scurrying beneath the roots of yews. The situation was unnerving, but Jack could feel a sense of adventure. He was like an explorer discovering a new land. He felt alive for the first time in years, as if his soul had been re-awakened.

He admired the beauty and serenity of this place, as the sound of water grew louder. After travelling a bit further, Jack noticed a clearing up ahead. Reaching the edge of the woodland, he came upon a field of blue flowers. Jack hesitated, staying behind the tree-line, scanning his eyes across the field. Then he caught sight of something unexpected.

Chapter 5

A BEAUTIFUL MAIDEN

About forty metres away a beautiful woman sat on the grass, facing a large body of water. Then Jack realised it was actually a river, full of large stones, producing a soothing sound as the water passed over them. He could only see the back of the woman from where he stood, but she was clearly young and had long, golden hair. She was also wearing an elaborate white dress, which glowed in the sunlight.

She had blue flowers in her hair, the same kind that were growing throughout the clearing. As he stepped out of the tree-line, Jack noticed a brown picnic basket beside her. Peering across the field he couldn't see anyone else. All Jack could see was more of the same green forest, which seemed to go on forever, except for a narrow path on the other side of the clearing, situated between the forest and the water's edge.

Jack couldn't keep his eyes off the strange woman. He couldn't remember the last time he had seen a lady wearing such a beautiful dress. Most of the young women Jack saw in the shopping mall were dressed in mini-skirts and tiny tops, or daggy sweat suits. This woman, however, was a total contrast. There was something enchanting about her.

She was dressed in an old-fashioned, modest and conservative way. Jack thought it refreshing. A sudden longing came over him. Despite not knowing who she was, he felt deep within his soul that she was a rare and precious jewel—it was like seeing a unicorn!

What am I doin'? This ain't right, Jack thought, with a sense of guilt, as if he were a peeping Tom. Then, without warning, as though she had sensed his presence, the maiden glanced back, looking directly at him. "Shit!" he gasped, jumping back into the tree-line, stumbling amongst the foliage for cover. "She saw me!"

Not sure what to do, Jack headed back through the forest, retracing his steps. Everything was still green, with no Australian bush in sight. It was completely silent. He couldn't even hear the sound of kookaburras in the distance. "Where'd all the friggin gumtrees go? Wait—my phone!"

Feeling the pockets of his pants Jack removed his phone, but for some reason it wouldn't switch-on. He repeatedly pressed the 'on' button, but the screen remained cold and lifeless. "Come on!" he growled. "This doesn't make any sense—the battery was full!"

Jack thought about the woman; he had to get back to her. She would know the way out. After shoving his phone back into his pocket he returned to the clearing. Jack was now conflicted between his fear of being lost, and his fear of meeting the beautiful, yet oddly-dressed woman. Stepping out of the tree-line, he looked towards the stream of water.

The beautiful young woman was still basking in the sunlight by the water's edge. He took a deep breath as he headed through the ankle-high grass. With the aroma of blue flowers swirling around him, Jack made his way towards her. The scent of the peculiar flowers could only be compared to that of bluebells; only they were shaped like daisies but with a deeper shade of blue and a purple stem. But Jack's main concern was the young woman. Thus far, she had remained perfectly still, and he was now less than ten metres away. *Should I yell? No—that might freak her out,* he thought.

Jack decided to approach her from the side, giving her plenty of time to see him. Still hugging the tree-line, he made his way towards her. When he got closer, Jack could see that she was sitting with her legs crossed, lying flat against the grass, her sandal-covered feet pointed towards the river. Her arms were resting behind her body, palms flat, with her head tilted towards the sunlight.

Jack was instantly captivated by her beauty. Her eyes were closed, so he walked with a bit of a stomp, in the hope that she would hear his approach. Then his attention was drawn to the sparkling river of water. Most of the creeks around Sydney were muddy and brown, but this river was so clean it looked good enough to drink from.

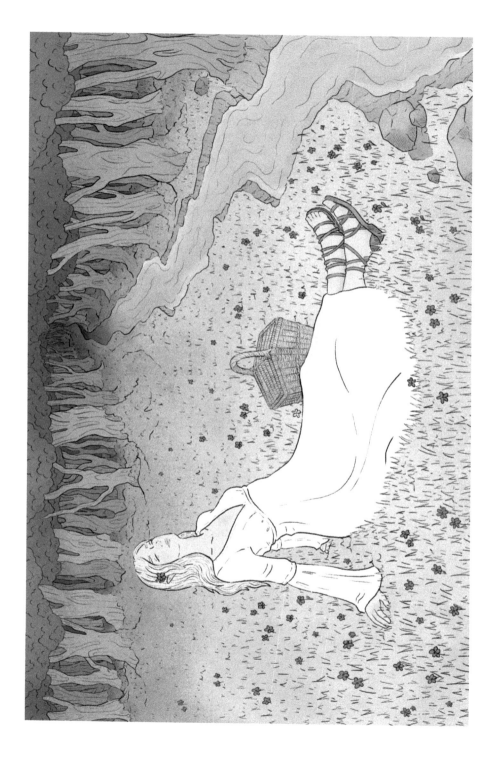

Turning his attention back to the young woman, Jack was now less than three metres away. He opened his mouth to speak, but the words wouldn't come out. Jack started to panic. He was worried that she would open her eyes and see him gawking at her. *What's wrong?* he thought. *Say something! She's gonna think you're a lunatic!*

Jack took a deep breath, but before he could speak, she said, "We've been waiting for you."

His jaw suddenly dropped! She'd been aware of his presence the whole time. She opened her eyes and smiled as Jack's body turned to ice. He couldn't understand why he was so nervous. He had dealt with life-threatening situations, but now he was lost for words. His heart pounded as he opened his mouth, but still the words wouldn't come out. "Um, I-I'm... hello," he finally managed.

"Your name's Hello?" she giggled.

"No! I mean—I meant to say my name's Jack."

"It's alright, Jack. I was just teasing you. Besides, I know who you are," she smiled again, exposing her amazingly white teeth.

She stood up and brushed off her dress, then glanced up at the sun before picking up her picnic basket. "Who are you? How'd you know my name? I think I'd remember if we'd ever met," said Jack, defensively.

Taking a step forward, she looked him up and down. "I'll explain on the way. But for now, you can call me, Sarina."

Jack was confused. "You want me to go with you? Where're we going? You see, I got a bit lost back there, and now I can't find my way home."

"We're going to the Sapphire City!" she said, with a burst of joy. "And you can't go home yet, so you'll just have to come with me."

"Sapphire City?"

"Yes, but we'd best be going."

This woman's nuts! She must be an escaped mental patient, he thought.

Jack would never make fun of someone who was genuinely ill, but he was now concerned for his own safety. "Sarina, are you okay? I mean, I know I'm lost, but I'm still in Sydney. We're obviously in some kind of nature preserve, right?"

"Don't you know why you're here?" she asked.

"I'm here because I'm lost," he replied.

"No. You're here for a reason; a reason which only a great wizard can reveal. It's not by chance you've found yourself here—it was destiny."

"Let me get this straight: you want me to go to a place called the Sapphire City, to meet a wizard, who'll reveal my destiny? You sure you haven't seen the Wizard of Oz too many times?" he chuckled.

"The Wizard of Oz? I don't know him," said Sarina. "There aren't any wizards in Eloria by that name."

Eloria? What's she on about? Jack thought, shaking his head in disbelief.

"We'll stop by the wizard's cabin on our way, if you like? And I daresay that once he's seen you—he'll probably join us," she added.

"Hmm... yeah, that makes sense!" said Jack, sarcastically. "Every city should have at least one trusty wizard. I mean, you never know when he might come in handy!"

Sarina burst out with laughter, her giggling so contagious that Jack couldn't help but join in. After calming down, she moved towards him with her eyes directed at the ground. Taking a step back, Jack was nervous as she drew closer. She softly pushed her body against his, in a playful, yet provocative manner. The scent of the flowers in her hair was intoxicating. Looking up, she stared into his emerald-green eyes.

Jack was stunned by what he saw; Sarina's eyes were like something out of a dream. They were not one colour, but many. In fact, they were every colour. Her eyes were like a rainbow! They glistened and morphed into different shades of red, orange, yellow; green, blue, indigo, and violet. They swirled with colour, and for a moment Jack feared that he would be trapped in her beautiful gaze. When she finally stepped back, Jack noticed something else, that Sarina's ears were rather... pointed. "Okay, what exactly are you?"

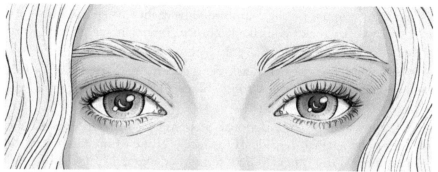

"I'm an elf," she said, with a hint of a smile.

Jack was unable to respond. But after weighing-up the evidence, he could only conclude that it was at least a possibility. "Look, I'm sorry, okay? I didn't mean to make fun of you. I just didn't want to accept that I was stuck in some parallel dimension?"

Sarina gave him another toothy smile. "You're not in another dimension, silly! You're in Eloria!"

"I'm where?"

"Eloria," she repeated. "Just think of your world as a room inside a house of many rooms, with Eloria being one of those. But you can only enter another room if the door's been opened from the other side."

Jack sighed, trying to make sense of his predicament. "Okay, then how'd I get here? Who opened the door?"

"We opened it for you. You can't go back—at least not for a while. Don't worry; a month in Eloria will only take up one day in your world. Your presence will soon affect all!" she said with a look of bliss.

"Are you sayin' I'm trapped here?"

Sarina looked at him in confusion. "No, you're not trapped here. We just need you for a while, that's all. We need your help with something."

"Why do you keep saying *we?* Who else knows I'm here?"

"The high council of the Sapphire City wishes to speak with you. They need you to make a difficult choice, one that will affect every Elorian."

"What could they possibly ask of me? I'm just a security guard. What happens if I make the wrong choice? They won't hurt me, will they?"

Her expression became serious. Stepping closer once more, she placed her hand against the side of his face. "None of my kin will harm you—neither will the others. There're many dangers in Eloria, but I'm willing to die for you, and I promise to always protect you."

Jack could hardly believe his ears! How could this seemingly fragile, and gentle elf-maiden, be willing to lay down her life to protect a stranger? "Are you nuts? Why would you do that? We don't even know each other. I could never let you die for me."

"You don't know me, but I've been watching you your entire life."

How could she have seen me if we were in different worlds? Jack thought. *Watching me my entire life? Impossible—she only looks about twenty!*

"I saw how hard you worked for that job you didn't get," she revealed, as his eyes widened. "And I've seen you lose faith in humanity, but it never hardened your heart. You're a good man—that's why you've been chosen."

"Wait a minute," said Jack, "if we live in different worlds or rooms as you claim, then how could you've seen those things?"

Sarina's eyes lit-up as a smile formed in the corners of her mouth. Leaning closer, for the third time, she whispered in his ear, "Wizard's magic…"

Stepping back, she peered across the clearing towards the flow of the river. "So, Jack, are you coming with me?"

Jack understood her meaning, but his sense of adventure was still hindered by his fear of the unknown. "To the Sapphire City, right?"

"That's right," she nodded, "we're going to the Sapphire City. And once you've been there for a while, you'll never want to leave. Trust me."

All he had waiting back home was a decade of regrets. If he didn't go to this Sapphire City, Jack knew he'd regret it for the rest of his life. "Would you like me to carry your picnic basket?" he smiled.

Sarina's eyes lit-up with excitement. "No thanks. But I'd like to hold your arm for a while, if you don't mind?"

It was an odd request, but looking into her rainbow-coloured eyes, Jack could sense a mutual attraction. However, Sarina was an elf, and Jack knew nothing about elf-culture. *Maybe they're just an affectionate bunch?* he thought, as he stuck out his elbow, inviting her to take hold. Wrapping her hand around his arm, they embarked on their journey together.

Chapter 6

JOURNEY TO THE SAPPHIRE CITY

Following the riverbank, they made their way across the clearing before entering the woods on the other side. Sarina kept a hold of Jack's arm, leading him down a dirt track through the forest of oaks. Jack was anxious and excited. Then a thought entered his mind: *I wonder if others have been here before?*

He didn't want to spoil the moment with questions but couldn't help himself. However, when he opened his mouth to speak, Sarina said, "Can I ask you something?"

"Of course," he replied. "You can ask me anything?"

"I want to ask you something about humans, but it's okay if you can't answer."

"Sure. We're a pretty weird species. You're probably just as curious about humans as I am about elves."

Jack waited in anticipation. "Why do humans kill each other?" she asked. "I've never had a problem killing orcs and goblins, but I would never kill another elf. That would be like murdering a family member."

"What the—did you say orcs and goblins?"

"Yes, but please answer my question."

He tried to focus, but Jack couldn't stop thinking about the orcs and goblins. "Um, well, not every human's a good human. I mean, some of us can be downright nasty at times. I guess the main reason we kill is to obtain power, wealth, or land. Sometimes people kill out of revenge, or because they've had a disagreement. Then again, perhaps they were drunk, or they acted without thinking. I s'pose it depends on the situation."

Sarina didn't look convinced, but how could Jack answer such a question, a question that he himself had struggled with? "I wish I could explain it," he continued. "But honestly, I have no idea why humans kill. It might just be part of our nature, or perhaps we've gotten so used to it that we've become desensitised. Most of us would never do such a thing. Men in power send the young to fight their wars—it's not like they have a choice."

After walking quite a distance, Jack noticed the river had widened. It was much deeper, and the current had slowed, but was still crystal clear. However, the question regarding humans in Eloria was still gnawing away at him. "Can I ask a question now?"

"Of course, Jack. You can ask me anything, too."

"How many humans have been here?"

There was a long silence. Then finally Sarina said, "Well, there was one man who came here before you. But he wasn't a real human—it was a long time ago."

Jack was disappointed, but Sarina's answer had raised another question. "Wait, what do you mean he wasn't a real human?"

"Sorry, Jack, I'm not allowed to speak of him. Only a member of Eloria's high council can tell you about that story."

Jack assumed there was a good reason for the secrecy. He didn't want Sarina getting into trouble on his account. He was about to change the subject when he caught sight of something enormous. The mossy-green wood was now filled with towering oak trees of immense size; some must have been over sixty metres tall! He looked across the river and could see more on the other side. It was a vast, expansive forest, and just on the horizon was a speck of white. Jack became excited. "Snow!" he cried. "I've never seen snow before!"

"That's ice," Sarina revealed. "It covers the peak of Sycamore Summit. It's taller than most mountains in your world—but not so tall by Elorian standards."

"Okay, but does it snow in Eloria?"

"Yes, but only one month a year in the Sapphire City. It always snows in the far-north, and north-east, but those lands don't belong to us—they belong to the dwarves."

"There're dwarves in Eloria too? Does Eloria have different seasons like my world? How many months a year do you have? When does it snow? Don't they get cold up there?" he asked, bombarding Sarina with questions.

"Slow down!" she laughed. "We have the same four seasons and twelve months a year. Our seasons are like those in the northern lands of your world. But time's different in Eloria—at least while you're here. In your world, it's September, but in Eloria, it's the middle of Góa, which humans call March. And it only snows in the month of Þorri. That's mid-January to mid-February in your world, so I'm afraid you're a few weeks late."

"Okay, but what about the dwarves? Don't they get cold up there?"

"Of course not, silly!" Sarina laughed again. "Dwarves were bred to withstand the cold, and their kingdom's underground, so it wouldn't affect them much anyway."

"I see," said Jack. "Then what about the year? Back home it's the year two thousand and nineteen."

"Eloria's in its four thousand, three hundred and twenty-third year. We're barely a third of the way into our fifth age, but I'm not supposed to talk about it."

"Okay," said Jack, scratching his head.

Following the path, Jack began to feel they were being watched. Amazingly, Sarina sensed what he was feeling. "Don't worry, this forest is quite safe. You might see some Elorians if you're lucky, but none of them will harm you."

Her words were comforting as they headed deeper into the labyrinth of oaks. "What kind of Elorian would live in these woods?" Jack curiously asked.

"Well, you might see a brownie or two—they're tiny—no taller than a foot. They often travel this way. They're resourceful and will journey great distances to sell their trinkets. Mostly, there're just faeries here. They can be difficult to see because of their glamour. They use it to camouflage. Faeries only reveal themselves if they wish to be seen."

"Have you seen one?"

"Of course," she replied. "This forest used to belong to them, but now it's imperial land. When the elves made peace with the faeries we allowed them to inhabit their old lands. That's why we call this place the Forest of the Faerie Queen. Oh, and Mugglegruffe lives here, too. He's a dwarf—he's the most powerful wizard in Eloria."

"I thought dwarves lived in the north-east?"

"Yes, but elves and dwarves have always been allies, not that they particularly like each other. Some visit the Sapphire City, but most live in the far north-east, beneath the snow-capped mountains. They have a mighty stronghold, called the Kingdom of Stonehill. It was one of the first places to be mined of gemstones for our city."

A city made of sapphires? Jack thought. *How could they build something like that?*

He was about to inquire, but noticed the forest was getting darker. His eyes darted all over the place as they journeyed beneath the twisted branches of oaks, looking for any sign of movement. Despite the dark atmosphere the forest was still lush and green. As they ventured further —the oaks became bigger. "I don't believe it," said Jack, "the base of that tree's gotta be the size of my house!"

"Beautiful, aren't they?" said Sarina, with a smile.

These trees were over one hundred metres tall and their gigantic limbs stretched far enough to form a web-like canopy, with their dense foliage almost blocking out the sun! All Jack could do was gaze up in awe. *If only I could climb one...* he thought.

Unlike the pristine forest in which he had first become lost, the ground of this fairy-forest was disturbed. The narrow path was wide and rough, and the ground was littered with the markings of hooves and the lines of a vehicle. Jack hadn't seen any cars or motorbikes around, and assumed the markings had been made by horse and cart.

They continued along the path, and again Jack felt they were being watched. Soon, they came to a point in the road where another path veered off, leading deeper into the forest. It was quite narrow, and Jack was surprised when Sarina stopped. "This leads to Mugglegruffe's cabin. I know he'd like to see you. Are you ready to meet him? I'll be with you, of course."

"Why?" Jack worried. "He isn't dangerous, is he?"

"Well, he can be a little grumpy at times. But I promised to always protect you, remember?"

Chapter 7

MEETING MUGGLEGRUFFE

Jack peered down the pathway. His curious mind longed for adventure. "Okay, I'll meet this wizard of yours."

"Yes! I knew you would!" said Sarina with joy. "And don't worry, you won't regret it. Mugglegruffe might be old and a bit abrasive, but he's one of the wisest beings in Eloria. He's also on the high council. Many have travelled far to seek his guidance. You're very fortunate."

"Okay," said Jack, "but why doesn't he live in the Sapphire City?"

"Sometimes he does, but these days he spends most of his time in the woods."

Jack followed as she led him down the pathway. As they travelled deeper into the forest, the oak trees were spread further apart, making the trail easier to follow. Yet, Jack still couldn't shake the feeling that something was watching them. He glanced back to see if anything was there.

"Something wrong?" Sarina asked.

"No. I'm fine—I just keep gettin' this feeling like we're being watched. It must be my imagination."

"You're just nervous, that's all. I know this's very strange for you, but like I've been saying: as long as you're with me, you have nothing to fear."

What could she possibly do if someone attacked us? Jack wondered. *Bash them over the head with her picnic basket?*

He then noticed that some of the trees were bearing leaves of red and gold. "Sarina, you said Elorian seasons were like those in the northern lands of my world, right?"

"Yes," she confirmed.

"And you said it was March—that would make it springtime?"

"That's right."

"Then why do all these trees have autumn leaves?"

"The day Mugglegruffe became a wizard was a special one. It was autumn when it happened. Some of the trees around his cabin never lost their leaves, and have remained that way ever since."

Jack wasn't sure what to make of her words, but after travelling a bit further they came upon a white picket fence. Beyond the fence, the area opened up into a beautiful garden full of wild, blue flowers, like the ones in Sarina's hair. Sarina opened the front gate, and there, sitting in the centre of the tiny clearing, was Mugglegruffe's cabin.

There were yellow flowers on the grass-covered roof, with a variety of coloured ones below, surrounding the exterior of the home. Bees and butterflies were flying about, and Jack noticed a yellow bird sitting in the fork of a tree, chirping away. The path beneath their feet was made of stone, leading all the way up to the steps of the porch. The cabin itself was made of wood, and was protected by a stone-walled base, covered in green moss. It was rustic and beautiful, and looked as if it had risen-up out of the earth. "It's like something out of a fairy-tale," Jack remarked.

"Wait till you see inside," said Sarina, leading him on.

As they approached the steps of the porch Jack noticed a brass, letter-slit in the front door, allowing the dwarf to receive mail. *They have a postal service?* he thought.

34

Just as he was about to approach, Sarina stopped him. "Wait here, Jack. I don't think he's had a visitor like you before. I'd hate for him to mistake you for something else. I'll knock first, okay?"

Walking up the wooden steps, Sarina lowered her head as she stepped onto the porch. She then approached the smaller-than-average door, which was about five-feet in height. She knocked three times; Jack's heart skipped a beat, as if something bad was about to happen.

Seconds later, they heard a loud clang, like someone dropping a pot, then a voice began to shout. "If you're trying to sell me those phoney trinkets I'll turn you into a spirit-light!"

Sarina glanced back and saw the look of concern on Jack's face. She gave him a comforting smile to ease his fears. "Mugglegruffe, it's *me,* Sarina! I've brought someone with me who I think you'll want to meet!"

They heard another clang, then some foot-steps, followed by the sound of a key turning. Sarina stepped back as the door opened. And there, standing in a cloud of smoke, was a dwarf no more than a metre tall, with a long grey beard and a pipe of burning tobacco clenched between his teeth. He was wearing an old blue robe, covered in purple triskelion and yellow triquetra designs, which Jack recognised as Celtic symbols.

It was striking, but the once vibrant colours had faded, and the cuffs and hem of gold were almost threadbare. The dwarf was also holding a wooden staff as he stepped onto the porch, and Jack noticed a blue crystal atop of it. The twisted wood was curled around the gem, resembling an eagle grasping its prey.

"Sarina..." he uttered, removing his pipe. "Oh, my sincerest apologies, milady. I wasn't expecting you back so soon. I thought you were one of those pesky brownies, who still think they can trick me into buying their phoney trinkets! They may've fooled me once, but they certainly won't a second time."

"No need to apologise. I know how frustrating brownies can be," said Sarina, kneeling down to give him a hug.

As they embraced, Mugglegruffe noticed the human in their midst. Sarina then turned and said, "Jack, this is Mugglegruffe, the most famous wizard in Eloria."

The wizard stared at him. *Why's he lookin' at me like I'm some sort of alien?* Jack thought, as the dwarf came towards him with his staff in hand. *I hope he doesn't turn me into a spirit-light—whatever that is...*

"I never thought in all my days I should live to see the last Shadar! Has he met the council, yet?" asked Mugglegruffe, glancing back at Sarina.

"No," she replied. "He's only just arrived. You're the first Elorian he's met, besides me. I thought it best if we called past."

"If you hadn't brought me the last Shadar, I'd have been very disappointed indeed."

What's a Shadar? Jack wondered, as the wizard approached. Instinctively, Jack knelt down to extend his hand. "Hello. I'm, Jack Campbell. It's a pleasure to meet you."

"No, boy, the pleasure and the honour are mine," he smiled. After shaking hands, Mugglegruffe pointed his staff towards the doorway. With a quick nod Jack headed towards Sarina, who was still standing on the porch.

"Wait," said Mugglegruffe.

He hasn't changed his mind already? Jack thought.

"We're not alone!" said the wizard, turning towards the forest.

Sarina stepped off the porch. "What is it?"

Mugglegruffe aimed his staff at the trees behind the open gate. "Who's out there?!"

They waited a few seconds but couldn't see or hear anything. Jack and Sarina moved closer to each other. She placed her hand on Jack's shoulder, preventing him from getting in the cross-fire if Mugglegruffe was forced to cast magic.

"I see you!" the wizard shouted. "Your glamour doesn't fool me! Come out from behind those trees or I'll start blasting holes through them!"

Strange figures began to emerge. They looked like women, their ears pointed like Sarina's, but they weren't elvish. Their skin was many shades of green, black, and brown, all mixed together. Jack thought they were camouflaged like modern soldiers.

As the creatures approached, Jack could see green moss growing from their arms and shoulders. They were each unique in minor details, such as hair colour. Some had brown, others black, and one in particular had long, fiery-red hair with yellow flowers sticking out of it. But they all had leaf-matter, flowers, or a combination of both, running through their locks.

As they drew closer Jack noticed their eyes were a luminous-green. However, what struck him most was that, apart from a few leafy vines covering their private parts, they were basically naked. "Grrr... damn faeries!" the wizard growled, lowering his staff. "Have you lot been spying on us?"

One of them stepped through the front gate. Despite her strange appearance, Jack was impressed by her beauty. She was wearing a beautiful wooden crown, which had white flowers growing from it, with more flowers spread throughout her emerald-green hair. "We meant no harm by our glamorous ways. We came to see the chosen one. We'd never harm a human; especially one in the company of Sarina Starborne and Mugglegruffe, the wise and powerful wizard of the woods."

"Flattery will get you nowhere with us, Queen Eleanor!" the dwarf scoffed. "The history of faeries hasn't been forgotten by the likes of me, and you know I hate unwelcome visitors. And since you've decided to walk on my land, without my permission, I'd be justified in assuming your intentions are sinister! So I suggest you and your kin go back to your own domain before I lose my patience."

The faerie queen wasn't acting in a threatening manner, yet Jack couldn't help but wonder why his friends were so wary of these beings? "Please, Master Mugglegruffe, has the Great War not been over for thousands of years? Have we not kept our word since the Winter Campaign? Violence is the last thing we desire."

"Then what do you desire?" he questioned.

"I wish only to speak with the chosen one. That is, of course, if he's allowed any say in the matter? Or do you now own him because he's on your land?"

The wizard smiled, then took another puff of his pipe. "Think before you speak, Queen Eleanor. For if what you say is true, wouldn't you also be my property? After all, you're standing on my land!"

The faerie queen pursed her lips, then looked into Jack's eyes. "Please, chosen one, we come in peace. I seek only to hold your hand for a moment, that I may bestow my blessings upon you. A blessing from a faerie queen's a rare gift; one which only a human can receive. It should never be hastily dismissed."

Jack looked at his friends. "It's up to you," said Sarina. "This's your decision."

"I know how deceptive faeries can be. But if you accept—it might protect you from dark magic," said Mugglegruffe. "Besides, Queen Eleanor knows that if she tries to harm you, my retribution will be swift."

"As will mine!" Sarina added.

Jack was getting the impression that faeries were not the benevolent beings found in children's books. He had always doubted the existence of magical creatures and would scoff at anyone who believed otherwise. But now his entire view on reality had been shaken to its core. These faeries were both respected and feared by his new friends, and the last thing he wanted, was to make an enemy of them.

Stepping towards her, Jack could feel the force of her radiating energy, giving him the sensation that he was in the presence of royalty. "Hello, Queen Eleanor. My name's Jack Campbell. I'd be honoured to receive a blessing from you."

"A wise decision, chosen one."

She knelt before him. Then, taking a hold of his hand, she brought it to her lips and kissed it. *This is awkward,* Jack thought.

She looked deeply into his eyes as her skin sparkled like shimmering diamonds in the sun! Her fiery-green eyes glowed and swirled with power. Jack was captured by her gaze and felt what could only be described as painless electricity running throughout his body. As the glowing in her eyes faded, she stood up and released her grip.

"Your bravery's served you well. I have bestowed two powerful blessings upon you. The first is the gift of faerie-sight—my kin will no longer be hidden from your gaze. The second is a gift of protection from dark forces, which dwell in both our worlds. No servant of evil shall be able to use dark magic against you."

What's she on about? Jack thought. *What dark forces?*

"You'll know soon enough," she said.

"Huh? Did you just read my mind?"

Without answering, she turned away and headed back towards the forest, where the other faeries were waiting. Jack could tell by the smile on Sarina's face that he had made the right decision about the blessing. Even Mugglegruffe gave him a nod of approval.

"One last thing," said Queen Eleanor, turning around.

"Yes?" said Jack.

"Because you've chosen wisely the faeries in this forest shall forever be your allies. If you find yourself in danger—seek us out. We will die to protect you."

Jack watched as the faeries retreated into the forest. *First Sarina—now the faeries are willing to die for me? What's wrong with these people? I hope Mugglegruffe can explain all this...* he thought.

Jack breathed a sigh of relief as he returned to the porch. He looked at his companions, but almost intuitively, they could sense his mind was full of questions. Before he could speak, Mugglegruffe said, "Right, you two, enough time's been wasted. Come inside and I'll put the kettle on—nothing like a cup of tea to settle the nerves."

The dwarf headed inside with Sarina following. Jack stood and watched as she placed her picnic basket inside the doorway. Glancing back, she could see how confused he was. With a reassuring smile, she jerked her head to the side, inviting him to enter.

Jack made his way into the cabin, ducking his head as he entered the doorway. Once inside, he was hit with the powerful aroma of freshly cooked bread. The interior was cosy; Mugglegruffe had made good use of the space. There was a dining table to his left, and a kitchen to his right, near the back wall. An open sack was lying on the kitchen bench, full of raw potatoes, with some odd-looking fruits nearby.

Between the kitchen and dining area was a fireplace made of cast iron, and on the far-left wall, Jack could see a bookshelf full of leather-bound books. In the far-right corner there appeared to be some kind of chemistry set. It was sitting atop an old wooden bench, covered with herbs, gemstones, and ancient swords.

"Welcome to my cabin of contemplation!" Mugglegruffe declared. "I have plenty of chairs. But if you're too big, you'll just have to use the floor."

They approached the dining table. Jack didn't want to risk breaking the dwarf's furniture, which looked very old, so he pulled-out a chair and offered it to Sarina. "You're such a gentleman," she said, in a playful tone.

Seconds later, Sarina was struggling not to laugh as he plopped himself down on the floor beside her. To Jack's surprise it was quite comfortable. Obviously, the furniture had been designed for someone of Mugglegruffe's stature. But despite having to sit on the floor, Jack was able to see across the table. He watched as Mugglegruffe moved about the kitchen, preparing a silver tray with cups on it; and when the kettle began to sing, Jack saw that it was sitting atop an old wood-burning stove made of cast-iron, but with a stone chimney.

"Sarina," he whispered, "you have to tell me what's going on? Why're you and Queen Eleanor willing to die for me? What makes *me* so special?"

"Sorry, Jack, I told you before I can't say much. I'd tell you if I could—honest. Wait for Mugglegruffe. He's a member of the high council."

"You're a special person in this world of ours, Shadar," said Mugglegruffe, apparently eavesdropping as he walked over and sat down. "Life has many paths, and your path has led you here. But I'm afraid your true purpose in Eloria is shrouded in mystery."

"What's that mean?"

"It means no one knows exactly why you were sent to us. I know you've been chosen, chosen by a higher power. Your arrival was foretold long ago; it's beyond our understanding."

I'm not buyin' this! Jack thought, but instead, asked: "What does Shadar mean?"

"Well, it's an ancient word—many thousands of years old. For some, it means you've been sent here by God, as a messenger."

Jack would've burst out with laughter if not for the look of sincerity on the dwarf's wrinkled face. "Come off it! You think God sent me here?"

"Come off what?" asked the wizard. "My chair? I'm sitting down, aren't I?"

"It's a figure of speech," Jack replied. "God's never spoken to me, and I certainly haven't spoken to him. So how could I be his messenger?"

"Being a Shadar is a sacred role. You may not hear the voice of God, but like it or not; you are now his instrument. Do you think your arrival was a coincidence?"

"Look, I don't mean any disrespect to your beliefs, but I stopped believing in God when I found out there was no Santa Claus."

The wizard abruptly left the table. *What's his problem?* Jack thought. *I don't have to believe this crap. I hate religion!*

Jack saw religion as the cause of all wars. Life had taught him the world was a cruel place. God either didn't exist, or didn't love people enough to intervene on their behalf.

"Don't worry," said Sarina. "After we've finished our tea, we'll go to the Sapphire City. Then you can meet with the high council. They will give you the answers you seek."

"That's right," said Mugglegruffe, returning with the silver tray in his hands. Sarina pushed some papers aside, so he could place it onto the table. As they were enjoying their warm beverages, Jack glanced at the papers. They were mostly old maps, but a few were drawings, and one in particular caught his eye. "What's this?" he asked, examining the depiction of a humanoid bird-like creature, which according to the script at the bottom, just happened to be made of fire.

"You needn't concern yourself with that!" said Mugglegruffe, before he snatched it out of Jack's hand and stashed it in his robe.

Jack was feeling rather annoyed as they continued to drink their tea, but he was soon struggling to hold the beverage down. Mugglegruffe's brew was extra sugary; Jack was starting to feel sick, but didn't want to offend the wizard. *I hope I don't spew my guts!* he thought, resting his hands on his stomach.

By the time they finished their tea, Jack had built-up enough courage to continue his line of questioning. But once again, Mugglegruffe beat him to it. "Right, you two, we'd best be off, or we'll never get there before nightfall."

Jack and Sarina proceeded to leave the cabin. They stepped onto the porch and patiently waited as the wizard grabbed his leather-satchel. After placing his pipe inside, he pulled the strap over his head, allowing the contents to dangle by his waist. He then removed a pointy hat, which was hanging from a hook, and placed it onto his head. It resembled the wizard's robe, having the same purple and yellow symbols.

Grabbing his staff, he stepped outside and secured the cabin using a brass key. He then passed between them without so-much as a glance. As they followed, Jack couldn't help but think of all the wizards depicted in films and literature, and thought the dwarf looked the part. Unexpectedly, Mugglegruffe led them around the right side of the cabin, towards a tall brown gate. Before Jack could ask where they were going, Sarina came up beside him and took a hold of his arm. "Can you hold this for me?"

"Sure," he replied, as the gate was being opened.

As she handed him the picnic basket Jack heard a loud clang. *That sounded metallic. Aren't picnic baskets s'posed to be full of food?* he thought, as

43

Sarina vanished through the gate. Jack wanted to peek inside, but just as he was about to open the lid, he was distracted by the sound of neighing. He watched as Sarina lifted Mugglegruffe into the air, before placing him onto a pony! Jack struggled not to laugh as the wizard rode past, but he genuinely felt that his mode of transport was slightly undignified.

"Come on, Jack," Sarina smiled.

She was now coming towards him, leading two large horses by the reins. The black horse was much larger than the white. *These horses were prepared in advance! How'd they know I'd be here? Sarina said she'd been watching me with wizard's magic. Maybe Mugglegruffe can see the future?* Jack thought, with a confused look on his face.

"Thanks," said Sarina, taking her basket.

Jack watched as she lashed it to the back of the white horse using leather straps, which were hanging from the back of the saddle. Before he could offer to help, Jack held his breath as the black horse trotted towards him. "Sarina!"

"It's alright, Jack, Midknight doesn't bite. He's a well-trained war horse!" she laughed, as the beast sniffed his jacket.

Jack had never ridden a horse in his life. He tried to put on a brave face but was terrified at the thought of placing his life in the hands (or hooves) of an animal. He watched as Sarina gripped the top of her saddle, placed her left foot in the stirrup, then climbed onto the back of her horse. *Piece of cake!* Jack thought, as he copied her actions and found himself firmly seated.

"Ah! There we go! Good boy, Midknight! I assume this big guy was born at the stroke of midnight!" Jack laughed, petting the horse's neck. He noticed a smirk on Sarina's face. "What's so funny?"

"I know you're scared," she teased. "Oh, by the way, your horse's name is Mid-knight with a silent *k*."

She reads me like a book! Jack thought, as Sarina positioned her horse beside him.

"It's alright," she whispered. "I know it's your first time on a horse. I'll go ahead of you, and Midknight will follow. Just don't fall off or do anything silly and you'll be fine."

Chapter 8

THE SAPPHIRE CITY

After hours of travelling, they were still riding along the main road, following the river. The path had become wider and easier to navigate, and Jack was feeling more confident on his horse. The road was well-used—there wasn't a blade of grass to be seen. Dozens of hoof-prints littered the ground, which meant civilisation was close.

"I don't mean to be a whinger but are we there yet?" Jack complained.

"Patience, Shadar," Mugglegruffe replied. "The journey's just as important as the destination."

After passing some yews, Jack glanced down and saw several boot prints. He looked around in the hope of seeing another of Eloria's inhabitants, but all he could see were more trees. Eventually, they came upon green hills that seemed to go on forever. "We call these rolling hills the Sea of Grass," said Mugglegruffe, slowing his pony's pace.

"Where'd all the trees go?"

"The Sea of Grass was once part of the forest. But you can't build a city without wood. The elves had to get it from somewhere," the wizard revealed.

Reaching the top of a large hill, Jack was both amazed and confused. He was expecting a city made of sapphires, but all he could see was silver. The huge mass was shimmering in the sunlight. There were hundreds of houses and a bridge across the river, leading up to the gate of the city. They brought their horses to a halt and took in the astonishing view.

"An incredible seven-hundred and forty-one, point three-one-six acres of city! That's three square-kilometres to be exact," said Mugglegruffe. "The surrounding walls are ten metres in height, fourteen metres if you include the watchtowers. Well, Shadar, what do you think?"

"I'm confused," he said. "I thought it was called the Sapphire City because it was made of sapphires?"

His friends laughed. "A city made of sapphires? Impossible!" the dwarf chuckled. "It was built from stone, quarried from Limestone Ridge, then the city walls and imperial buildings were coated in moon-dust."

"Moon-dust?"

"That's right. They call it silver in your world."

Jack glanced at Sarina, who gave him a nod of confirmation. "But if the city's made of stone, why's it called the Sapphire City?"

Sarina pointed towards the city. "Do you see those three towers in the centre? Look closely at the tip of the tallest."

Jack stared at the tower. A few seconds later, he caught a glimpse of what appeared to be a flash of green light. "Is that what I think it is?!"

"Yes," Sarina confirmed. "It's the largest green sapphire in Eloria, big enough to reflect the sunlight."

"Wow! That's impressive!"

"Sapphires aren't the only jewels down there," said Mugglegruffe. "Gemstones are the heart of Eloria's wealth; the city's teeming with them."

Sarina moved forward. "Come on, Jack. They're waiting for you."

"Yes! Let's go, Shadar! Your destiny awaits!" the dwarf cried.

Galloping down the hill, it didn't take them long to reach a small village, situated outside the city. As they entered the main street Jack could see dozens of elves. They were buying goods, crafting furniture, thatching cottages, and making clothing. Unlike the elves Jack had read about in books, they weren't all tall and fair. Most were fair-skinned, and had blonde hair and blue eyes, some were olive-skinned, and a few dark-skinned. They all had pointed ears, like Sarina, but the vast majority weren't nearly as beautiful. Some were short and plump, others were rugged and rough.

As they moved about, Jack could sense a unity he had never seen in the human world. Suddenly, he heard the sound of metal being struck and saw an elf to his right, hammering away at a red-hot blade. Jack was curious about the forge. He was about to inquire, but the elves had

caught wind of his presence. They whispered amongst themselves, staring at the stranger in their midst.

"Um, is this part of the city?" Jack nervously asked.

"Yes," Sarina replied, "this's where the farmers bring in their crops. It's essential for the city and supplies most of our food. The village of the silver bridge was the original cornerstone—a construction town. The city became overcrowded, and many chose to live outside the city walls. It gave them more space to work; and before long, the village had become a town in its own right."

"The city's overcrowded?" Jack assumed. "That's how it is in my world."

"Not quite, Shadar."

"Huh?"

"What Mugglegruffe means is that we don't have the technology your people rely on. If the machines in your world failed, a lot people would be in trouble. We prefer to live more simply. But the Sapphire City's always busy. Travellers and merchants come from all over, seeking work and prosperity."

After passing through the rest of the village they arrived at the silver bridge. Standing either side of the entrance were two, green sapphires, at least three metres in height. They were also engraved with symbols, much like the ones on Mugglegruffe's robe and hat.

"Fair dinkum!" said Jack. "One of those'd be worth millions back home."

"Come, Shadar. It's getting late," said the wizard.

After crossing the silver bridge, Jack could see two elves guarding the entrance to the city. They were dressed in silver, medieval-style armour, holding tall spears and broad shields, with swords attached to their belts. Moving closer on their trusty mounts Jack noticed a tree symbol embossed on their shields. They also had three green sapphires affixed to their breastplates, positioned horizontally in a straight line. Each gemstone was about the size of a bottle cap and shaped like a three-pointed star.

He then noticed the enormous entrance gate which consisted of two wooden doors, hinged at each side. *They must be two feet thick!* Jack thought. As they approached, the guards looked at him curiously, then glanced at Mugglegruffe before giving them a silent nod. Without speaking a word they passed through the open entrance.

Jack was amazed by the city's beauty and grandeur. Many of the buildings and walls were covered in silver, and the streets had been crafted using black and white stone. The masonry was impressive. The white stone made up the bulk of the paving, and the black stone had been used to create a floral pattern. However, the black stone wasn't just for decoration—it lined the intricate pathways, which were decorated in green sapphires. *These people are insane! Why would they pave their streets with gemstones? Aren't they worried about thieves?* Jack thought. He would have inquired, but his mind was racing with questions.

As they headed towards the heart of the city, he found most of the elves were dressed in green tunics and woollen vests, going about their daily business. Jack noticed a group of children, or elflings, laughing and chasing one another as they played. When they saw how different he was, they stopped and whispered, pointing in his direction. But there was no evil in their innocent eyes, they were just naturally curious.

"Hey, shouldn't those kids be in school?" he asked.

"Why?" said Sarina. "Parents teach their children what they need to know. Most of them will learn a trade or craft, which are passed down from generation to generation."

Jack could hear a lot of commotion coming from the eastern part of the city. He peered down the road and could see large crowds gathered around market stalls. Hundreds of elves were trading goods, most of which were food-related. Others were selling swords, bows, and armour, which were hanging from wooden beams like decorations.

Reaching the heart of the city, most of the elves were dressed in fine armour. Some were wearing silver, like the guards at the city gate, but most were wearing green armour. Unlike the guards at the city gate, the green-armoured elves had the tree symbol embossed on their breastplates. Few were carrying shields, but they all had swords around their waists.

50

"Isn't it beautiful?" said Sarina.

"I've never seen anything like it," Jack admitted.

Unexpectedly, a group of elves on horseback approached. They were all wearing green armour with the tree symbol on their breastplates. The only difference between them was they were each holding a tall spear, featuring a different flag. Each flag was firmly attached behind the tips of their spears, which Jack assumed was a form of heraldry. The troop stopped in front of them—blocking their path! Jack nervously watched as the troop's leader came forward.

He was the only soldier among them not wearing a helmet. His green breastplate was glistening in the rays of the sun as his powerful steed champed down on its bit. The elf's short hair was chestnut coloured, his white skin had a golden tan, and his eyes were hazel. He wiped the sweat from his brow. Jack wondered if the troop had just returned from battle.

"Mugglegruffe," the elf began, "General Starborne's been anxiously awaiting your return. Please make haste to the tower of the high council."

"Why, thank you, Sir Tyrus. But we must take our four-legged friends to the eastern stables. They've had a long journey and could use a good night's rest."

"You needn't bother. We're on our way to the armoury. We'll keep them in the imperial stables."

"Well, if it won't inconvenience you, we gratefully accept."

"It's no trouble," Sir Tyrus confirmed.

Dismounting her horse, Sarina started to remove her picnic basket. Jack wasn't sure what to do, but when he saw her about to help Mugglegruffe down from his pony, he got off his horse. As he went to her aid, Jack could hear the elves whispering to each other as they observed. Once the wizard's feet were firmly on the ground, the troop began to move off. Jack could see the curiosity in their eyes. But they were now riding away, with a few staying behind to take their horses, including Mugglegruffe's pony, before heading off after the rest.

"Who were they?" asked Jack.

"Elorian knights, Shadar," said Mugglegruffe. "They happen to be some of the finest warriors in the world. There aren't many foes who can withstand the charge of Elorian knights on horseback."

With Mugglegruffe leading the way, they journeyed deeper into the heart of the city until they reached the very centre. Before them was a courtyard of stone, surrounded by small trees, finely shaped hedges, and colourful flowers. In the centre of the courtyard was the tallest tower in the city, with two smaller ones, positioned either side.

Gazing up at the central tower, Jack could see oriel windows of bright silver and stained-glass evenly spaced throughout the column. Between each window were holes of bellowing chimney smoke— giving the building an industrial look. It was the same tower he had seen sparkling in the distance, like the beacon of a lighthouse. "Ah, here we are at last!" said Mugglegruffe. "Welcome, Shadar; welcome to the tower of the high council."

Ascending the stone steps of the entrance they went inside. Jack followed as they proceeded down a long hallway, which had a beautiful greenstone floor, mixed with silver floral decorations. On the ceiling above him the decorations were repeated, but with the added luxury of green sapphires. Further on, the walls on both sides were covered with swords and shields. They appeared to be decorative, and Jack noticed that every shield was either engraved or painted with the same tree symbol.

As they reached the end of the hall, it opened up into a large room, featuring a giant staircase of oak. Standing beneath the stairs, Jack glanced up to see they went all the way to the top of the tower, and he couldn't help but wish they had elevators.

He looked at Mugglegruffe, who had a smirk on his face. "Don't worry, you won't have to climb too far," he chuckled. "Now, you two wait here while I go see if the council's ready to receive our guest."

Before ascending the staircase, Mugglegruffe whispered something in Sarina's ear, then hurried away. *What did he say?* Jack thought. *Maybe I should—what the heck is that?*

Jack's eyes were drawn to something above his head. At first glance he didn't know what to make of it. But as he looked closer, Jack saw it was different technology to that of his own world. The diamond-shaped object was emanating a beautiful white light, but not from any electrical globe. "Sarina, what's this light above my head?"

"All the lights in the city are made of crystal. It's an ancient technology. It's been around for at least a thousand years," she revealed. "Come with me, Jack. I want to show you something special."

She led him past the staircase and into another room, before placing her basket on the floor. The room was large and there were elves congregating near the centre, all dressed in fine robes with gold trim. Sarina didn't pay them any attention; she just led him up to a large mural on the back of the far wall. It was a design of a large tree, identical to the ones featured on the armour and shields of the elves.

It was greyish-brown, with seven branches and seven leaves on each branch. The leaves were made of green sapphires, which must have been set in the wall with great care. The tree had three roots, pointing downward, and the entire wall around the outline was decorated with a silver floral design. Sarina gazed up at the mural with a sense of reverence and pride, becoming lost in the glorious image. "This is the symbol of our people, and of the Sapphire City. It's called the tree of life."

"Don't some of the cultures in my world have a symbol like this?" Jack asked.

"Yes, but this symbol's very special. It was given to us by the most powerful being in the universe. He came to Eloria almost two thousand years ago. He's our High King… and one day he will return."

Jack wondered if Sarina was talking about the only other human to enter this world. He remembered her saying that he wasn't exactly human, and that she wasn't allowed to speak of him. "I thought you couldn't tell me these things?"

"I wasn't before, but Mugglegruffe gave me permission."

"When he whispered to you?"

"Yes, but I can't tell you everything. He just said I could tell you about our symbol, and the tree of life is very sacred to us."

Jack was frustrated by the secrecy. He was about to inquire further, but was distracted by the sound of footsteps. They turned around, expecting to see Mugglegruffe, only to see a male elf with fair skin, golden blonde hair, and bright blue eyes. He was wearing green armour, with the tree of life on his breastplate; and even though he wasn't wearing a helmet, he had a sword attached to a belt on his left hip. "Albion! Where've you been?!" Sarina cried, leaping into his arms.

"Nowhere really," said the elf, giving her a hug. "I've just returned from my patrol near the border of Darkwood Forest."

Sarina stepped back with a shudder. "Darkwood Forest?! Your patrol was only to go as far as Peniven! Why in the High King's name would you enter the forbidden lands?"

Whoever this Albion fellow was, Sarina was fond of him, and Jack couldn't help but feel a bit jealous. "Relax," he replied. "We didn't actually cross the border. The wildwood rangers reported that orcs have been using the forest to cross into our lands, but we saw no sign of them. There have also been whispers throughout the city that the last Shadar's entered our world," said Albion, looking at Jack.

"The whispers are true—the last Shadar has indeed come forth," Sarina smiled, as she stepped closer to Jack and took a hold of his arm.

"I thought so."

"Albion, this is Jack Campbell, the last Shadar," said Sarina, gracefully holding out her arm in a regal manner. She then looked at Jack, and said, "Jack, this's my brother, Albion Starborne; he's a captain of the imperial army."

Jack was relieved to learn that Albion was Sarina's brother. "It's an honour to meet you," he said, extending his hand.

"No, Shadar, the honour's mine. I vow to defend you with my life, to the last breath," the elf replied, making a fist with his right hand, then resting it on the left side of his chest. Then, with his arm still in place, he bowed his head in respect.

Jack could barely fathom his words. *Why does everyone I meet in this world seem so eager to die for me? I'm just a security guard,* he thought.

He was about to ask why, but again they were interrupted. "If you lot are done exchanging pleasantries, the council's ready to receive our new guest," said Mugglegruffe.

Jack turned to see the wizard tapping his boot on the floor with an impatient look on his face. "We can't go with you," said Sarina, "but you must go with Mugglegruffe. Only a member of the high council can take you into those chambers of wisdom."

"Don't be afraid. We'll be waiting for you," Albion encouraged.

Following the wizard towards the big staircase, Jack glanced back. "Wish me luck."

"Come on, Shadar. Don't be so nervous. I'll be there with you," said Mugglegruffe, leading him upstairs.

Chapter 9

THE FIRST COUNCIL MEETING

Jack's heart was beginning to flutter. *I feel like I'm going for a job interview! Which floor's he takin' me to? There must be about thirty?* he thought.

Mugglegruffe stopped as they reached the third floor, giving Jack a sense of relief. He followed him down a hallway towards a large double door made of solid oak, with the tree of life carved into the wood. Standing either side were two guards, who quickly opened the doors as they approached.

"Alright, Shadar, this is nothing to worry about. Just be yourself, only speak when spoken to, and be sure to keep your words truthful."

Jack could hear raised voices as they entered the council chambers; and he was shocked to see a round table, surrounded by five angry elves and a loud dwarf. It was impossible to interpret what they were saying. It looked as if they were about to come to blows. *I thought these chambers were s'posed to be full of wisdom?* he thought.

Mugglegruffe stopped and let out a deep sigh. He then headed towards the centre of the room as Jack followed. Two of the elves weren't quite as angry, remaining in their seats. But the rest were standing up, shouting back and forth, pointing their fingers at each other.

Like the table, the room was also circular, and there were seven doors, spread-out in a half-circle around the back of the far-wall. Each was marked by a gold number, displaying one to seven in numerical order. The council members continued to argue, having failed to notice their presence. Three of the elves seemed to be soldiers, or knights, one of which was arguing with the red-bearded dwarf. The dwarf was clad in silver armour and had a golden crown upon his head, encrusted with three purple jewels.

With Jack by his side, Mugglegruffe stood in front of the table waiting to be acknowledged, but they continued to argue. Irritated, the wizard raised his staff and banged it on the floor three times! The council became silent as they turned to Jack, the only stranger in their midst. "My friends," said Mugglegruffe, "I bring you the last Shadar!"

That got their attention! Jack thought, as the council took their seats.

Struggling to climb atop a wooden stool, Mugglegruffe motioned for Jack to sit beside him. With sweaty palms and a pounding heart, Jack quietly sat down. The council members stared at him, as if he were some sort of extra-terrestrial being.

Seconds later, an elf in green armour stood. His armour was the same as two other elves in the room, except for one difference: he was wearing a crimson-red, Roman-styled sagum, attached to the back of his shoulders, flowing down like a cape. Jack assumed he was an elf of high stature. "Greetings, Shadar. Welcome to the high council of Eloria, and of the Sapphire City. I am Godfrey Starborne, General of the imperial army, and Steward of Eloria. We've been expecting your arrival for almost two-thousand years. We consider ourselves honoured by your presence," he said, then sat back down.

Starborne? Sarina's father? Two thousand years—I've only been alive for thirty-three! He sounds Irish. Everyone else sounds English, Jack thought, struggling to comprehend.

The council members stared at him with fear and curiosity, as if expecting him to say something profound. *I better introduce myself,* he thought. "Um, hello, my name's Jack Campbell, and from what I've been told, only a member of this council can answer my questions. So if you could tell me why I'm here, I'd really appreciate it."

Some of them looked at each other, then suddenly burst out with shouting and arguing. "Did you hear that?! He doesn't even know why he's here!"

"Well, that went better than expected," Jack whispered to Mugglegruffe.

The dwarf banged his staff on the floor a second time; again the room became silent. "You'd best remember it was I who was given the great revelation! Just because he's unaware of his purpose, doesn't mean he hasn't been chosen!" the wizard scowled. "He comes from a different world. It's his world we're trying to save. He's a stranger, not unlike some of you were once, and he should be given time to adjust."

One of the elves sprung from his seat! He was wearing green armour and had short black hair and blue eyes. "For thousands of years we've waited for humans to change. They can't be trusted! Shadar or not!"

Again the council erupted. "I didn't know Elorians argued so much," said Jack.

"Don't take anything they say to heart. Just remember that I believe in you. And so do many others throughout this city," the wizard softly replied.

For a third time Mugglegruffe was forced to bang his staff. "My friends and fellow councilmen, clearly there's much to discuss. Having a human in our world is not something to be taken lightly. I suggest we reconvene at a later date, after our guest has spent some time with the people of our great city."

"I say we send him back to his own world!" cried the dark-haired elf.

"I second that motion! Let's take a vote!" the angry dwarf agreed.

With the council whispering amongst themselves, Jack realised his time in Eloria might be short-lived. But as he was looking to Mugglegruffe, in the hope of being spared the humiliation of deportation, someone tapped him on the shoulder. Jack glanced to his left to see an old elf, wearing a green robe with golden floral decorations on the cuffs and collar. His face was pale and wrinkled, and the rest of his long white beard was hidden beneath the table. He was also wearing brass-rimmed spectacles, firmly seated upon his ears, which were longer than those of any elf Jack had seen so far. "Don't worry, lad," he struggled to whisper, in an old raspy voice. "I know you've got the numbers. You're not going anywhere."

At least someone else's on my side, Jack thought.

General Starborne arose once more. "It's time to vote. May wisdom and grace guide this fateful decision."

As the General sat back down, Jack saw a glance exchanged between him and Mugglegruffe. Godfrey then looked around the table. "Those in favour of allowing the human to stay, please place your medallion white side up," he instructed, before flipping a large circular coin.

Jack hadn't noticed the green medallions, which every council member had in front of them, but he was hoping to see at least four of them flipped. The council was composed of seven members, and when the fourth medallion was finally turned over he breathed a sigh of relief. The members who hadn't voted for him were the red-bearded dwarf, a brown-haired elf, and of course, the dark-haired elf, who seemed particularly agitated by his arrival. The General arose for a third time. "This council has voted—the Shadar will stay. We'll review his progress in three months' time."

With the meeting over, Jack was faced with another problem as a feeling of sickness began to grow in the pit of his stomach. *What am I gonna do for three months?* he thought. *What did Mugglegruffe mean? How could they help a world as divided as mine?*

Jack watched as the two elves who had voted against him stormed out of the chambers without saying a word. He then felt someone tapping his shoulder again. To no surprise, it was the elf in the green robe. "See, lad! I knew you weren't going anywhere!"

Before Jack could thank him for his vote, the old elf turned away and left the room. Jack looked at Mugglegruffe. He was about to ask if they could leave but was distracted by the sound of raised voices on the other side of the table, where General Starborne was having a heated discussion with the red-bearded dwarf. A moment later, the red-bearded dwarf stormed away. He was about to leave, but suddenly came back and stood in front of Mugglegruffe. "Sorry, my old friend, I just can't do it! I've given Godfrey my notice. If I stay any longer, my son will try to claim my throne!"

The wizard sighed. "You gave me your word, Brutus. You said you'd leave the past behind. Does a king's word count for nothing? What are the troubles of one kingdom, compared to the fate of an entire world?"

"I tried!" the dwarf snapped. "You may be able to forgive humans for what they did, but I cannot! I will not! Elves can meddle in their affairs if they wish. But I'll not jeopardise what I've built for the sake of those murderers. I return to the halls of Stonehill where no human shall ever be welcome!"

With that, the angry dwarf turned away and left the room. "What was that about? He doesn't even know me. How can he judge me like that?" said Jack.

"Don't concern yourself with King Brutus Brutalan. He's an ill-tempered dwarf who's still trapped in the past. Long ago, humans committed terrible crimes against dwarves. But I'd never blame you for the actions of your people, and neither should he. A mind full of hatred and vengeance makes it difficult to let go. It's an anchor for some, a chain that'll never be broken."

"Look, I don't wanna cause any trouble. I know some of these guys hate me, but what am I gonna do about the rest of the elves? What will they think of me?" Jack worried.

"Make no mistake, your presence will cause a rift. Like the humans in your world, the elves, too, are afraid of change. But you also have a lot of supporters. Now, there's a couple of elves waiting for you downstairs, so we'd best not keep them in suspense."

They left the chambers and headed downstairs where Albion and Sarina were patiently waiting. As Jack began to approach, someone was heard to shout, "It's an insult for a human to be in our city!"

The two elves from the council meeting were also in the room. *What is it with these guys?* Jack thought, glancing at them as they proceeded to walk past.

Just as he was turning his attention back to his friends, one of them shoved him in the back, using his armoured shoulder! Jack spun around to see the brown–haired elf glare at him as they passed by. Jack took a deep breath. As he went to approach his friends, he was shocked to see Albion struggling to hold Sarina back!

"Calm down!" said Albion, locking his arms around her waist.

Jack hurried over. "It's alright, Sarina! I'm fine! It didn't even hurt, okay?"

"No, Jack—it's not okay! I promised to protect you. He's a guest here, Albion! Those idiots should be removed from the high council!"

"Look, if Fergus or anyone else lays a hand on him, I'll pound them into dust!" said the captain, before releasing his hold.

Jack was captivated by Sarina's protective instincts. A member of the opposite sex had never defended him in such a way. "Look at me guys; I'm perfectly fine. I know how volatile a situation can get, but it's over. The last thing I want is for a fight to happen over me. There's always opposition. Can't we just let it go?"

"Well said, Shadar," the wizard agreed.

"No worries," Jack replied. "But why do they hate me so much? Did humans hurt them, like they hurt the dwarves?"

Albion and Sarina were hesitant to answer. "The elf who shoved you, was Sir Fergus Crouse," said Mugglegruffe. "He's a follower. He does what the other one tells him to do. And that particular elf just happens to be Sir Julius 'troll slayer' Santorean. His rhetoric has been ruffling a few feathers as of late. There's a group of elves who doubt the prophecy, an anti-human sect, and Julius's influence has only added fuel to the fire. He may be a knight, but he's a prideful, arrogant fool. Of course, he's only been that way since the loss of his father."

"Don't worry, Jack. They'll come to believe in you as we do. They just need a bit of convincing. Besides, you've got three months to prove them wrong," Sarina encouraged.

"That's true. Wait—how'd you know that?"

"Surely you didn't think we'd let them send you home?" Mugglegruffe chuckled.

"Look, you guys can play politics if you like, but there's something I must know…"

"Yes, Jack?" Sarina smiled.

"You mentioned orcs before, Albion. And Mugglegruffe, you just called Julius a troll slayer, so I'm guessin' there're some pretty dangerous creatures in this world? If you guys want me to stay, then I need to know, is there anything you haven't told me about?"

Rubbing his chin, Albion looked at the wizard, as if seeking permission to answer. "Why are you looking at me? Speak your mind, Captain!" the dwarf barked.

"Well, we didn't want to worry you on your first day," said Albion. "Your presence in Eloria won't go unnoticed by the darker forces; they're constantly trying to get a foothold in both our worlds. I won't lie to you, Shadar; there are real dangers in this world. But as long as you stay inside the city, you should be safe."

Jack's face turned pale as he remembered his nightmare. Sarina could sense his anxiety. "What's wrong, Jack? Did something happen? If something's wrong, you should tell us. Don't keep us in the dark."

"I had the worst nightmare this morning. It was really vivid. It seems strange to have it the same day as finding myself here."

The elves were a bit concerned, but Mugglegruffe's eyes were wide open. He didn't believe in coincidence. "Tell me what you saw?" he said.

"Okay. I was in a black forest, and was being chased by a dark figure. He had red glowing eyes, big hands, and sharp talons. He was super-fast and caught up with me in no time, cackling like a maniac. I woke up before he could get me."

They all stood there in shock. "What?" said Jack.

"Impossible!" Albion gasped. "He couldn't have known the arrival of the last Shadar. What if he followed him?"

"W-what do you mean?" Jack struggled to ask. "Can one of you please tell me why you're so upset about a dream?"

"It was no dream, Shadar," said Mugglegruffe. "The creature you described is known to us. He's an infernal spirit; a demon, by the name of Barbatus. In your world he's known as the Shadow Man. He's the prince of chaos—a powerful sorcerer, and high-ranking Lieutenant of the Red Dragon, with multiple legions at his disposal."

Jack was starting to feel faint. "Don't say his name out loud!" Albion warned. "If that thing's entered our world it could summon him!"

"Don't be superstitious, Captain. It would take more than that to summon a demon of such power. And giving in to fear is like ringing the dinner bell! But in light of this, it makes no difference. The ancient evil from days of old has found a way in."

"Then why haven't we seen him? Why didn't he attack us on the road?" Sarina asked, as Jack struggled to keep up.

The wizard ran his fingers through his long grey beard. "He may not have entered through the Southern Gate, but used a portal, and according to their physical laws, no creature of darkness can cross over without being weakened. Perhaps he is here, but he wouldn't be capable of mounting an attack until he's regained his full strength. Still, not even the Shadow Man would attack this city alone. Right now he would be looking for help. Those rumours of orcs entering Darkwood Forest may not be a coincidence."

"Those rumours are weeks old," said Albion.

"Yes, but they have their mystics and diviners; they could've foreseen this. You know how powerful an orc sorcerer can be."

"Fine," said Albion. "I'll inform my father and advise him to double the guard. It might be excessive, but at least we'll sleep at night."

"Very wise, Captain," Mugglegruffe nodded. "I'm sure he will approve."

Albion proceeded to leave as the wizard turned his attention to Jack. "It's been a long and troublesome first day for you, but now I must take my leave, for I have other business to attend to. Sarina will take you to your quarters," he said, then left the room.

"Come on, Jack. Let me show you your quarters," Sarina smiled. "Don't worry about our enemies—the city's well-guarded. Besides, my room's right next to yours. I won't let anything happen to you."

Upon hearing her gentle words Jack's nausea faded. He followed her back to the big staircase. As they ascended the tower he wondered how many flights they would have to climb. Reaching the third level, Jack saw the guards stationed outside the council chambers. Sarina continued until they reached the seventh floor. "This looks nice," said Jack, admiring the hallway.

There were nine doors, each of which was marked by a golden number. But even a five-star hotel didn't have green walls lavishly decorated with sapphires. *This is weird—the doors in this place are all labelled in English numerals, and everyone I've met has spoken English. I wonder if they have their own language...* Jack pondered.

"Here we are!" said Sarina, stopping outside a door with a gold numeral '7' in the centre, surrounded by a floral-design.

"What do those markings mean? I've been seeing them everywhere."

"They're mostly decorative," she replied, opening the door with a gold-plated key. She led him into a glorious room, and Jack was surprised to see the lights already on. Someone had prepared his quarters in advance. The floor was made of greenstone, and the walls were covered in light-green wallpaper, which was decorated in green sapphires and silver floral designs. *Not even wealthy people have rooms like this!* Jack thought.

In the lounge room to his left, Jack could see a pair of green cushioned chairs; a two-seater lounge chair, and a table of oak, situated in the centre of the room. To his right, there was a closed door, but his gaze was caught by the paintings on the far-wall. The largest painting was a rendition of the tree of life. It was identical to the one downstairs, but on a much smaller scale. Then he saw a painting of a great battle between the elves, and some nasty-looking creatures. Their hides were grey, and their red eyes were larger than a human's. Their armour and weapons looked inferior compared to those of the elves. "Hey, what're those ugly lookin' buggers?"

"Those are orcs," she replied. "They're cruel and violent beasts, lacking empathy and compassion. Their nature is to kill and devour, but that's a mercy compared to the other crimes they're capable of."

Jack didn't know what to make of her words. Looking closer, he noticed something in the corner of the painting. It appeared to be an oversized orc but was different to the others. Based on the size difference it was at least twelve feet tall!

Unlike the orcs, whose bodies were hairless, except for their heads —the creature was covered head-to-toe in thick, shaggy black fur. It was wearing brown armour, but unlike the orcs, its blood-red eyes weren't oversized. "What kind of orc is that?"

"That's not an orc, that's a troll," said Sarina. "They're bigger and stronger than orcs. Sometimes trolls hunt and devour orcs. But when united against a common enemy, trolls will lead them into battle."

"Did Julius really kill one of those things?"

"He's killed a lot more than one," she revealed. "Julius once lived in his family's home. It was a cabin, near the village of Peniven—a lonely farming town. One day, a group of trolls broke down the door and killed his mother. Consumed by vengeance, he tracked the beasts down and killed them one by one. It was a terrible time. His father had already been lost in the Great War, long ago. After losing so much, I don't think Julius has faith in anything. He's full of anger and sorrow."

"I feel bad for him," said Jack, "but that doesn't explain his hatred for humans. Mugglegruffe told me that humans committed crimes against dwarves. What about the elves? Did they commit crimes against them, too?"

"Even if that were the case, Julius's hatred runs deeper. I have no doubt that humans did bad things. But when you're someone like Julius, it's easy to find something to be mad at. Do you know what I mean?"

"Yeah, I think so. By the way, I still haven't thanked you for sticking up for me down there. You were really something..."

"It was nothing," Sarina blushed. "Besides, I did promise to protect you."

"Yes, but—"

"Come on! I haven't shown you the rest of the place yet," she interrupted. "Let's look at the kitchen, shall we?"

Jack followed her into the kitchen, which resembled the look and style of an old English one. There didn't seem to be any modern appliances, but there was a wood-burning stove, like the one in Mugglegruffe's cabin. The pots and pans were made of cast-iron, and the sink was made of steel. Above the sink was a brass tap, with two oddly-shaped handles. "Do I have running water? I thought this city was medieval? What's the bathroom like?"

"Yes. You've got indoor-plumbing as well. We're not as backward as you think," said Sarina, with a hint of sarcasm.

"I didn't mean anything by it. I was just surprised, that's all."

"I know—I was just teasing you," she laughed.

Jack suddenly felt a cool draft; there weren't any windows that he could see. Then he noticed a ventilation pipe above his head. It was made of steel, with a brass grate, and was producing a nice air flow.

"You should have everything you need," said Sarina as she moved about, opening various cupboards. Jack could see plenty of crockery, bread, biscuits; some odd-looking nuts, even a slab of cheese. And sitting by the pantry, on the kitchen bench, were several flasks of wine, a bowl of red grapes, and some silver chalices.

"This's way better than my place!" he remarked.

Leading him back to the closed door, Sarina opened it to reveal the bedroom. Jack followed her inside and saw a large bed, with a bedside table, and a second door, which led to the bathroom. There was a wardrobe against the wall, opposite the foot of the bed, and a wooden chair in the corner. The bed was made of oak, and the four bed posts were engraved with floral patterns. "This bed's big enough for three or four people!" Jack exclaimed.

"I know you get lonely at night," said Sarina, with a cheeky smile.

"How would you know?" said Jack.

"I've been watching you a long time."

With her cheeks turning red, Sarina tried to hide her smile as she tossed something onto his bed. Jack glanced down to see the golden key. He stared into her eyes until she could no longer look at him with a straight face. "Goodnight, Jack. I'll see you in the morning."

She gave him a playful wink, then left his quarters. Jack listened to the sound of the door closing behind her, and when he felt that he was alone, Jack couldn't help but say, "I knew she liked me."

Always security conscious, Jack used the golden key to lock his quarters, then returned to his bedroom. He opened the wardrobe and found seven sets of elvish clothing. Not only were they beautiful and well-made, they were also his size! Taken aback, Jack rummaged through the wardrobe until he found a bed-robe, which he changed into, curious to see how it would feel. "This's better than my boxer-shorts. How'd they do this? I can't even pick the right size when I shop for myself!"

Jack yawned and rubbed his eyes. By force of habit, he found himself looking around for a clock, and his eyes were drawn to something hanging on the wall. "I don't believe it—a clock! Crystal technology and Elorian clocks, what else can these people make?" he laughed.

He examined the odd-looking machine. It was some type of gear-operated clock, but it didn't seem to have a keyhole or winding apparatus. *It can't be battery-operated,* he thought. *It must use the same technology as the crystal lights.*

With his mind fatigued, Jack finally gave-up and retired for the night.

Chapter 10

CELEBRITY STATUS

Jack was awoken the next morning by the sound of someone knocking on the front door. He took the key from his bedside table, and when he opened the door, there stood Albion with a silver tray in his hands. It was covered in toast, fruit, biscuits, and a cup of tea. "Come on, you've slept long enough," said the captain, handing him the tray.

"Thanks," Jack replied. "I'm pretty hungry."

"You didn't eat last night?"

"No," he replied, his stomach rumbling.

"Why didn't you grab something from the kitchen cupboard?"

"I was so excited I forgot about food. Boy was I buggered! It was about five o' clock when I went to bed, but it felt like I'd been up for days."

"What time was it when you came to Eloria?" Albion asked.

"It was mid-afternoon," said Jack. "We walked to Mugglegruffe's cabin, then rode the rest of the day. I don't know what to make of it…"

"Sarina said you found her in the morning. You came through the Southern Gate just after dawn. Didn't she explain that Elorian time would be different for you?"

"Sort of," said Jack. "She said that while I stay here, one month in Eloria would only be one day in my world. What's the Southern Gate?"

"It's the gateway between your world and ours."

"How far is it from there, to the Sapphire City?"

"It's at least a days' ride. You must've been up for twenty-four hours."

"Okay," said Jack, "that makes sense. But why didn't we stop to eat? All I had to drink was some of Mugglegruffe's tea—it was horrible!"

"I don't have time to explain now, but we don't eat as often as humans."

"Really? What about dwarves?"

"They don't have to eat as often either, but eat as often as they can!" he laughed. "Anyway, have some breakfast, get dressed, then come downstairs to the hall of the great tree—it's where we met yesterday. I'll be waiting."

Before he could reply, Albion stepped back into the hallway, closing the door behind him. Jack carried the tray to the kitchen and placed it on the dining table, situated in the centre of the room. He was looking forward to the day ahead. *I hope they let me explore the city. Mugglegruffe said I have to spend some time with the people,* he thought. *I wonder if they'll let me climb onto the roof, so I can see that giant sapphire.*

Devouring his breakfast, Jack was amazed by the aromas and flavours. Each bite was more flavoursome than anything he'd ever tasted. The fruit was perfect and shiny, like something out of a television commercial. After scoffing down some cinnamon toast, a red apple, an orange, and a handful of grapes, Jack had consumed the entire tray of food. He left the tray on the table, went back to his bedroom, and opened the wardrobe. "What am I gonna wear?" he mused to himself. "I don't wanna stick out like a sore thumb."

Since the clothes were all his size, Jack didn't think it would matter what he chose to wear, but he was worried about being a laughingstock. After all, how often had they seen a human wearing elvish clothing? He carefully looked at each set; one of which included a waistcoat with golden floral designs, but Jack didn't know what Albion had planned. After examining each item, he finally decided on a pair of pants with a matching long-sleeved shirt. Both the pants and shirt were light-green, featuring a dark floral pattern. The style was somewhat Japanese—the elves had influenced many cultures in Jack's world.

He placed the clothes onto the bed, then opened the drawer at the base of the wardrobe. It was full of green socks and underwear. "What is with these elves and green?"

"Good morning," he heard a female voice say.

Sarina was standing in the doorway, and Jack's eyes widened when he saw her attire. Yesterday, she was wearing a beautiful white dress, but now she was dressed in green armour! The tree of life was embossed on her breastplate and she had two green-handled daggers— one on each hip, attached to a belt around her waist. "Good morning to you, too!" Jack smiled. "I hope we're not fighting any orcs today?"

"No—this is my uniform!" she laughed. "I'm not just a pretty face, you know. I'm a vital piece of the imperial army."

"I see. Then why don't you have a sword?"

"I'm an imperial ranger; we track down our prey. We don't fight like knights and foot-soldiers. Rangers engage the enemy at a safe distance. My bow's in the armoury, but I always keep my daggers close. They were a gift from my father. Anyway, you'd best get dressed if I'm going to make a ranger out of you."

"You want me to be a ranger? I don't know anything about daggers and stuff. The most I've ever carried was a baton."

"Relax, Jack. I'm just teasing you. Albion's going to teach you the way of the sword; you get to be his squire. My brother hasn't taken on a squire for a very long time, so consider it an honour."

"I have to use a sword?"

Despite wishing he knew how to use one, the reality of actually wielding an instrument of death was not to be taken lightly. Sarina could sense his anxiety. "You've only got a few months to learn the basics. That's why we're taking you to the armoury. Trust me, as soon as you start, you won't want to stop. I'll meet you downstairs in five minutes. Don't be late or I'll have to come find you," she teased, before leaving his quarters.

A few months to learn the basics? Shouldn't I be spending time with the people? Jack thought, putting on his elvish clothes. He also found a pair of green boots, which were tucked away in the back of the wardrobe. Everything was a perfect fit. It was like the elves had snuck into the human world and did a fitting as he slept! Dressed in his new attire, Jack left his quarters and headed down the big staircase towards the hall of the great tree. He passed a couple of elves, who looked at him strangely, then gave him a silent nod. "At least they didn't laugh," he whispered to himself.

Jack stepped into the hall of the great tree. Many elves were standing about, most of whom were gazing up at the tree of life. In the centre of the room, Jack saw Albion and Sarina talking to another elf. He was young and handsome with olive skin, brown eyes, and wavy brown hair. He wasn't wearing armour, but a brown leather apron, long pants, and a long-sleeved shirt, with the sleeves rolled up to his elbows. Lastly, he appeared to be holding a red leather-bound book, and a white ink-feather. Jack recognised the elf as a member of the high council who had voted for him.

He approached as they all turned towards him, and just as he was about to say, 'good morning,' Albion beat him to the punch. "Morning again, Shadar. This is Marshall Tucker, our Master Blacksmith."

Extending his hand, the elf dropped his book. "Oh! I-I'm so sorry! Please forgive my clumsiness!"

"It's alright, no need to apologise." Jack picked up the book and shook the elf's hand before passing it back to him.

"Ah, thank you."

Jack glanced at Albion and Sarina, who were struggling to contain their amusement. Marshall opened his red book and began flipping through pages. When he found the right page, the blacksmith looked up and smiled. "Um, I just have two questions."

"Okay," said Jack. "Fire away."

The elf licked the tip of his ink-covered feather. Jack was disgusted by the trace of blackness left on his tongue. Marshall then coughed to clear his throat. "What's your favourite colour? And which animal do you most relate to? Wait—it doesn't have to be an animal! You can choose a mythological creature if you like? Like a gryphon, or maybe a pegasus... or perhaps something else?"

Is this guy weird in the head? Why's he askin' me this? Jack thought.

"Take your time, Shadar," Albion advised.

"Well, my favourite colour's blue. But I can't think of an animal..."

"Think back to your childhood," said Sarina. "When I was younger, I wanted to be a hawk, so I could soar above the clouds."

He thought back to his childhood. All Jack could remember was playing with a stuffed monkey before his stepfather tore it to pieces in a drunken rage. "Well, I saw this documentary about the wolves of Yellowstone National Park. And I remember thinking that I'd love to come back as a white one when I die."

Marshall looked at Albion, who gave him a nod of approval. "The Elorian snow wolf's a powerful animal. It has great strength and endurance," the captain stated, as Marshall jotted down the information.

Closing his book, the blacksmith suddenly raced out of the room without saying goodbye. Jack was very confused. "Why'd he ask me those things? Did you see how fast he ran? He moves like the wind!"

Albion covered his mouth, struggling not to laugh. "It's for your armour. Marshall's going to make you something special," said Sarina.

"Okay," said Jack. "Is he always so enthusiastic?"

Unable to contain himself, Albion burst out with laughter. Jack stood there in bewilderment as Sarina began to giggle, shaking her head in amusement. "What's so funny?" he asked. "And why'd you say snow wolf? I never said anything about snow."

Albion was laughing so hard that he was struggling to hold back tears. Finally he wiped the moisture from his eyes. "I've never seen him act like that! I don't think he's ever been so excited to make a suit of armour!"

"He's excited because of me?" asked Jack.

"That's right," Sarina confirmed. "Word travels fast, and now every elf in the city's curious about you. Marshall's a Master Blacksmith. And from this day forward, he'll be remembered as the elf that made the armour of the last Shadar."

"Why am I the last?" Jack inquired. "What happened to the others?"

"Only a human can be a Shadar," Sarina replied. "I don't know much about them, but there hasn't been one in your world for a thousand years."

Jack was about to inquire further, but then noticed some of the elves looking in his direction. "Don't worry about them," said Albion. "Just be yourself. Everything'll be fine."

Upon hearing his words, Jack was reminded of what Mugglegruffe said to him before the council meeting: *Just be yourself, and be sure to keep your words truthful.* Then Jack realised the dwarf was missing. "Hey, where's Mugglegruffe?"

Sarina bit her lower lip as Albion rubbed his chin. "Mugglegruffe's a solitary dwarf. He's probably back at his cabin checking on his tobacco leaves," he said. "Or he could be rummaging through old books, looking for a way to defeat the Shadow Man."

"What if something's happened to him?"

They stood there in silence. "What's wrong?" said Jack. "Sarina, last night you told me not to keep you in the dark. Don't you think I deserve the same?"

"You're right, Jack," she replied. "But we don't know his intentions. Mugglegruffe's the most powerful wizard in Eloria. He would never want us to go looking for an enemy that he couldn't handle. He can be eager at times, especially when it comes to facing a foe. But he wouldn't fight Barbatus unless he was certain of victory."

"You think he's gone to fight the Shadow Man?!"

"No. I think Albion's right—he's back at his cabin or something. Mugglegruffe's not a sociable character, in case you didn't notice?"

"Oh, I've noticed," said Jack. "To be honest, when I first met him —I thought he was a bit of a nutcase. But if it weren't for his support yesterday, I don't know where I'd be."

"Well, I'm glad he's growing on you," Sarina smiled.

"Come on, Shadar. Don't worry about Mugglegruffe. I once saw him kill a water-dragon, and that's no easy feat! It would take an army just to slow him down."

"You mean there really are dragons in Eloria? What's the Red Dragon he spoke of?"

"Relax, my human-friend," Albion chuckled. "The Red Dragon's one of a kind; it's a vessel of pure evil. The Dragon's just an illusion; it's not his true form. As for Elorian dragons, well, they're all but extinct—at least the flying ones are. No one's seen a flying dragon in Eloria for five hundred years."

"That's not entirely true," Sarina argued. "You're forgetting about ice dragons; they still inhabit the Snowy Mountains. And you forgot about the beast of Dragon's Crest."

"The beast of Dragon's Crest hasn't been seen since the Great War!" Albion scoffed.

"True. But you wouldn't question King Brutalan, would you? You know he saw an ice dragon last year, right?"

"Okay, fine—maybe they still exist. But it's not like they're flying around, burning up livestock and villagers anymore, is it?"

"What about the water-dragons?" Jack curiously asked. "Are they still around?"

"Yes, but water-dragons don't have wings, they have fins instead. That means they're better-suited to water environments, like rivers and lakes. They rarely go out to sea though, because then they'd have to contend with sea-serpents and the krakens of the deep. Krakens are the most destructive; only a fleet of ships would be daring enough to take on one of those."

"Well, if I come across any, I'll be sure to keep my distance."

"Come on. Let's get going," said Sarina. "By the way, Jack, I think you look very handsome in your new clothes."

"Thanks," he replied.

Heading past the big staircase, they made their way down the hall of shields. When they stepped outside, Jack noticed the statues of elven warriors. They were surrounded by colourful flowers and small trees, reminding him of an English garden.

"Can I look around for a bit? I've never seen a garden like this."

"Sorry, we're running late," said Sarina, "but I'll take you on a personal tour one day, if you like?"

"Sounds good," he replied.

Making their way into the city streets, it wasn't long until Jack noticed something odd. One of his duties, as a shopping mall security guard, was to pick up small pieces of rubbish and alert the cleaners to any spills. "Where're all the rubbish bins? This place is immaculate. I've seen towns smaller than this, and they were like garbage dumps!"

Albion and Sarina laughed. "We don't need bins. Every elf's proud of our city, we all do our part to keep it clean," she revealed. "The Sapphire City's like the circle of life; nothing gets wasted."

Jack was amazed. "Do you have any homeless elves or beggars?"

"Homeless elves and beggars?" Albion laughed. "Not in the whole of Eloria would an elf beg for anything! The only time an elf would be homeless is after an orc raid. It doesn't happen very often these days. But if it did, we would open our homes to those in need. They'd be well-cared for until new homes were built."

The cities in Jack's world were full of homeless people begging on the streets, as those who passed-by would ignore them like they didn't exist. *Most of the wealth in my world's owned by the elite. I bet they wouldn't part with a single coin to save a life. Big time bankers and captains of industry, who think they're gods. Most of 'em are no better than the scumbags who sell guns and drugs to kids. Hang on—what about criminals? Even Eloria must have them?* he thought. *Or maybe the only criminals around here are the orcs and trolls?*

Walking through the streets, Jack saw elves opening their stores. They immediately noticed his presence; and when he saw a group of children playing near a bakery, he was half-expecting them to curse at him, like the delinquents at the shopping mall would back home. But as the trio were passing by, they waved in his direction with smiles on their faces. Jack gave them a wave back, and they suddenly cheered and clapped their hands with joy!

It was a very different reception. Jack thought about the times he had caught kids stealing, spraying graffiti, and destroying property. As he looked around, however, they weren't doing anything of the sort.

He was truly impressed by their behaviour. But there was still a question on the tip of his tongue. "Do you get much crime in the Sapphire City?"

They glanced at him with raised eyebrows. "Don't you remember the paintings in your quarters?" said Sarina.

"Wait, what do you mean by crime?" Albion asked. "An attack by orcs?"

"No. I'm talkin' about the elves. Do they ever steal from each other?"

"You mean do elves break the law?"

"Yeah," said Jack.

"Can you remember if any of our kin have broken one of the seven laws?" said Albion.

Sarina thought about the question. "Um, no, I can't recall the last time one of us committed a crime against another elf. There was that terrible episode during the Great War, and afterwards, also, but that was a long time ago."

"No one's broken a law? How's that possible?"

"There's no need to," said Albion. "Most elves are content; and if they weren't, we'd find a way to help them. The office of imperial commerce deals with such things. The only time I've locked someone in the dungeon, was because they'd had too much to drink, and were a danger to others, including themselves. It's a rare condition, but some imperials have battle-stress, and can get a bit violent in their drink."

A city without criminals—it's a miracle! Jack thought. "Okay, but what about disputes? It got pretty heated at the council meeting, and I did get shoved in the back."

"Elves like Julius and Fergus are a drop in the ocean," said Sarina. "We'd help them if we could, but they fear the prophecy and the change it could bring."

"But still, you must get the odd dispute from time to time?"

"Yes," Albion confirmed. "Disputes happen, but they're mostly about pride and personal honour. Our lawkeepers are trained to deal with those situations. If an argument can't be resolved, then those involved are given the option of sorting out their differences in the ring of honour. It takes place in the jousting arena. Disputes are a rare spectacle, but are always followed by a handshake."

"What's a lawkeeper?" asked Jack.

"See him?" said Albion, pointing to a soldier in silver-armour.

"Yes. There were two like him outside the city gate. Then I saw two more outside the council chambers."

"Well, if you see a soldier wearing silver armour, with three green sapphires on their breastplate, then he or she is one of our lawkeepers. The three star-shaped sapphires represent our God, who gave us the seven laws."

"Can you—"

"We'll teach you our laws another time, Jack," Sarina interrupted. "We're almost at the training grounds."

"Okay, but what about the ring of honour? What happens?"

"The weapons are blunted, like the ones we use for training," said Albion. "If an elf wants a bit of ancient justice, he can face down his opponent in the ring of honour and beat it out of him. Plate-armour has to be worn, so it's quite safe. Of course—accidents do happen. But like I said, it's always followed by a handshake."

"Has anyone died?"

"No," Albion chuckled. "It's more like a battle of wills."

"What about the city?" said Jack. "It must've taken a lot of stonemasons to build it?"

"They came from a town called Zintathu," said Sarina. "Some chose to stay when construction was complete. They opened market stalls, taverns, or emporia where they could sell and trade jewellery. They've done well for themselves."

"They're still required for maintenance," Albion added, "especially after an orc-raid. It might surprise you to know that some of our best knights are former-stonemasons. We take care of our own."

Jack was glad to hear that each individual was cared for, and that alternative work was always available. "There it is, Shadar!" said the captain.

Jack looked up to see a castle of bright silver. As they approached, he could see two lawkeepers standing either side of the open archway. Passing through the open doors, Albion gave them a nod of respect. Jack could hear shouting as the cavernous archway opened up into a stone courtyard. "These are the training grounds," Albion revealed.

Dozens of elves were sparring, while others were attacking wooden statues, shaped to resemble orcs. "Stay close," said Sarina, "you don't want to get hit by mistake."

They headed towards the end of the training grounds. Jack could see a wooden door with a sign above it which read: *Imperial Armoury*. As they approached, Jack suddenly felt threatened when he locked eyes with the dark-haired elf, Julius Santorean! He was about twenty metres away, training against three other elves. Amazingly, Julius was getting the better of them. "Hey, Julius' kickin' the crap outta those guys."

Albion gave a quick glance. "Be careful around him, Shadar. He doesn't like you, and he's one of Eloria's most respected knights. He also happens to be the third greatest sword-master in the city. Don't do anything to antagonise him. Just stick with us and you'll be fine."

Who're the top two sword-masters? Jack wondered, before he was faced with another problem. Julius and his sparring partners were now staring at him as Albion and Sarina came to an abrupt halt. Jack was observing them so carefully that he almost bumped into the back of Sarina, catching the scent of vanilla as his nose touched her golden hair!

Looking back, Jack saw that Fergus Crouse, the elf who had shoved him in the back, was now standing with the rest of the group. They were all having a great laugh at his expense. Albion was having trouble with the door, so Jack was forced to stand by as Julius and the elves pointed and whispered amongst themselves. *Yeah, I know you're all talkin' about me,* Jack thought. *I feel like I'm back in high school.*

Albion finally pushed the door open. "Someone needs to look at that thing!" he said, as they went inside.

Chapter 11

LEARNING THE WAY OF THE SWORD

"Welcome to the armoury," said Sarina, as they entered the large room. Jack was expecting it to be dirty, with mud and straw covering the floor, like the armouries depicted in films. But the floor was made of beautiful greenstone, and the silver walls decorated with swords and shields. A statue which was made of white stone, possibly marble, stood in the centre of the room.

"That's amazing!" said Jack, staring at the statue.

"Read the inscription," said Albion.

It was a statue of a warrior battling a ferocious dragon. Engraved on the base was an inscription: *In honour of General Godfrey Starborne — in his victorious battle against the great Red Dragon… the beast of the West.*

"I met him at the council meeting," said Jack. "He's your father, right?"

"Yes, indeed," Albion confirmed.

"You must be very proud of him?"

"Of course!" said Albion. "It was his battle against the Red Dragon that made him famous. The Starborne name is known throughout the whole of Eloria. Our father's courage and leadership during the Great War is the stuff of legend. When the war was ended, he was made General of the imperial army."

"The Red Dragon's defeated?"

"No, Shadar," Albion chuckled. "Only when the prophecy's fulfilled will the Red Dragon be caged forever."

"Come on, Jack. It's time to start your training," said Sarina.

It was every man's childhood dream to wield a sword, yet Jack found himself daunted at the prospect of using one in battle. Albion led them towards a wooden rack full of razor-sharp swords, and Jack breathed a sigh of relief as they passed by the glistening steel. The captain stopped in front of an empty rack. "Take your pick, Shadar."

"Huh? I can't see anything."

Sarina reached into the rack and retrieved a wooden sword. Having both been made of wood—they were well-camouflaged. "Oh! I see! That's more like it! I can use one of those!" Jack exclaimed.

Albion looked at him in confusion. "Surely you didn't think we'd have you training with a real one?"

"Well, to be perfectly honest, I did. But these training swords'll suit me better!" said Jack, removing one from the rack.

He theatrically waved it around as Albion and Sarina shook their heads in amusement. "Come on," Sarina laughed, "it's time you learnt the basics."

When they entered the next room Jack saw other elves using the same wooden swords. "At least I'm not the only amateur," he smiled.

"Stay with Albion," said Sarina. "He'll teach you everything you need to know about wielding a sword. I have to go to the range and practice with my bow."

"Will I get to use a bow as well?" asked Jack.

"Once he's taught you the sword, I'll teach you the bow." Sarina then looked at her brother with a stern expression. "Don't you dare let him get hurt."

"Don't worry. I won't beat him up too much," Albion laughed.

"I'm serious, Albion," she smiled. "You know I'll get you if you do."

As soon as Sarina left the room, Albion suddenly cried, "Alright, Shadar! Show me what you're made of!"

Shit, Jack thought, *this guy's gonna break me in half!*

"Wait—stay here! I forgot something."

Albion hurried back to the other room. When he returned he was carrying a padded jacket. "What's that?" Jack curiously asked.

"It's called a gambeson," he replied. "It's very protective; this one's seen a lot of use. It might be hard to squeeze into. It was never made for a human."

"It looks a bit stretched—I think it'll fit," said Jack, before handing the captain his wooden sword.

Taking the gambeson, Jack was surprised by how light it was. He managed to pull it over his shirt and place his arms through the sleeves. It was tight, but he still had plenty of mobility. The jacket was dark-green and covered in dirt stains. It also featured leather straps, with steel buckles.

Now that he was ready Albion started to teach him the basics of sword fighting. The captain first taught him how to stand properly, then how to follow-up with a strike. He also taught him the art of counterattack, by learning to block and parry an opponent's blade. Albion was impressed by his progress.

"You're a natural, Shadar! I'm surprised you haven't used a sword before."

The hours flew by like minutes, and before Jack knew it the day was over. "I think that's enough," Albion advised. "We'll start your training again at first light. Make sure you get a good night's rest."

"What about food? My stomach's rumbling. Why didn't we stop for lunch?"

"It's my fault. Elves can go a long time without food. When we do eat, we only eat twice a day—morning and night. I'm sure there'll be some food in your quarters. I'll bring you a big breakfast in the morning."

Jack removed his gambeson and followed him back into the other room. He waited while the captain returned their training gear. After leaving the armoury, they made their way into the city streets. The atmosphere had dramatically changed. The sun was almost down and the paths were now lined with crystal lights. The city was glowing with white light! There were lampposts of silver throughout the streets and laneways, which Jack hadn't noticed in the daylight, and they gave the city a Victorian look. And like the lampposts, there were lights emanating from the windows of the buildings which clearly used the same crystal technology.

"Wow!" said Jack, seeing them reflect the silver coating of the imperial buildings. "And I thought this place looked good during the day!"

"Beautiful, isn't it?" said the captain.

Peering down a street leading northward from the armoury Jack saw something that reminded him of Mugglegruffe. It was a wooden sign, painted with a grey-bearded wizard. The figure was holding a staff and wearing a pointy blue hat, with his eyes hidden beneath the brim of his lowered head. The sign was hanging from a wooden beam attached to one of the buildings, and the words on the sign read: *The Wandering Wizard.*

"What's that place?" said Jack, pointing towards it.

"The inn of The Wandering Wizard," Albion replied. "It's a place for merchants and travellers to stay when they need a good night's rest. Elves drink there, too, but if you want a real drink, The Pluming Puffin's where we go to knock back a few. Best damn ale in the city! There's nothing like a mug of ale after a training session. I'll take you there someday, but after you've earned the respect of the knights. Outsiders aren't welcome in The Puffin—it's only for imperials."

"I don't just want the respect of the knights; I want the respect of the whole city. It's starting to get dark—what the hell?" Looking up at the night sky, Jack saw something amazing. "I've never seen so many colours!"

"Aren't there any luminaries left in your world?"

"Luminaries? You mean stars?"

"In Eloria, we call everything above the clouds luminaries," said Albion. "The sun is the greatest luminary—his name is Orjares—after the sun in your world."

"I see," said Jack. "Well, we've got stars, or luminaries as you put it, but nothin' like this. There are no colours like these, I can promise you that!"

"They're all silver, right?" said Albion.

Jack pointed to a cluster in the night sky. "The stars in my world are like those."

Albion looked disappointed. "So the tales are true... are you sure you don't have any blue or gold ones?"

"No," Jack sighed.

"What about red or green?"

"Nope."

"You at least have some purple ones?"

"Sorry, we've only got the silver ones. But I wish we had some of those..."

Jack's eyes were then drawn to a blue star of immense size. It appeared to be solitary, and was shining brighter than the others. "What's that big one?" he asked, pointing up to the large celestial body.

Albion stared at the object as if lost in a dream. "That's the blue star of the prophecy. They say that when the last Shadar appears, the blue star will fall, lighting-up the night sky with a great flash and sea of blue."

Why's he tellin' me this? Jack thought.

"Something wrong?" said the captain.

"I don't want to cause you any trouble, but can you tell me more of the prophecy?"

"I'm afraid not. I've already let my tongue slip. Don't tell anyone, okay? I wish I could answer your questions. Truly I do."

"Your secret's safe with me," said Jack, gazing up at the night sky. "Hold on, something's missing. Where's the moon?"

"We don't have one," Albion revealed. "I've read about them in the imperial library, but the blue star's been our guide for as long as I can remember. Her name is Benase, which is one of many names for the moon in your world. I've never seen a moon. They're like the blue star, only white, aren't they? My father says the moon in your world is called Erae, and that she's the same size as the blue star. I've always wanted to see her. Would you say she's the same size?"

"I think so…" Jack replied. "I've never paid much attention to it back home."

"Our worlds must be very different," said Albion.

"They sure are," Jack confirmed. "Millions of coloured stars and not a single moon—talk about ironic!"

When they reached the tower of the high council they proceeded inside; and when they arrived at the big staircase, Albion stopped. "You did well today, my friend. Make sure you get some rest. That is, if you wish to continue your training?"

"Hell yeah! It was more fun than I thought. But aren't you going up as well?" said Jack, pointing his thumb at the stairs.

"This tower's mostly reserved for council members and lawkeepers. My sister stays here because my father wants to keep an eye on her. But as a captain of the imperial army, I stay in the imperial tower, with the knights."

"Imperial tower?" said Jack. "Do the soldiers and rangers live there, too?"

"Most of the foot-soldiers live in the barracks. Only the knights and foot-soldiers that have attained a high rank stay in the imperial tower. As for rangers, well, they're just a small outfit. They don't have a place of designation."

"That means I could bump into Julius on my way upstairs? I can give him your kindest regards, if you like?" said Jack, sarcastically.

"Careful, Shadar. I've told you not to mess with him. He's greatly respected by all the knights, including my father. So keep your nose clean," Albion advised, before turning away.

"Wait! Why does your father have to keep an eye on Sarina?"

"She hasn't done anything wrong. It's just that sometimes her southern blood gets her into trouble. I don't have time to explain now. Ask me about it some other time."

"Okay. See you tomorrow," he said, before heading upstairs.

Reaching the seventh floor, Jack entered his quarters using the golden key. He then went to the kitchen to find the empty silver tray filled with food! Instead of breakfast, it now contained a plate of vegetables, a venison steak, and a side of baked potatoes. "Hang on," said Jack, "how'd this get in here? I thought I had the only key?"

It was a mystery, but that didn't stop him from consuming the delicious meal. After finishing his dinner, Jack went into his bedroom and found that someone had also made his bed. "I guess they must have housekeeping." He placed his dirty clothes in the basket on the bathroom floor, then had a quick bath and went to bed.

Jack completed the same cycle of training each day. The days soon turned into weeks, and the weeks became months. Albion would sometimes take him to the sea of grass, so he could learn to ride and fight from horseback. The council had said that Jack was to spend time with the people. Yet, each morning, he would go with Albion to the armoury and learn the way of the sword. Sarina would join them, but she also had other duties, which often kept her away.

She did keep her word, however, and gave him a personal tour of the imperial gardens. It was a lovely day. They walked arm-in-arm together as she explained the different properties of each plant, and the name of each flower. Her knowledge of all things Elorian was profound. Jack's fondness for her had grown into something stronger than friendship, and he sensed the feeling was mutual.

But whenever he tried to move close to her, Sarina would look around to see if they were being watched. Jack realised that anything other than friendship was strictly forbidden, so he kept himself occupied with his training.

Albion's constant encouragement was of tremendous value. By the end of the first month, Jack had completed the basics; a feat, which no elf had accomplished. And for almost two months Jack had been using a blunted sword and was training in the open courtyard. Julius and Fergus kept a watchful eye on his progress. But Jack still hadn't spoken a word to either of them, and was doing his best to stay out of trouble.

Chapter 12

A CHALLENGE FROM JULIUS

Almost three months of training had made Jack lean and strong. He was in the best shape of his life. He was still concerned for Mugglegruffe, who hadn't been seen or heard from since hearing about Jack's nightmare. Albion had learned from his father that Mugglegruffe did indeed go back to his cabin, but anything beyond that was speculation. Sarina said it was nothing unusual, that he would often disappear for months at a time.

Jack and Albion had become good friends. The captain would often refer to him as little brother, which didn't make sense to Jack, since the elf only looked about twenty! At the end of another hard day's training, they were about to leave the courtyard when a loud voice bellowed, "Where are you going, human?! Why don't you have a sparring session with me?"

Jack turned to see Julius standing there with a grin. Before he could reply, Albion stepped in front him. "What's wrong with you, Julius? You know he's just a squire. I'd be happy to fight you instead!"

Fergus Crouse pushed through the crowd of onlookers. "Too late, Captain! The challenge has been made. Your Shadar has to accept, or have you forgotten about law six?"

Albion looked at Jack with concern. "You're wearing plate-armour, Julius. Jack doesn't have any, so it wouldn't be a fair fight according to the laws of chivalry. Surely you wouldn't break those?"

"Relax," Julius smirked. "It's just a little sparring challenge. We'll use wooden swords if that makes you feel better? I wouldn't dare kill your chosen one."

Several onlookers began to chuckle. Albion didn't know what to do. He had promised to protect Jack, but dozens of elves were now gathering in anticipation. Jack knew there was no escape, and he didn't want to let Albion down. "Well, Captain? Is your squire going to accept or tuck his tail between his legs?" said Julius, making the elves laugh.

Albion was about to respond when a firm voice echoed across the courtyard. "Okay, Julius, I accept your challenge!"

"What are you doing?" said the captain, as Jack boldly stepped forward.

Julius's friends gave him some friendly slaps on the back, but the rest of the knights appeared to be insulted by the charade. They knew the squire didn't stand a chance, which made Julius's challenge a farce.

"You've got courage, human, I'll give you that! But for the good of this city, I'm gonna make an example out of you. And after I've left you broken, I expect to see you trudge back to that dung-heap of a world you came from."

Dung-heap? Don't elves know how to swear? Jack thought, as Fergus retrieved two sets of training weapons.

Fergus gave Julius a sword and shield, then tossed the other set at Jack's feet in a shocking display of disrespect. As Jack went to bend down a knight quickly retrieved them. The elf looked familiar as he handed him the weapons. "Thanks," said Jack.

Stepping closer, the elf whispered in his ear. "No matter what happens, remain calm. Everyone knows you can't beat him. His goal is to humiliate you. You only get to win if you keep a cool head. Don't show any signs of anger."

Jack recognised his voice. It was the elf who had taken his horse to the stables, after speaking with Mugglegruffe, the day he arrived in the city. "Thank you, Sir Tyrus," said Jack.

"Come on, Shadar, you're gonna be fine," Albion encouraged.

With butterflies dancing in his stomach, Jack focused on breathing as he stood opposite his opponent. News of the challenge spread like wildfire, hundreds of elves were pouring into the training grounds. *I feel like a gladiator!* Jack thought.

"Let's make it first to three strikes," Julius smirked.

A lawkeeper stepped out of the crowd holding a red flag attached to a wooden pole. He held it up high as the courtyard fell silent. Julius widened his stance, raising his sword and shield. "Wait—what are the rules?" said Jack.

"When I wave the flag, you try and survive!" the lawkeeper replied.

"Get ready, Shadar," said Albion.

The flag was waved and the elves began to cheer and shout! Jack kept his focus on Julius, who was now circling him, bobbing up and down in a mocking fashion. The crowd laughed again. Unexpectedly, Julius took a swipe at his head, and Jack barely got his shield up in time to stop the blow! He staggered back, but was able to stand firm.

The crowd roared with laughter as Julius wobbled his legs. "What's the matter, jelly-legs? Can't stand on your own two feet?"

Bring your face a bit closer and we'll see who gets the last laugh! Jack thought, as the elf continued to mock. Julius lowered his sword and took a step forward. Jack's moment had arrived! He knew the elf was overconfident, and seized the opportunity by charging forward. Before Julius could react, Jack delivered a powerful strike to his shoulder, knocking him to the ground! "Strike one for the human!" said the lawkeeper, as the crowd erupted in disbelief!

"I don't believe it! You got him!" Albion cried.

The elves were going crazy with excitement. The look on Julius's face turned to anger as he rotated his shoulder. Making it back to his feet, he glared at the human and came charging forward! He used his speed to outmanoeuvre the squire and strike him on the leg!

"Aaargh!" Jack gritted his teeth.

"Strike one for Sir Julius!" the lawkeeper yelled.

Looking like a silly kangaroo, Jack was forced to hop up and down a few times to shake away the pain. "Think you can take me, huh?" Julius barked.

The elf was too fast for him, but Jack didn't care. *I can't leave this courtyard with 'em thinking I'm a coward,* he thought.

With his pain subsiding, Jack gave a loud battle-cry and lunged at his opponent! But once again, Julius used his speed to side-step and hit him on the back, knocking him to the ground. "Strike two for Sir Julius!"

Jack picked himself up and took a deep breath. Julius had struck Jack's gambeson, and, to his astonishment, he didn't feel a thing. "Come on! Is this all you've got? Haven't you learned anything?" said Julius.

He attacked again, but with more self-control. Julius avoided the strike, but this time Jack blocked the elf's counterattack as the crowd went wild. Hearing their reaction, Julius became unhinged and struck out with greater ferocity! Jack was able to block his attacks; he even managed a counterattack of his own.

Back and forth they duelled! Strike after strike, block after block! The melee was endless and the crowd was lapping it up. Finally, the elf's speed was too much, and with a swift counterattack, Julius landed the final blow to Jack's arm! "Strike three, and winner of the challenge, Sir Julius Santorean!" the lawkeeper declared.

With a deep breath Jack begrudgingly extended his hand. You could have heard the sound of a pin drop as the crowd fell silent. Julius glared at him with hatred, before turning his back! The crowd booed as the elf tossed his weapons. He then stormed out of the courtyard with Fergus trailing behind.

"Well done, little brother!" cried Albion, who came out of nowhere and wrapped his arms around Jack's shoulders, giving him a bear-hug.

"I lost…"

"Who cares!" he laughed. "Didn't you hear the crowd? Not only did you knock the great Julius Santorean, right on his ass, but you gained a ton of respect! Trust me. The crowd wouldn't have shamed him, otherwise."

Surprisingly, a few of the knights approached and offered to shake Jack's hand. He tucked his sword under his arm. Each knight shook his hand and said, "Well done."

"I'll take those!" said Tyrus, taking the sword and shield. "Go get some rest—you did well for a squire. Nothing out of time."

"Thanks for your advice," said Jack.

"Don't mention it," he smiled. "You fought with courage and humility. Julius has never been shy of any courage, but he still lacks a knight's humility."

"Thanks guys!" said Albion, as the knights headed back to the armoury.

"Wow… I wasn't expecting that."

"See!" said Albion. "I said you'd earned some respect. Now, come on, let's get out of here! It's time for a drink!"

"Okay, but what did Tyrus mean when he said: nothing out of time?"

"That's the ancient war-cry of our ancestors. It means to be patient, but not lazy. And, for imperials, it means to never allow thoughts of revenge cloud our judgment. Wait for the perfect moment to strike. There's a time to plan, and a time to act—the timing must be right. It can also mean to wait for God's timing. God is all-knowing; His timing is perfect."

"I think I understand," said Jack, nodding his head. "But there's something else I've been meaning to ask."

"Then ask away."

"You said Julius was the third greatest Swordmaster, right?"

"You want to know who the first one is, don't you?" Albion smiled.

"I bet it's your father?"

"No. Believe it or not, my father's the second best. A knight by the name of Destrian Dare is the greatest," Albion revealed. "He's known as Eloria's greatest knight. And to tell you the truth, he puts the rest of us to shame."

"I'm surprised I haven't met him," said Jack.

"Destrian was sent to the fishing village of Henki. The villagers keep getting attacked by a sea monster. Fishing's their way of life. If they can't fish—they can't eat. So my father sent Destrian, along with a troop of knights to take care of it. If anyone can kill the beast, it's Eloria's greatest knight."

"He's that good, eh?"

"Are you kidding? He once took down a thirty-two-foot giant. The battle took place near the Kingdom of Stonehill, and Destrian killed it single-handedly."

"Wow, I hope I never get a challenge from him!" said Jack, as they both laughed.

"Anyway, it's time to celebrate! You've earned it after surviving your first challenge. Follow me," said Albion, as they left the training grounds.

Chapter 13

A WIZARD RETURNS

When they entered the tower of the high council Jack remembered that Albion's quarters were in the imperial tower. He was starting to wonder what the captain was up to, then Albion said, "I've arranged something special for you, my friend."

"Really?"

"You've done well these past few months, better than anyone expected, so there's a little surprise waiting for you upstairs."

They headed up the big staircase. When they reached Jack's quarters the captain stopped outside and put his finger to his lips. "Shhh... listen... can you hear anything?"

Jack placed his ear against the door. "Yes! I hear voices! How'd they get into my quarters without my key? Did housekeeping let them in?"

"They wouldn't have to. My father's got a key to every room in the tower," Albion revealed, before opening the door. "Go on, Shadar. They're waiting for you."

As they stepped inside Albion closed the door behind them. Jack followed him into the kitchen as the voices fell silent. Sitting at his dining table, was General Godfrey Starborne, Sarina, and Marshall, the Master Blacksmith.

Before Jack could speak the General rose from his chair. "We've gathered here, tonight, in honour of *you,* Shadar. My children have kept me updated on your swift progress, and I must admit—I'm impressed. The high council has also been informed about the positive effect you've had on our people."

With a slight bow, he motioned for Jack to sit beside him. Jack walked around the table, and glanced at Sarina before taking his seat. She gave him a smile. Jack was about to wink, but changed his mind as Albion approached. The captain pulled out a chair and sat beside her. Jack desperately wanted to speak to Sarina, but if the others got wind of their mutual attraction, it could prove to be troublesome.

After adjusting to the shock of Albion's surprise, Jack could now feast his eyes upon the banquet of food. There was a roasted lamb, duck, chicken, baked potato, vegetables, and several grains of bread; and at the end of the table were two barrels of wine. Lastly, Jack noticed five silver chalices around the table that were all filled to the brim. "I can't believe you've done this."

"I hope you're hungry?" the General asked.

"I don't know what to say..." said Jack. "I'm just grateful for the acceptance and kindness you've all shown me. All I can say is thank you, thank you to you all."

Albion was about to speak, then someone said, "Ah-ha! You're having a party and didn't invite me?!"

Standing by the kitchen entrance was a dwarf with a grin on his face. "Mugglegruffe!" Jack blurted out. "Where've you been?!"

Jack went to stand, but the wizard raised his hand. "Don't move, Shadar! I almost forgot something."

They remained in their seats as he went back into the lounge room. A few seconds later, they could hear a grunting noise, like someone shifting furniture. Finally, Mugglegruffe reappeared, dragging the same wooden stool he had used at the council meeting. The dwarf pushed aside one of the chairs and moved it into place. They watched with fascination as he climbed atop and wobbled around. Then, looking up with a big smile, he burst out with laughter! Like a contagious joy they immediately joined-in!

"How'd you drag that thing upstairs?" Albion cackled, spilling his wine.

"There's nothing Eloria's most powerful seer can't accomplish... as long as he puts his back into it!" Mugglegruffe chuckled.

"I was worried about you," said Jack. "Where've you been? I was startin' to wonder if you'd ever come back."

The wizard gave another hearty chuckle. "Worried about *me?* I left, because I was worried about *you.* I went back to my cabin of contemplation, where I keep my oldest books of knowledge, so I could find a way to defeat you know who."

Jack knew he was referring to the Shadow Man. Before he could ask about it, Sarina stood up. "It's nice to have you back, Mugglegruffe. But tonight's about Jack and we have a lot of celebrating to do."

"Then let the celebrations begin!" the wizard declared. "Where's my chalice? Hurry! Pour me some wine!"

They laughed at his antics while Sarina retrieved another chalice from the cupboard and filled it to the brim. "Ah! Thank you, milady!" said Mugglegruffe, taking the silver cup.

General Starborne rose again, with chalice in hand. "To our new friend and ally… Jack Campbell, the last Shadar."

"To the last Shadar!" they toasted.

They feasted and drank for several hours, telling stories of old. Stories of great battles, heroic knights, and foes they had vanquished. Marshall was now asleep in his chair, having consumed too much wine. Jack listened to the tales of courage, valour, and chivalry. Then he waited for Albion to finish telling his story about a creature in the sewer, and said, "Excuse me, General, can I ask you something?"

"Of course, you may."

"You know that statue of you fighting the Red Dragon, the one in the armoury?"

"Yes," he nodded.

"Well, I was wondering… how did you defeat the beast?"

The elf's demeanour became solemn; the kitchen was now silent. *Oh, no,* Jack thought, *I hope I haven't made a mistake.*

Leaning forward, Godfrey put down his chalice and took a deep breath. "Many dragons once dwelled in Eloria, but no foul beast was more dangerous than the Red Dragon, for he was no mere beast. He was something more terrifying. In truth, he's an ancient entity who can take many forms. The Red Dragon was to be his form when he entered our world."

"What do you mean?" asked Jack.

Godfrey became lost in thought as he laid his hands on the table. "Before your world was formed, the King of the Law created powerful beings of light. They were his company, and obeyed without question. But when he created mankind, the most beautiful of them became jealous, desiring to be equal with God. His rebellious heart blackened. He convinced man to sin, and creation itself was corrupted. He was made formless for his lies, cursed to wander the earth as a spirit, along with his followers, a third of the Angelic host. He vowed to take the King's throne of Araboth—the most beautiful world—the centre of all creation. He swore to create man in his own image. Free will was both a blessing and a curse to humanity, but the King would never forsake his children."

I've been waiting months to hear this! But who's the King of the Law? Is he the same as the High King? Jack thought, as Godfrey continued.

"Almost five hundred years later, two hundred beings of light saw how beautiful the daughters of men were, and lusted after them. They rebelled against the King and took for themselves human wives."

"They came to my world?" said Jack.

"That's right," he confirmed, "and their wives bore abominable children. Some bore the first dragons, faeries, spriggans, nymphs, and many others, but the Nephilim giants would become the most favoured. The Arabothians taught their wives the making of charms and enchantments, and taught their offspring how to make weapons. But they soon lost control of the giants they'd created, and after consuming the riches of men—they turned against them. The Nephilim defiled and devoured men and women; they even sinned against the animals, creating numerous tribes of abominations. They built kingdoms of darkness, teaching men to consume the flesh and blood of their enemies. Meanwhile, their Arabothian fathers, having the ability to assume many forms, led the nations astray into sacrificing to demons as gods."

"It must've been terrible," said Jack.

"Yes, it was," the General replied. "When the goodness of man was all but gone, the King of the Law's hand was forced; he sent a great flood to cleanse the earth of wickedness. As punishment for taking human wives, the fallen two hundred were caged in a realm of fiery darkness, to be kept there until judgement day. A realm called the Dark

Abyss. A seer foretold that every sinner—those not found in the book of life—would be cast into the lake of black fire. From that day on, the Arabothians that fell, whether formless or not, were called Abyssians, for that would be their fate. But many tribes, both good and evil, sought refuge beneath the earth, escaping the great flood."

"Then what happened?" said Jack, with much anticipation.

"Guided by the dreams and visions of a powerful seer, the elves re-emerged; and after scouring the earth for those loyal to the King of the Law, they were led to a new world, the world of Eloria. But some of those tribes, who worshipped demons as gods, sought to destroy them before they could escape the world of man, known as Midland. Eventually, the elves and dwarves made it to Eloria, but not without many sacrifices. Four years later, back in the human world, the giants emerged from their caves to continue the work of the Abyssians. They taught humans the art of dark magic. But with little resources, they were forced to battle each other for the remnants of Midland, a war which lasted many decades. By the time it was over, man had repopulated the earth; and with the covenant of the King of the Law, they were invincible! Their strength and wisdom covered the earth. Without their Abyssian fathers, the giants were outmatched and corrupted humanity from the shadows, preying on the weak. For hundreds of years they interbred with humans, teaching dark magic, just as their fathers had taught them. And again, creation was corrupted, giving rise to the orcs and trolls."

"Some of the worst..." Albion whispered.

"But the covenant of the King of the Law had made man strong enough to battle the giants and their abominable offspring. With God on their side, man could no longer be convinced to worship trees and stones, and demons as gods. Out of desperation, the giants summoned many Abyssians, including the most powerful, called Abaddon, to help them gather up an army and open a portal to Araboth, the King of the Law's heavenly realm. Abominations from all over the world answered the call to war, including orcs, trolls, goblins, ogres, dark elves, and many others. Only thing was, because the Abyssians were formless, they had to rely on the magic of giants to open the portal… and their skills were far from perfect."

"Like pouring water onto Greek fire," Mugglegruffe remarked.

"But the events that followed would be a costly mistake for them… and for us."

"Huh?" said Jack.

"You see, the Abyssians didn't know that when the earth was flooded, it splintered into seven realms. Pieces of the earth had broken away, creating an additional six, smaller worlds, one of which was Eloria. When the giants tried to open the portal to Araboth, it led them here instead. But the portal was weak. Many abominations made it through, but only a handful of smoke-demons were able to enter before it closed. Unfortunately, Abaddon had also made it through; the Abyssians were no longer bound by the formlessness placed upon them in the human world, and could once again take physical form," the General sighed.

"It's alright," said Jack, "you don't have to continue."

"No, Shadar, I must. This knowledge has been hidden from mankind for far too long."

"Thank you, Sir."

"Abaddon could take the form of anything he desired. He took the form of a winged serpent, a great Red Dragon. His army had landed in the north-west, and with the first attack on a small village… the Great War had begun. The beast then laid siege to the kingdoms of the dwarves: Ironfall and Silversmith. We tried to aid them but suffered many casualties, yet we were able to wipe out the dark elves, which caused many to defect from the Red Dragon's army, some of which were his most valuable allies. It was a small victory, but not enough to save the north. With the fall of the northern kingdoms, the Red Dragon set his sights on the Kingdom of Stonehill, a dwarf stronghold in the north-east, and Eloria's capital in the south, the Sapphire City. The Red Dragon sent his most destructive allies, the last of the Fomorian giants, to wage war against the Kingdom of Stonehill. Destrian Dare, who was a knight of Tarakona at the time, led a fearless troop of knights to aid them. Despite suffering many losses, the giants were defeated and the kingdom was saved. But the orcs were heading southward, towards the capital, with their Master flying overhead. They were carving-out a path of destruction as they burned every village, sparing no one."

"That was just the beginning of our dark times," said Mugglegruffe.

"Indeed," the General continued. "I was just a captain back then, but it was General Balinor Santorean, who led the army into battle. He was a fine general, but made the fateful decision of splitting the army in half."

"Sorry for the interruption," said Jack. "Did you say Santorean? Was he related to Julius Santorean?"

"Yes. Balinor was his father. Have you become friends with Julius?"

"No. Actually, I just lost a challenge to him," Jack replied. "He made the challenge, and I couldn't refuse. It was first to three strikes, but I only landed one."

"Oh, my God!" Sarina blurted out. "Albion! Why didn't you do something?!"

"It's alright," he replied. "They were only using wooden swords. You should've seen the crowd go nuts when Jack knocked him on his ass! I mean, he still lost, but at least the crowd was on his side by the end of it. They booed Julius out of the training grounds. He wouldn't shake hands after the challenge, so they let him have it!"

Sarina sat there in shock as Mugglegruffe began to chuckle and shake his head in amusement. "Sounds like you did well for a human! Getting one strike on Julius is more than a worthy accomplishment!"

"You should've been there, father," Albion smiled. "Tyrus Wynter and some of the others came up to him after the fight and shook his hand. He lost the challenge, but won the respect of the knights."

The General looked at Jack with a sense of pride. "You just keep surprising everyone, don't you, Shadar. I'm proud of you for holding your own. Never back down from a challenge—that's the imperial way!"

"Thank you, Sir," said Jack, "but can I hear the rest of the story?"

"Yes, where was I?"

"You'd just finished saying that General Santorean split the army in half."

"Ah, that's right," he said, taking a sip of wine. "I was given command of half the army and ordered to attack the orcs and trolls, while he led the remaining forces against the Dragon. With my knights on horseback, we charged into their defensive lines and crushed them into oblivion. Once they had fled into the wilderness we looked to re-join the main army. The General's men were being decimated by the beast—its breath was a firestorm! It would take more than strength of arms to kill a beast of such power. So, upon the advice of a wise and powerful seer, I sent what was left of my troops to aid them. Then I rode south, into the forest, seeking a reclusive dwarf."

"This's where I come into the story," said Mugglegruffe.

"Yes, and who knows what would've happened that day if I hadn't found you, my old friend," the General smiled. "When I arrived at his cabin I didn't know what to expect. You see, Mugglegruffe wasn't exactly known to us at the time. We thought of him as an unsociable eccentric. Nevertheless, his knowledge and talents were known far and wide, including the human world... once upon a time."

"You were in my world?" Jack glanced at the wizard.

Taking a swig of his wine, Mugglegruffe rolled his eyes. "I'll tell you about my adventures another time, Shadar. Let Godfrey finish the story."

Jack sensed that Mugglegruffe was hiding something but he didn't want the story to end at such a pivotal moment. "I'm sorry," he said. "Please continue."

"Never have I met such a brave dwarf," the General revealed. "He gave me a sword of magic, which held incredible power. We returned to the battlefield to find the Dragon feasting on the ashes of the dead. General Santorean had ordered the retreat; only he himself had stayed behind. He was half burnt and barely alive, but like a phoenix rising from the ashes he made one final charge at the beast. Sadly, the Dragon saw him coming; and in one fell swoop, the beast opened its jaws, snatched him up, and devoured him."

Visibly shaken, Godfrey rubbed his forehead. "I let out a cry of shame. Eloria had lost its first and greatest general. I charged down the hill, and when the Dragon came for me, Mugglegruffe used his staff to fire bolts of blue lightning from the hilltop. With the beast distracted, I used the magic sword to open a portal into the human world. In Midland, the beast would again become formless, and Eloria spared its wroth."

"I wish I could've been there, father," said Albion.

"Trust me, son, you don't," he replied. "Anyway, I picked up a spear and threw it at the beast, piercing its left eye. With a great bellow, it staggered back towards the portal. But when it realised what was happening it came for me again. It bore down and I barely escaped its jaws but was able to drive the magic sword into its wounded eye. Then I grabbed the shaft of the spear and held on for dear life as the beast raised its head, lifting me in the air! I pulled at the sword, twisting, as the Dragon roared in pain. When it finally came free, I fell to the ground. Losing its balance, the beast was cast back into the sinful world of Midland, with the portal closing behind it."

With a deep sigh, Godfrey leaned back in his chair. "With Mugglegruffe's aid I was able to save Eloria. But the real heroes died on the battlefield, along with the greatest hero—Balinor Santorean. Their names are inscribed on a wall of honour inside the hall of the dead. There's also a mural of the battle, and a statue of Balinor's last stand. We only enter that hallowed place to remember our history, so that we do not repeat it. By the evil works of the Red Dragon, humans lost their precious gift. Now the world of Midland's become a dwelling place for demons. Darkness has slithered back into the hearts of humanity. The scales of justice are unbalanced, but all things must come to pass…"

Mugglegruffe raised his chalice. "To our dead!"

Everyone held up their chalices, except for Marshall, who was still asleep in his chair. "To our dead," they solemnly toasted.

"Thanks for telling the story," said Jack. "I know it must've been difficult."

Without taking his eyes off Marshall, Godfrey nodded his head. He then reached over, grabbed the elf's shirt, and shook him awake. Marshall sat up with a glassy look in his eye. "I-Is the party over?" he choked.

"It's time for you to present our gift to the guest of honour," Godfrey demanded.

"Oh," said the elf, "please forgive my rudeness! I've consumed too much wine."

The General rose from his chair as the others followed suite. Albion went to Marshall's aid, who was struggling to stand on his own two feet. When they entered the lounge room, Jack noticed a sheet of blue silk covering something on the table. "It's now... m-my distinction... to bestow... this," said Marshall, wobbling back and forth.

"Sit down, you fool! Or you'll do yourself some damage!" Albion laughed.

Marshall sat in one of the lounge chairs and appeared to instantly pass out. Godfrey shook his head in frustration. He then walked up and pulled away the sheet, revealing a suit of blue armour. "This's our gift to you, Shadar."

"Wow! It's the best uniform I've ever seen!" said Jack, stepping forward.

It was royal-blue, and the armour was shining in the light. On the breastplate of the cuirass, complete with tassets, was a white tribal design situated around the head of a white wolf, featuring blue sapphires for the eyes. In fact, there were blue sapphires on every piece of the armour. *It's like a functional piece of art,* he thought.

Included with the cuirass was a matching set of blue greaves and bracers, both of which had the same tribal design. The shoulder-pauldrons, too, were blue, and shaped like the head of a wolf. There was also a lighter-blue, sapphire-studded belt, with an attached blue scabbard; a royal-blue gambeson with a matching set of blue clothes, and a pair of blue, leather-boots. There was even a pair of blue, steel-plated gloves, in the form of gauntlets. Lastly, there was a chainmail shirt and matching pair of pants to complete the set.

"I don't know what to say…" said Jack. "I have no words."

"You don't have to say anything," said Sarina.

Jack looked at the faces around the room. "I'm just so grateful for everything."

Unexpectedly, Marshall leapt out of his chair as if awoken from a dream! He stumbled forward to see his creation. "I haven't had time to make you a helmet or shield, but I'll finish them soon enough. The steel has to be thicker. You humans have such big bones! That means it takes longer to make," said the blacksmith, struggling to stand.

"Don't worry, I'll take good care of it," said Jack. "You've done an amazing job. You truly are a Master Blacksmith."

Taking a hold of Marshall's shoulders, Albion gently directed him back to the lounge chair. "Here, take another nap."

Marshall plopped down and closed his eyes as Sarina opened the draw of a small table by the lounge. She removed a folded blue cloth and approached Jack with her arms held out. "This is from me," she smiled. "I made it myself, so I hope you like it."

Jack unravelled the cloth to reveal a triangular-shaped blue flag, with gold trim around the edges, and the head of a white wolf in the centre. "It's your banner," she revealed. "If you ever become a knight, these will be your House colours to fly with Elorian pride!"

She must've sewn it by hand! I wish I had something to give in return, Jack thought.

"Well? Do you like it?"

"Are you kidding?" I'll cherish it always! Thank you, Sarina."

Mugglegruffe examined the armour. "Wait a minute, something's not right. Something's missing…"

"What do you mean?" said Jack.

The wizard reached into his robe and magically produced a sword. "You can't go walking around in armour without a sword!"

With the blade resting on the dwarf's tiny palms he graciously presented it. "I told you I had to figure out a way to defeat the Shadow Man, and that sword is the answer!"

Examining it closely, Jack was amazed by how light it was. It was a hand and a half sword with a silver cross-guard shaped like the heads of two wolves, positioned back to back, facing away from the double-edged blade. The pommel was bronze, and also shaped like the head of a wolf, with two blue sapphires for the eyes.

The blade was razor sharp, but quite distinct from an elvish one. It seemed to have been reforged from an older blade, giving it a beautiful Damascus pattern. The fittings had clearly been made to match the armour, yet Jack sensed something unusual about the weapon. "I don't know why, but this sword feels like it came from some distant age that's long been forgotten. I've seen a lot of blades these past few months, but nothing like this. Isn't Damascus steel more common in my world?"

"The origin of the steel makes no difference," said Mugglegruffe.

"Then how's it gonna help me defeat the Shadow Man?"

With a gleam in his eye the wizard smiled at him. "Oh, I think I know what's goin' on," said Jack. "Is this sword magic?"

"Indeed," Mugglegruffe chuckled. "It was given to me long ago, by a seer of the human world, who once counselled a great king. Do you remember the second blessing the faerie queen gave you?"

"A gift of protection," said Jack. "Dark magic can't be used against me."

"Exactly! The blade of that sword was forged to repel dark magic. If the sorcerer tries to cast magic on you, he'll wish he hadn't! The power of that sword will repel his sorcery, and you'll be protected. You wouldn't stand in the path of a forest fire when facing a strong wind! It should give you the time you need to land a killing blow. Decapitation's the only way to kill the father of shadow demons; that's what the books say. Even one as powerful as the Shadow Man has a weakness. With his magic useless, he'll have to resort to unarmed combat. But with that sword and the faerie queen's blessing, you shall prevail."

"Um... okay, but what about his talons?"

"Don't worry, you'll be fine. You've got armour and he doesn't—simple!"

Has this dwarf gone mad or is he pulling my leg? Jack thought.

"You alright, Shadar?" Albion asked. "You look a bit pale."

"Well, I'd rather leave the fighting to powerful wizards. But if I'm forced to fight him, I'll send him back to the human world!" said Jack, holding up the sword.

Everyone clapped, except for Marshall, who was still asleep in the lounge chair. "Alright, alright, it's getting late," said Godfrey, "and we've got another big day tomorrow. I think we'd best call it a night."

As they began to leave, Godfrey noticed that Mugglegruffe was struggling to drag his wooden stool. "Give it here, then," he said, taking it from him.

"Why, thank you, Godfrey, but I could've done it myself, you know," the wizard chuckled, as they headed out the door.

Albion wasn't far behind. Jack struggled not to laugh when he saw him carrying Marshall over his shoulder. "Need a hand?"

The captain smiled as he stepped into the hallway. "Oh! I almost forgot," said Albion. "Stay here in the morning. I'll come up and help you with your armour. You won't be able to put it on by yourself."

"Okay, thanks."

With Albion carrying Marshall away, Jack noticed that Sarina was going to be last to leave. She walked up and kissed him on the cheek. "It almost feels like you're one of us, Jack Campbell."

"I'm still only human, Sarina, but if I could choose any life, it'd be one with you."

Struggling not to blush, she left his quarters as Jack closed the door behind her. He then went into the kitchen and filled his chalice with wine. "Here's to you, Sarina Starborne, the only woman I want, but can probably never have."

Jack sighed and shook his head. "If I could choose any life, it'd be one with you... what the hell was I thinking?!"

It was too late to take back his words. But somewhere deep within his soul, Jack was glad to have said them. He took his new clothes back to his bedroom and stowed them in his wardrobe. That night, as he slowly drifted away, Jack wished for the first time that he could stay in Eloria forever.

Chapter 14

THE SHADOW MAN

Jack awoke the next morning to a pounding hangover. Sitting on the edge of his bed, he heard someone enter his quarters. A moment later, Albion appeared in the bedroom doorway, ready to put him through another hard day's training.

"What are you still doing in bed? How many wines did you have last night? You need a bath!" coughed the captain, covering his nose.

Albion placed Jack's arm over his shoulder and lifted him off the bed, then carried him into the bathroom. "You drank too much, didn't you? Elorian wine's pretty strong, you know. You might want to stick to ale in the future."

When Jack managed to stand on his own two feet he realised that Albion was still in the bathroom. "Albion, don't take this the wrong way, but I can manage on my own."

"Alright, little brother," the captain laughed. "I'll be in the lounge room. Just give me a shout when you're ready."

"No worries."

After taking a quick bath, Jack opened his wardrobe to find a blue coat with the head of a white wolf in the centre. "Albion, come 'ere a sec!"

"You ready?" said the captain, entering the room. Albion saw that Jack was wearing his bath robe, and was standing by the wardrobe. "What are you doing?"

"Before I went to bed last night, this wasn't in my wardrobe," said Jack, tossing him the coat. "And as far as I know, I don't sleepwalk. So how'd it get in here?"

Albion carefully examined it. "Oh, this's your surcoat. Sarina was supposed to give it to you last night. She must've forgotten. That means she came back during the night…"

"Are you sayin' she came back while I was asleep?"

Albion looked at him suspiciously; Jack knew what he was thinking. "Whoa—wait a minute! I didn't even know about this! That's why I called you in here!"

"It's alright," he replied. "Sarina likes to sneak around at night. It's got something to do with her ranger training. One time, she got really mad at me—angry-troll mad. She snuck into my quarters and stole my clothes. I had to walk around in my bed robe!"

"That's pretty funny," Jack laughed.

"I told you she had too much southern blood. Fortunately, I didn't inherit those traits, but she certainly did."

"Oh, yeah, I forgot to ask about that," said Jack. "What exactly is it?"

"Well, our father's a northerner, but our mother was a southerner. Southern elves are wilder than their northern cousins, preferring to live in forests. They have a deep desire for adventure, and can't remain in one place for too long. Luckily, she's only half a southerner. But my father worries that one day her southern instincts will kick-in, and she'll run off with the wildwood rangers."

"Who're they?"

"They guard the border to the Forbidden Lands. It begins at Darkwood Forest and stretches up to the far north, near Glacier Pass. They look the same as us but can't stand towns or cities for long. Sarina's the only imperial ranger to have passed their training course. They're fast and agile, experts with a bow. They can also hunt, track, and walk through a forest without making a sound. They're closer to nature than we'll ever be. Most of the orcs they've killed never heard the sound of the arrow until it pierced their heart."

"Do you think Sarina'll disappear?"

"I hope not—I'd miss her too much," said Albion, placing Jack's surcoat onto the bed. "Now, hurry up! We're running late again as usual."

Once the elf was gone, Jack put on his blue clothes and went into the lounge-room. Albion started to help him with his new armour. "How do I become knight?" said Jack.

"You don't even know how to joust! It takes more than skill with a sword to become an Elorian knight. You must be battle-hardened just to be eligible."

"Battle-hardened?" said Jack.

"I'm talking about combat experience. The only danger you've faced was a sparring challenge from Julius. To be a knight, you must survive a real battle, against real foes. You're definitely not ready for that. Remember: nothing out of time. Your time will come soon enough, just be patient."

It took roughly ten minutes to get the armour on. Despite being a bit heavy, Jack didn't think it would affect his mobility. "It's truly the work of a Master Blacksmith. How'd Marshall get the paint so shiny?"

"There isn't a drop of paint on the armour. That's the colour of the gemstone he added to the steel," Albion revealed.

"What? That doesn't make any sense. How can steel be blue, or white for that matter? It's impossible," Jack questioned.

"It depends on which gemstone he uses in the forging process."

"Huh?"

"Most of the gemstones in Eloria have been exposed to firestone, giving them magical properties," Albion began to explain. "They're crushed into a fine powder, then combined with charcoal, before being added to the crucible. Think of them as a form of dye."

"Look, I've accepted a lot of crazy things in this world, but you can't possibly expect me to believe this nonsense. You're describing a form of alchemy, and alchemy's just a fancy word for chemistry. If what you say is true, then how do you explain the white wolf and tribal designs? They're white, not blue. You can't put two colours in the same steel."

"They're two separate steels. Marshall forges them individually using a layering method. Once he's created the design, the steels are re-heated and hammered onto the base layer. He continues this process until the steels become one. After the quench, they'll be one piece; he based the design of your armour on the snow wolves that live in the north."

"Hey, that's right. When Marshall asked me those questions you said the snow wolf was a powerful animal. I wish I could see one. What's firestone?"

"Never mind—we're running late. At least you look like a knight," said Albion, with a sense of pride. "Of course, if you need mobility, you can always wear the chainmail and surcoat without the armour. It's a good option if you're going into a situation that requires quick manoeuvring. Then again, Marshall's blend of Álfur Stál was made especially for you. You'll have to figure out what works best."

"What's Álfur Stál?"

"They're words from our native language. Roughly translated, it means Elf Steel. Oh, we forgot your sword!"

The captain sheathed the sword and showed him how to tie the belt around his waist. With his armour complete, Jack was feeling ten feet tall and bulletproof. *This's weird,* he thought, *I feel like I'm back in my security uniform.*

They left his quarters, made their way downstairs, and left the tower of the high council. As they were heading towards the training grounds they heard screaming in the distance! Albion's eyes widened as Julius and several knights came running towards them. "What is it?!" the captain yelled, as they ran to meet them.

"Orcs and trolls are attacking the village of the silver bridge!" Julius cried. "The horses are asleep and we can't wake them—there's sorcery at work! We can't take down trolls without cavalry! Where's the General?!"

"Calm down! Give me a second to think!" said Albion, before he turned to Jack. "Get back to the tower and tell my father! Tell him we've got no horses and are gathering reinforcements. We'll meet him at the silver bridge!"

"Okay," Jack replied.

Running towards the tower as fast as he could, Jack glanced back to see hundreds of elves pouring out of the training grounds. Albion and Julius appeared to be joining them as they charged towards the city gate. Jack was aware of the carnage that orcs and trolls could inflict; every second was going to count.

When Jack reached the tower he ran inside. "Orcs and trolls are attacking the village of the silver bridge!" he cried.

Several lawkeepers raced out of the tower. As he reached the end of the hallway, Jack went straight into the hall of the great tree. *Sarina! Oh, thank God she's safe!* he thought.

Sarina and her father were standing in the centre of the room, talking to the old elf in the green robe, who was also a member of the high council. Jack wasn't used to the weight of his armour and was struggling to catch his breath. "General!" he cried.

They knew something was wrong. He was about to speak, then they heard the sound of a horn blowing. "The horn of war!" Sarina gasped. "The city's under attack!"

"What's happened?!" said Godfrey.

"Orcs and trolls are attacking the village of the silver bridge. Albion and Julius went to gather reinforcements, but Julius said the horses were asleep and couldn't be woken. Then he said something about sorcery. Albion wants you to meet him at the silver bridge."

"I must go!" said the General, turning to the old elf. "Professor Hobblestone, make sure we have enough medicine on standby. Without horses, I fear hundreds may be wounded."

Like a flash of lightning, Godfrey raced out of the room with Jack and Sarina in tow. As they were running down the hall of shields, Sarina said, "What about the horn, father?"

"We don't have time to worry about that!"

"What is it?" said Jack, trying to keep up.

"The horn of war's never been late," Sarina replied. "Someone, or something, must've taken-out the guard."

They hurried out of the tower and made their way into the streets. Jack had never seen them so empty. "Stop!" Sarina cried, as she came to a halt. Stopping late, they turned towards her. "Something isn't right! This feels like a—" her eyes widened with terror, "—trap..."

Sarina raised her arm, pointing to something in their path. Jack and Godfrey glanced at each other, then faced forward. Standing in front them was the dark figure. It was the Shadow Man! The demon sorcerer —Barbatus! He was about forty feet away, shrouded in black smoke. His eyes were glowing red and his black talons were at the ready. Suddenly, the demon let out the most evil laugh they'd ever heard, "Aaarghhahahahaha!"

Without thinking, Jack drew his sword and marched towards his enemy. "No, Shadar!" the General shouted.

Unfazed, Jack walked towards the demon. "No!" Sarina cried, stepping forward as the General quickly grabbed her.

Sarina once said she was ready to die for him, but Jack wasn't going to let her. He stopped about twenty feet away from the demon, who was smiling with glee as red light emanated from his mouth. "I know who you are, Barbatus!" Jack growled. "And I'm not gonna let my friends die for me. It's *me* you want, so here I am!"

The demon stared back at him with the same menacing smile. Barbatus was toying with him, but Jack didn't have time for a stand-off. Albion was out there and needed his help. "You wanna kill the last Shadar? Now's your chance!" he yelled, raising his sword. "Come on! What're you waitin' for?!"

"Aaarghhahahahaha!" the demon cackled, before gazing over Jack's shoulder.

He's not here for me! Jack realised. "Sarina, get your father out of here!"

"What are you talking about?!"

"He was sent by the Red Dragon to kill your father! He was never here for me! Your father's the one he wants!"

"I made you a promise, Jack! You cannot die!"

"Don't you get it? The horn of war was late! Someone's helping this bastard, one of our own! You have to find the traitor!" he warned. "This whole thing's a setup! Get to the village! Albion needs you both!"

Barbatus continued to cackle as they tried to make sense of his words. The General knew the horn was late for a reason, but couldn't imagine an elf being responsible. "You can't fight this enemy alone!" said Godfrey. "My son can handle what's out there!"

"I've only had three months training," said Jack, "but neither of you stands a chance! I think you're forgetting that I have something you don't!"

"What is this madness?!" Godfrey shouted."

"Have you forgotten about the blessings? Don't you remember Mugglegruffe's words?" said Jack, holding up his blade. "The knights are horseless! There're families with children out there, they need your help! Do you really wanna keep arguing about this?!"

Gritting his teeth, Godfrey remembered that Jack was protected from dark magic. So he reluctantly gave him a nod as Sarina looked at her father with tears in her eyes. She then stared at Jack, who was about to fight the demon alone.

"No!" she cried, drawing one of her daggers as she stepped forward. But the General grabbed her once again before she could run to his aid. "I made you a promise!" she screamed, with tears rolling down her face. "You can't die!" she wailed, as Godfrey tightened his arms around her, pulling her away.

"Send him to hell, Shadar!" the General cried.

With Sarina and the General gone, Jack tried to focus on Barbatus, but after witnessing Sarina's reaction, he was comforted by a feeling of peace. *I didn't know she cared so much,* he thought. *What's death compared to love?*

Barbatus stepped forward, seemingly amused. "Clever, little Shadar!" he scowled. "Think you can save Godfrey from my wroth? For meddling in my affairs I'd normally grant you a slow and painful death, but since time is of the essence—I'll finish you quickly!"

Jack readied his sword, waiting for the demon to use magic. The Shadow Man let out a high-pitched scream, causing Jack's body to tremble! Then he held up his taloned hands and began to conjure red fire. In a swift burst, the demon let out another shriek, casting an inferno of red flames! Jack was covered in fire! At first, he thought he was being burned alive as the fire engulfed him. *Wait—I feel no pain— the blessing's worked!*

The flames disappeared as Barbatus roared in frustration. "Well, well, well, the little Shadar's protected by magic, I see! Guess I'll have to finish you the old-fashioned way… by tearing you apart!"

With a deafening scream, the demon charged forward, its taloned-fingers outstretched! It was like Jack's nightmare, but this time he couldn't run! He charged at Barbatus with his sword held high, bringing it down upon the demon's head in a slashing motion. With supernatural reflexes, Barbatus dodged the strike and slashed at Jack's throat! Amazingly, he was able to block the attack using his arm as a shield.

The blow struck his bracer! There were scratches on the steel from the demon's talons. Jack slashed at his opponent but failed to land a single blow! The Shadow Man tried to attack his face, which wasn't protected by armour. Jack parried away the demon's hands, with the creature's talons barely missing his vulnerable throat.

Despite the parry, the demon was unharmed as he retreated backwards. Jack felt that he was gaining the upper hand. He continued to charge, slashing wildly as he tried to land a killing blow. In doing so, however, Jack had left himself open to attack. It was like leading a lamb to the slaughter. Barbatus drew him closer and closer, lulling him into a false sense of security. Then, with a sudden burst of speed, he struck Jack in the chest with such force that it knocked him to the ground! As he hit the white stone, Jack's sword fell from his grasp and slid away, stopping several feet out of reach!

Before he could get up, Barbatus screamed with glee and jumped on top of him! The demon's claws were aimed at his vulnerable throat, but Jack was able to grab a hold of his wrists, preventing his attack. With his heart pounding, Jack struggled to keep the demon at bay. He had to get his sword, but it was too far away.

"Ahahahaha!" Barbatus cackled. "Come on, little Jacky! Let me get under your skin! I just wanna bathe in your blood! I'll take you to my black forest! Hahahaha!"

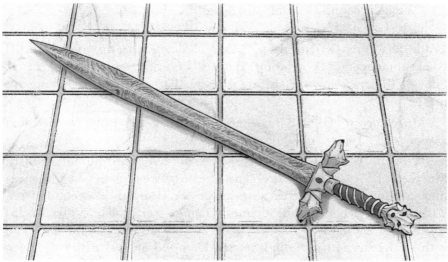

Jack couldn't hold on forever. "Time to die now, little Shadar! Don't worry, this's just a dream! When you wake up, you'll be back in your own world, where you can live out your pathetic, pointless existence!"

He's actually enjoying this! Jack thought.

Barbatus opened his mouth, blinding Jack with red light! He could barely see, and the demon's teeth were edging closer. Jack was centimetres away from having his throat torn out! He tried to squint through the blinding light, but it was useless. Suddenly, Jack heard a clap of thunder as a bolt of blue lightning struck the demon's head, throwing him off! "It may be a good day to die, Shadar, but you'll not die on this day!"

Rubbing his eyes, Jack looked across the ground to see Mugglegruffe standing there with his staff! The wizard looked down at him. "Get up! Get your sword!" he cried, as Barbatus continued to writhe in pain.

Jack scrambled across the floor and retrieved his weapon. As he tried to stand, however, a tearing pain was felt along his ribcage. He was struggling to breathe. "Damn! I think my ribs are cracked!" he coughed.

"What's wrong?! Get up!" Mugglegruffe shouted.

Jack looked around; the demon had now recovered. He felt helpless as the Shadow Man stood up, "Aaargh! I'm gonna rip your head off your shoulders and shove-it up your ass! You ruined my master's plans, but you'll never stop me! Eloria's destined to be mine! It belongs to me!"

Mugglegruffe readied his staff. "Failure's the only destiny that awaits you!"

With a great roar, Barbatus casted red fire! Simultaneously, Mugglegruffe casted blue fire! The streams met together in the air as they continued to cast, trying to out-power each other! Seconds later, Barbatus was laughing; the demon's flames were pushing the wizard back. With Barbatus distracted, Jack circled around behind him, and with all the strength he could muster, he stood up and struck the back of the demon's neck, "Aaargh!"

His cast was broken! Mugglegruffe's flames were flying towards them! Jack dropped to the ground and covered his head as the blue flames engulfed the demon. Covered in fire, Barbatus stumbled back, tripping over him as the wizard stopped casting. Jack forced himself to stand as Mugglegruffe slumped to the ground in exhaustion. Jack limped towards him, but despite his best efforts he had failed to cut off the demon's head. As Mugglegruffe raised his head off the ground, something caught his eye. "Get down!"

Jack kissed the ground as red flames flew over his head. Mugglegruffe, too, was forced to roll to the side, barely avoiding them! Without thinking, Jack stood up into the flames. The dwarf had forgotten that because of the faerie queen's blessing, dark magic had no effect on him. Fortunately, it'd also slipped Barbatus's mind. Jack stood inside the flames, glaring back at the demon, who was screaming in frustration. He then raised his sword into the fire, holding it in front of him. He watched as the blade turned red, absorbing the magic that was being cast; and, raising his sword high, Jack brought the blade down with the tip aimed directly at the fiend. Suddenly, the red flames turned blue as they backfired on the demon, engulfing him, like a raging inferno!

Barbatus screamed as he burned with blue fire! Falling to the ground, he began to cackle until his body was nothing but ash. All that remained was his laughing skull and red glowing eyes, staring up at Jack. A moment later, the last remnants crumbled to dust as the flames evaporated.

Jack collapsed in agony. Leaving his sword he crawled towards Mugglegruffe. The wizard was exhausted from the battle but managed to sit up as he approached. "Are you alright, Shadar?"

"I can breathe again, but my ribs are bloody killin' me!"

"What did you think you were doing, fighting him alone?"

"You saved my life," said Jack. "You saved me, like you saved the General when he fought the Red Dragon."

Mugglegruffe looked at him in disbelief. "No, Shadar. It was you who saved me! If it weren't for your courage, we'd both be dead. You truly are the chosen one."

Jack cried in pain as he forced himself to stand. "And just where do you think you're going?" the dwarf asked.

"You don't know, do you?" said Jack. "Orcs and trolls are attacking the village of the silver bridge. Albion gathered reinforcements—I must go."

Struggling to get up, Jack helped the wizard to his feet until he could lean on his staff. "You can't come, my friend. You can barely stand. Anyway, I need you to find out why the horn of war was late. Barbatus came to kill Godfrey, so I sent him away with Sarina. They'd be at the village by now."

Mugglegruffe looked confused. "You'll need my help! I may be tired, but I'm more than capable of blasting a few trolls."

"Don't worry. I'll be fine."

"You don't know what you're up against!" he cried. "What you just did was short of miraculous, but you've never faced orcs or trolls before. Trolls are an even greater threat to you than Barbatus. They don't need magic to kill you. A punch from an angry troll can cave the skull of an elf!"

"Look, Sarina might be out there!" said Jack. "I'm going no matter what you say, but someone must've let Barbatus into the city. Someone's betrayed us."

"Alright, Shadar. Since I can't stop you from going back into the fray, I'll investigate the matter. Just be careful out there. Don't take any chances!"

"No worries," said Jack, retrieving his sword.

Leaning on his staff, Mugglegruffe headed towards the southern watchtowers as Jack made his way through the rest of the city. Albion was like a brother to him, and Jack didn't think he'd be safe with Julius watching his back.

Chapter 15

THE SILVER BRIDGE

As he got closer to the entrance, Jack could hear the cries of battle and the clashing of steel in the distance, but the entrance gate appeared to be locked. He approached the wooden doors and was shocked to find the guards dead!

Jack could hear women and children banging on the other side. Someone had murdered the guards and locked the villagers out to be slaughtered. "They've been stabbed! Barbatus didn't do this!" he said to himself.

The doors were secured by a large crossbeam. It was designed to be removed by two elves, but the screaming voices gave him a sense of urgency. With a cry of pain, Jack removed the crossbeam as the doors burst open, knocking him to the ground. "What happened? Who locked you out?!" he shouted, as the elves ran past with children in their arms. "There were kids out there! What kind of sick bastard—"

Jack picked himself up and limped through the entrance gate towards the silver bridge. He came upon dozens of bodies, elves and orcs, littering the ground in a bloody mess. They were mangled beyond recognition and the stench was indescribable! Plumes of smoke were rising in the distance, in the direction of the village. After navigating his way through the broken heap, Jack noticed a figure in the distance. Someone was standing in the middle of the silver bridge holding a sword. As he got closer Jack recognised him. "Marshall!" he cried.

Seeing the human's limp, the blacksmith rushed to his aid. "What happened? Did you kill the traitor?"

"I didn't see anyone," said Jack. "Mugglegruffe and I barely survived Barbatus. I came to help, but the entrance was locked. Someone murdered the guards."

"You fought the Shadow Man?! Is he dead?"

"Yes, but who killed the guards and locked everyone out?"

"It was the traitor!" Marshall replied. "The orcs found the secret ford to cross the river and cut the villagers off from the city. It was a massacre until reinforcements arrived. The knights drew them away, then someone locked the gate. I didn't see who did it, but Julius went back inside. I heard him say something to Albion about finding horses."

"Why're you just standing here? Why aren't you out there fighting with the others?" Jack questioned.

"I *was* fighting with them—I'm not a coward! Albion sent me back, along with half a dozen foot-soldiers, to protect the village."

"Foot soldiers?" said Jack, looking around.

"I think they're dead," the elf sighed. "I would've heard back by now if they were still alive. Some of the orcs defected from the main battle and flanked the village. I was the last line of defence, but the foot-soldiers kept them at bay."

"Where's Albion?"

"He's still out there."

"Okay. You stay here, like Albion ordered. Don't let any orcs or trolls get past," said Jack, before limping across the bridge.

"Wait! I can't stop a troll by myself!" Marshall yelled. "You're hurt! There're too many orcs! It's suicide!"

Ignoring his pleas, Jack crossed the silver bridge and started to make his way through the village. Several homes had been torched by orcs and were burning out of control. Jack's nose was hit with the stench of corpses. He came upon more bodies and was starting to feel queasy. Then, to Jack's ultimate horror, he came upon the bodies of innocent children; and, most disturbingly, they were partially eaten. "Those bloody savages! I swear I'm gonna kill every one of 'em!" he growled.

The cries of the battle were getting louder. Jack desperately wanted to run towards them, but the faster he moved—the harder it was to breathe. He was then taken aback when he came upon the body of a troll. It was at least eight feet tall! Its muscles were gigantic, and its features resembled a silverback gorilla. Just the creature's head was almost the size of Jack's torso! He hurried past, and it wasn't long until he found himself closer to the front of the village, bordering the sea of grass.

The sounds of the battle were getting further away. The imperials had driven their enemies into the rolling hills, keeping them away from the village. As Jack was nearing the border, something caught his eye. He watched in disbelief as a grey and bloodied figure rose from the dead—it was an orc! It was bleeding profusely from a wound on its leg. When it saw Jack, the creature suddenly picked up an axe. "Human meat!" the orc cried, as it came stumbling towards him.

As the creature swung, Jack parried the axe and struck the orc's neck, severing its head! A spray of blood hit his face as the orc's headless body fell to the ground. Examining the corpse, its forehead was painted with three yellow stripes. The same stripes were also painted on every piece of its leather armour. "Son of a bitch was fearless!" Jack stammered.

He wiped his cheek and saw a red stain in the palm of his gauntlet. For some reason, despite having seen numerous dead orcs, he expected its blood to be green. But orcs bled the same as any other mammal. He made his way up a large hill and entered the sea of grass, listening intently as he tried to locate the battle. Situated less than two kilometres from the village, Jack saw it taking place. It wasn't a battle—it was a war!

There were thousands of elves, clashing with thousands of orcs, and spread throughout the field, were at least ten trolls. He pushed towards the battlefield, but Jack was still limping and struggling to breathe. Fighting off the pain, he charged into the ranks of the enemy with a loud battle-cry, landing blow after blow! Each swing of his sword was a tremendous effort as he stabbed and slashed at every orc in sight. After killing several of the foul creatures, Jack's face and armour had turned crimson red. When the elves noticed his presence they shouted with pride. "The Shadar's with us!"

With the chosen one fighting by their side, the elves received a boost of confidence as the battle turned in their favour. Orcs were being massacred left and right, but the trolls were still decimating the elven ranks. The orcs quickly retreated behind them; the trolls were now on the frontline. Without thinking, Jack charged towards them. "Don't stop! Don't give these bastards a moment's rest!"

Rallying to his cries the elves charged into the beasts. They swarmed them, attacking from all sides, while the rest pushed forward to attack the orcs. The imperial rangers fired arrows at the heads of the trolls, keeping them distracted while the knights targeted their vulnerable legs. The orcs were separated from the trolls, which were being engulfed by a sea of armoured elves. Despite the superior numbers, the trolls were still wreaking havoc; Jack now understood why the knights needed the strength and speed of their horses.

With the knights and foot-soldiers battling the behemoths, the archers picked their targets, trying to land a killing blow. The trolls were slowly succumbing to the overwhelming odds. Several minutes later, the skills of the imperial rangers had taken down four of them. Without the trolls, the orcs didn't stand a chance. They pushed forward, and it wasn't long until the battle became neck and neck once more.

As the orcs pushed them back, one of the trolls came stomping towards Jack. It was almost eight-feet tall and was holding a giant mace! Jack was in no condition to fight the beast one on one, but there was no escape. *What the hell am I doing?* he thought, standing his ground. *I'm just a security guard!*

He readied his sword as the beast tore through the elven ranks, swatting them with its giant mace! Suddenly, an elf pushed him out of the way and threw a spear into the troll's stomach. Jack picked himself up and was shocked to see Albion! "You shouldn't be here, little brother! Where's my father? Did you tell him where to meet us?"

Unbeknownst to the captain, the troll had pulled the spear from its stomach and was charging towards him. "Look out!" Jack cried.

Albion raised his sword as the beast struck the side of his arm with its giant mace, knocking him down. Standing over its prey, the troll was about to crush him. But Jack quickly ran up and drove his sword into the creature's back. He pierced through its leather amour, ripping its flesh as the beast roared in pain. Turning around, the troll smacked him in the face with its giant hand, "Aaargh!" Jack fell to the ground.

Shaking, he touched his face with his gloved hand. Blood was gushing from a broken nose, and a cut above his left eyebrow. The beast had struck him with such force that Jack had been thrown several feet away! The pain in his ribs was unbearable as his body surged with adrenaline. Albion was still lying on the ground, clutching his arm in pain. Once again, the troll turned its attention to Jack.

Despite the hard knock, Jack had somehow managed to hang on to his sword. Using it as a crutch, he mustered the strength to stand. As the beast came for him, several arrows pierced its left arm and shoulder. Somewhere, the imperial rangers were trying to take it down, but the arrows seemed to have little effect. "Come on, ya big bastard!" Jack cried.

With a great bellow, the beast swung its mace at Jack's head. He avoided the strike, and followed-up with a counterattack, by slashing the troll's arm. The beast roared in pain as his blade went through its flesh like butter, creating a deep wound! Enraged, the troll swung its mace, wildly. Jack was able to avoid the heavier strikes, but each time he was forced to block, shockwaves were sent running through his sword.

Jack was amazed by his sword's ability to take such abuse. His arms rattled with each new strike; he couldn't hold on forever. As the troll was bringing its mace down for another blow, it suddenly dropped its weapon and yelped! Jack didn't know what had happened, but taking advantage, he slashed at the troll's legs, which weren't protected by armour. The beast fell to its knees, giving him the opportunity to land a killing blow, and Jack didn't hesitate to violently slash its throat!

With a loud groan, the beast fell on its face with a tremendous thud! Jack saw Albion's sword buried in the troll's back, and when he saw the captain standing behind the corpse, he retrieved it for him. "Nice job!"

"You're either brave or just plain mad, Shadar!" the captain remarked, as Jack kindly returned his weapon. "Come on! Let's finish this!"

Albion pushed forward with the rest of the elves, and it wasn't long until they heard the sound of thundering, followed by the blow of a trumpet! The elves looked back and erupted with cheers! Jack stood on top of the dead troll to see what was happening. It was General Starborne! He was riding a beautiful white horse with hundreds following behind. "My brave knights! Gather yourselves! Join with me!" Godfrey cried, as the elves ran and jumped onto the passing horses with incredible timing.

Jack desperately wanted to join them, but he didn't have the speed or agility to jump onto the back of a running horse. His breathing was becoming increasingly difficult—it was like sucking water through a wet sponge. He coughed into the palm of his gauntlet and stood there in shock at the sight of his own blood. "Shit, I think I'm dying…"

With panic and fear setting-in, a terrible sensation of light-headedness began to overwhelm him. "What've I done to myself?"

Chapter 16

SARINA'S PROMISE

He tried to recuperate as the elves charged ahead with General Starborne. Jack watched as they stormed into their enemies, driving spears through their hearts. However, just as he was feeling a sense of relief, Jack was struck from behind! He was thrown several meters away, landing in a pool of blood—he knew it was a troll! Struggling to find his bearings Jack was surrounded by the corpses of the dead.

With no open ground he was forced to use the bodies around him as he dragged himself away. Standing on one knee, Jack saw the troll coming towards him. It looked very angry. It was the only one still alive; and since the infantry had pushed forward with the knights, Jack was alone. The beast was bleeding from several gaping wounds, and Jack knew it must've been taken down, but not killed. "Where's my sword?!"

When the beast had struck him Jack's sword was lost. The troll wasn't carrying a weapon either, but Jack was the size of a child by comparison. His body was aching as the blood from his forehead was starting to blind him. With the beast stomping towards him, Jack frantically searched for a weapon. Finally, he grabbed an elven sword from amongst the dead and stood up, "Alright! Come on, you big gorilla!"

Jack swung his sword as it lunged at him. The troll caught the blade with its bare hand and ripped it from his grasp! The blade had cut into the troll's hand, but the beast tossed it like a toothpick and grabbed him by the throat. Its fingers coiled around his neck, like a snake constricting its prey. He punched the troll as hard as he could. Each strike only aroused the beast as it bellowed with glee. Jack's bones rattled as its deafening roar echoed across the sea of grass. "I hope someone's hearing this?" he choked.

With his legs starting to buckle, Jack sensed he was about to lose consciousness. He dropped to his knees as the beast continued to roar. He then felt something on the ground beneath his fingers. When he

touched a sharp point, followed by a wooden shaft, Jack knew it was an arrow! The troll pulled him closer and bellowed as saliva and blood spewed from its mouth. Its teeth were bloodied and rotten, like a ravenous bear, and its breath smelled like decay. With his last ounce of strength, Jack drove the tip of the arrow into the troll's eye!

The beast shrieked, releasing its hold before stumbling backwards! Jack coughed, struggling to catch his breath. With an angry yelp the troll pulled the arrow from its eye, and while Jack was trying to recuperate the beast fell upon him! It grabbed him by the shoulder and punched him repeatedly in the chest. He tried to fight back, but it was useless. With each block, Jack felt as if the bones in his arms were going to shatter like glass!

The armour was doing its job, but his breastplate was now covered with dents, and was beginning to crack. Suddenly, the beast punched him square in the face! Avoiding the strikes was impossible. Jack was being mangled like a dog chewing its toy! Each strike was breaking his face. Unexpectedly, the troll released its grip; Jack fell to the ground in agony. He could barely see through all the blood. The troll stood over him and roared. It then kneeled down and grabbed a hold of his breastplate, pulling him closer. Balling its hand into a fist, it raised it up high, preparing to finish him off.

In a last act of defiance, Jack spat blood in the creature's face. But the beast just smiled, and licked it from the corner of its mouth. As the beast flexed its muscles to strike, Jack heard the sound of bone being pierced as the expression on its face went blank. The troll became lifeless. Its muscles turned to jelly and its arm dropped like a brick. Through a bloody mess, Jack saw the tip of a blade sticking out of its throat. Someone had snuck up and stabbed it from behind!

The sound of crunching bone may've been heard as the blade was being removed. And when the troll fell dead on its side, there stood Sarina with her daggers! Her eyes were full of tears as she threw herself upon him. "Jack!" she cried. "What've they done to you?!"

Her mouth was moving, but he couldn't hear her voice. With tears landing softly upon his bloody face, Jack looked into her rainbow coloured eyes. If this was to be his final moment, Sarina's face was all he wanted to see. His vision was getting hazy, and as he tried to say goodbye... his mind fell into darkness.

She draped herself over his motionless body, weeping uncontrollably. A moment later, she heard the sound of hooves coming towards them. Though it was rare for an orc to be riding a horse, she stood up with her daggers at the ready. But when she saw her father and his knights approaching, she knew the battle was won.

"Father!"

Godfrey jumped from his horse and wrapped his arms around her as several knights rushed to Jack's aid, fearing the worst. To everyone's astonishment, one of them yelled, "General, he's alive!"

"Impossible!"

"He has a heartbeat!" the knight confirmed, as Sarina's eyes lit-up.

With the rest of the army behind, Albion quickly approached. He pushed his way through the crowd and ran towards his fallen squire. "Watch his neck!" he yelled, as the knights were lifting him up. "Make sure it's supported! And don't even think about putting him on a horse —it's too dangerous! Look for a wagon!"

"What happened to your arm?" the General asked, as the knights were carrying Jack towards the village.

"A troll hit me with its mace, father. Jack saved my life."

Godfrey gave him a nod, pondering his next course of action. He turned to his weeping daughter. "Don't cry, my child," he whispered. "We'll do everything we can to save him—that's a promise."

Sarina managed to smile, but she knew Jack's chances of survival were slim to none. "Sir Tyrus!" Godfrey shouted.

"Yes, General?" said the knight, stepping forward.

"Ride back with haste! Tell Professor Hobblestone his skills will be needed for our wounded, and though it may sound callous, make sure the Shadar's first to be seen. There's only one human in Eloria."

"Yes, Sir!"

"Come, Sarina," said Godfrey, remounting his horse. "You must stay by his side. I'll drop you off at the tower, then I have to find

Mugglegruffe. The boy will need seer's magic if he's going to survive."
Without hesitation, she jumped onto the back of her father's horse,
holding him tight. "Captain Starborne!"

"Yes, father?"

"I know you're hurting, son, but I need you to stay behind and see
to our wounded. Bring them home. Enough have died this day."

"Of course," Albion bowed.

Without saying another word, Godfrey took off down the hill. At
any moment, the human might draw his final breath and Eloria would
lose the last Shadar...

Chapter 17

The Horn of War

With Godfrey riding back to the city and Albion searching for wounded warriors, Mugglegruffe had reached the south-west corner of the battlements. Leaning on his staff, he climbed the steps and entered the watchtower, where the guard was stationed. Someone had left the door open, leading to the horn of war. With his staff at the ready, he stepped inside to find the guard dead, lying in a pool of blood. He cautiously approached the horn of war. It was a large, trumpet-like instrument.

Someone had smashed it to pieces, rendering the early warning system useless. The horn of war had sounded late, but he couldn't understand why someone would then go to the trouble of destroying it. Searching for clues he made another discovery. The fallen guard had managed to write his attacker's name on the stone floor using his own blood! The dwarf kneeled and moved the guard's hand to reveal the last few letters. Mugglegruffe sighed before whispering the attacker's name. "Fergus Crouse…"

He then rolled the guard over. Someone had stabbed him twice in the neck and once in the armpit, piercing his heart. "You were facing him, weren't you?" Mugglegruffe said to the dead guard, as if he were still alive. "He looked you right in the eye when he stole your life. You poor, brave soul! May the winds of Araboth take you swiftly to your father's house, where all grievances and sorrows be vanquished, where all things are made new."

The dwarf had no doubt that Fergus Crouse, a member of the high council, was at least one of the culprits responsible. It was sad to know the guard had been slain by one of his own, yet he admired his courage for using his final moment to record his killer's name.

Mugglegruffe heard someone approaching from behind and spun around with his staff at the ready! He breathed a sigh of relief as Godfrey appeared in the doorway. The elf quickly raised his hands. "Could you lower that thing? You know it makes me nervous."

"What good's a shepherd without one?" said the wizard, lowering his staff.

"The guard's been killed?"

"Yes," he confirmed. "Where's Julius Santorean?"

"Why?" Godfrey asked.

"This guard wrote down his murderer's name in blood."

"And he wrote Julius?" the General assumed.

"No, but he did write Fergus Crouse," Mugglegruffe replied. "That's why I asked you where Julius was—those two are thick as thieves! Fergus doesn't have the brain capacity to pull off something like this, at least not alone."

"Why would you jump to such a conclusion? Fergus has always been handy with a sword. He's more than capable of taking a life."

Mugglegruffe shook his head. "Fergus is a fighter—he's no leader. He's always looked up to Julius; he would follow him even to death."

"Look, you're probably right, but we don't have time for this!"

The wizard sensed his urgency. "What is it?"

"It's the Shadar; I'll explain on the way," said Godfrey. "All I can say for sure is that he was attacked by a troll. I should've been there!"

"Calm down, and tell me what happened?" said Mugglegruffe, leaning on his staff as they proceeded to leave the tower.

"When my daughter escaped my clutches, I chased her back to where the Shadow Man appeared, but the boy was gone. I saw the pile of ash, and assumed that with Barbatus dead the horses may have awoken from their spell. I went to the stables and found them awake. Then I rode out to the battlefield with every horse I could find," the General struggled to say, feeling responsible for Jack's safety.

"Don't stop now," said Mugglegruffe.

"With the strength of our horses we charged down the rest of the filth, or so we thought. It wasn't until later I found the poor kid had been left alone with one of the brutes. If it weren't for my daughter's infatuation, he surely would've died. Then again, he may've slipped away by now…"

"You're not to blame," said Mugglegruffe, "the Shadar made his choice. It may have been a foolish one, but he was determined to keep fighting without my consent. Don't be disheartened—the last Shadar's not going to die."

They returned to the tower of the high council with haste. In Jack's quarters, where Professor Hobblestone convinced Albion to take him, Mugglegruffe remained at Jack's side for three days and three nights, until nothing more could be done.

In a strange way, this was a blessing, as Jack would not have to witness the events that took place during his absence. He didn't have to see the grieving mothers wailing over their dead children. He didn't have to witness the burial of fallen soldiers whose families were inconsolable. It was a blessing he didn't have to witness such things, things no one should ever see. Nevertheless, by sunrise, on the fourth day, the others were summoned.

Jack slowly opened his eyes and blinked a few times. The room was spinning as he looked around. He was still in pain, but there was something warm in his hand. He glanced to his right, and saw Sarina, who was sitting in a chair beside his bed. Her eyes were full of tears. She was holding his hand, which is why it felt so warm. Struggling to look around, Jack saw three more faces.

The swelling around his eyes made them difficult to identify. As they adjusted, he noticed Albion nursing a broken arm, which was in a sling. Godfrey was the easiest to identify, because of his red sagum; and the smallest person in the room was, of course, his favourite dwarf, Mugglegruffe. He tried to sit up, but Mugglegruffe and Sarina stopped him. "Easy, Shadar," said the wizard. "You've been asleep for three days, and you've cheated death in a way that few could imagine."

"Sarina," Jack managed to whisper. Leaning over, she placed her ear next to his mouth. "You s-s-saved me... you k-kept your promise..."

"Thank you for saving us, Jack," she said, with tears rolling down her cheeks.

Jack closed his eyes for a moment and fell asleep. The pain and exhaustion was too much for his body to handle. When he awoke the next morning, he was surprised to find that his friends were still watching over him. "I think he's awake," Albion whispered.

Jack looked at the captain, whose arm was no longer in a sling. Sarina was by his bedside, Godfrey was standing at the doorway, and Mugglegruffe was now perched on his wooden stool by the left side of the bed. "How long was I out?" he croaked.

"About twenty-four hours," the wizard replied. "How are you feeling?"

Jack pondered for a moment. "I can't feel much pain. My chest is a bit sore, but I can breathe like normal again. What'd you guys do to me?"

"Elvish medicine heals quickly, broken bones included. In fact, we've discovered that our medicine works better on humans, or at least it heals quicker." Mugglegruffe revealed, before taking a puff of his pipe and blowing a few smoke rings.

"You're lucky to be alive," Sarina revealed. "A few of your ribs were broken, your nose and jaw, and your right arm was broken in two places. You also had a fractured eye socket, not to mention those lacerations. If it weren't for divine intervention—you'd be dead."

"What're you talkin' about?" Jack coughed.

"When your ribs were broken, one of your lungs was pierced, but you kept on fighting. You even stayed conscious for hours, with blood filling-up your lungs. It was a miracle…"

Jack didn't know what to make of her words. Miracles and divine intervention were not something he believed in. He believed that God's voice was silent in his world, that life was nothing but a game of chance. It was a roll of the dice, or a card game, where some were dealt a good hand and others weren't. *How could God exist in a world like mine?* he thought. *Why would he condemn us to live in such a cruel and evil place? Yet we're s'posed to believe he loves us? Wait—I'm not in my world—I'm in Eloria. Maybe they're right? Maybe there is a God in this world?*

His strength returning, Jack pulled away the covers to find that someone had changed him into his bed robe. He curiously looked around the room. Sarina gave him a tiny smirk. "Don't worry, I didn't change you," she smiled, glancing at her father.

The General rolled his eyes as they quietly chuckled. Albion moved his chair closer to Jack's bed. "That troll would've made a meal out of me if it weren't for you. No one but my father ever rallied our kin the way you did. Many lives were saved because of you, both civilian, and imperial. It was an honour to fight by your side, little brother."

"We all did our part," said Jack, "and I think I understand why elves are so content. It's because you're a family. That's why you refer to each other as kin, even when you don't have family ties."

"Yes," Albion nodded. "We're a family, and there's nothing worse than being betrayed by one of your own…"

The captain squeezed his hand into a tight fist. Jack knew he was referring to the traitor. "It was Julius, wasn't it?"

"Yes," said Albion, gritting his teeth.

"Has he been brought to justice?"

"They would've faced justice by now, if we could find them," said General Starborne. "No one's seen them since the battle. Julius's closest friend and ally, Fergus Crouse, killed my guard in the watchtower. The guard wrote down his attacker's name before he died. It was his job to sound the horn of war. Fergus killed him, then took an axe to our early warning system. And we know it was Julius who killed the guards at the main gate, thanks to my son and Marshall Tucker."

"Okay, but who locked the villagers outside? That beam was heavy; I could barely lift the damn thing," said Jack. "Could Julius have done it himself?"

"Marshall heard Julius talking to my son. He was the last to go back inside the city. But moments later, the civilians were locked out. That's what we know to be fact."

"I'm sorry, father," Albion sighed. "He said he was going to look for horses. It seemed reasonable at the time. I thought he was going to check the eastern stables. I didn't know they were under the same spell. I shouldn't have trusted him!"

"It wasn't your fault—no one's to blame. Julius fooled everyone, including the council, including myself."

"Who blew the horn?" said Jack. "And why'd Fergus smash it with an axe? Isn't that a bit pointless if someone's already sounded the alarm?"

"That's what I've been trying to figure out," said Mugglegruffe. "We know Barbatus came to kill Godfrey. If they were in league with him, then Fergus may've blown the horn himself. That way, the army would be outside, leaving our General unprotected."

"I see," said Jack, "but something else doesn't make sense. The horses were already asleep before the guards at the gate were killed. If they were alive when Barbatus appeared, how'd he get past them?"

"That's the most disturbing thing of all," said Mugglegruffe, taking a slow puff of his pipe. "Somehow, some way, Barbatus was already in the city. For how long, we have no way of knowing. The city's entrances are manned twenty-four hours a day, seven days a week. A brownie couldn't get past our lawkeepers undetected, let alone a fiend, like Barbatus. For now, it remains a mystery."

"Those lawkeepers knew Julius well. I can't imagine how they must've felt when he turned on them," said Albion, shaking his head.

If I run into Julius, he's gonna wish he'd never been born! Jack thought. "Did anyone else leave the city, besides them?"

"Not that we know of," said Albion. "Julius had many friends, but I don't think they're fond of him anymore. All he has now is Fergus. With both of them on the run, they shouldn't be hard to find. Word travels fast in Eloria. They won't have any friends to aid them, and will be forced to live in the wilderness, like the beasts they are!"

Jack sighed as he tried to get up. "Easy, Jack! It's been less than five days. Don't push yourself if you're not up to it," Sarina advised, as Albion proceeded to help.

I can't believe I had broken ribs and a punctured lung! My eye-socket, my jaw, if it weren't for elvish medicine I'd be dead, Jack thought.

"You won't be doing any training today, my friend," Albion smiled.

"Then, what can I do?"

Mugglegruffe took another puff of his pipe. "You'll meet with the high council again. We wish to thank you for aiding the city. We're also going to tell you why you were brought here. Your questions will finally be answered."

Jack's eyes lit-up. "Well, if you ask me, it's about time."

The wizard hopped off his stool, and just as he was about to start dragging it, Albion said, "Give it here! I'll take it back to the council chambers."

"Why, thank you, Captain Starborne. Elves are always so courteous —they have such good manners—not like us dwarves!" he chuckled, as they left the room.

General Starborne was about to follow, then changed his mind. "You defeated a highly dangerous adversary in the form of Barbatus. If it hadn't been for your quick-thinking, I'd probably be dead. So when you meet with the council, there won't be any arguing or shouting. You'll be treated with the respect you deserve, but always be on your guard. The enemy knows what you're capable of; if Barbatus ever returns, he'll be looking for vengeance."

"I thought I killed him?" said Jack.

"According to Mugglegruffe, you sent him back to the human world. You failed to cut off his head, which's the only way to send his spirit to the Dark Abyss. That's where all infernal spirits shall one day be imprisoned. In your world of Midland, it's known as Hades, or Hell. But whatever the name—the destination's the same."

"He's in my world?"

"Yes, but he can't take physical form. He won't be back in Eloria any time soon, so you needn't be worried. This city owes you a great debt. Your efforts will soon be rewarded."

Before Jack could speak, the General bowed his head and left the room. Jack was stunned by his words. He never imagined that someone in his position would be so respectful. *If only I'd swung a bit harder!* he thought. *Physical form or not—Barbatus is still dangerous. I hope I don't see him in my dreams. Who knows what mayhem he's getting up to...*

Sarina stood up. Once again, she was going to be last to leave. Jack approached the doorway. "Seems like forever since we've been alone," he smiled. "There're so many things I wanna say to you. I just hope I'll get the chance to say them, before it's too late."

She looked into his eyes with a deep longing. Jack could sense the fiery passion waiting to be unleashed, but something was still holding her back. His heart was telling him their love could never be truly expressed. "I, too, have things I wish to say, but now isn't the time," said Sarina. "You must go and see the council. Listen to what they say, and I'll meet you downstairs by the great tree." She then kissed him on the cheek, wrapping her arms around him in a brief embrace, before silently leaving his quarters.

Chapter 18

THE SECOND COUNCIL MEETING

Jack opened his wardrobe and looked in the mirror on the inside of the door. He was glad to see that his face was still in one piece. Apart from being a little pale and thin, he couldn't see any serious disfigurement.

There was, however, a tiny scar above his left eyebrow, and another by the hairline of his temple. They were barely noticeable, yet Jack was glad to have some battle scars. They would always remind him of the day Sarina saved his life. He looked at the side of his chest, where his ribs had been broken, and could see another tiny scar. Jack had lost a lot of body fat thanks to Albion's training program. His body was toned and muscular. Lastly, he opened his mouth and was surprised he hadn't lost any teeth.

Despite all he had been through, Jack wasn't the least bit hungry or thirsty, so he put on his green pants and long-sleeved shirt, followed by his green socks and elven boots. The high council was waiting. Just as he was about to leave, Jack realised his blue clothes were missing. He curiously went into the lounge room to find that his sword and armour were missing too. "Where's my stuff? Damn, I lost my sword on the battlefield…"

Jack left his quarters and went downstairs to the third floor. When the lawkeepers saw him approaching, they opened the large double door. As he entered the council chambers, they proceeded to give him an elven salute. They made fists with their right hands, placed them against the left side of their chests, and bowed their heads in respect. *Albion did that when we first met, but no one else ever has. Maybe they also fought in the battle?* Jack thought.

He gave them a silent nod and entered the chambers. Jack was optimistic when he failed to hear any shouting; he approached the round table, where the council was already seated. Once again, he sat in the chair beside Mugglegruffe, and was half-expecting the wizard to say something. But the dwarf appeared to be deep in thought as he sat there rhythmically puffing his pipe. Jack's eyes were soon drawn to the two empty chairs, in which the traitors once occupied. He was about to ask Mugglegruffe where his armour had gone when a knight entered the room.

General Starborne pulled out the empty chair beside him, directing the knight to sit. Once he was seated, Godfrey began to speak, "My fellow councilmen, allow me to introduce, Sir Griffin Lockhart, who'll be taking the place of Fergus Crouse. I know this is unexpected, and under usual circumstances we'd delay before choosing a new member. But in light of recent events, this council's grown thin. I hope you'll embrace Sir Griffin, for he is a knight of the highest calibre; some of you may recall his exploits during The Winter Campaign."

"Your word's good enough for us," said Marshall, as the council nodded their heads.

Godfrey was about to continue, but Professor Hobblestone interjected. "I apologise for the interruption, but before we proceed I would like to ask if anyone's been successful in contacting King Brutalan? I'm aware that he submitted his resignation three months ago, but I was hoping he may've reconsidered? I've sent several messages to Stonehill, but as of yet I've received no reply."

"Well, he's not coming back if that's what you're asking?" said the General.

"We don't need him!" said Mugglegruffe. "He broke his oath to this council! Besides, the dwarf king's got enough to worry about in his own lands."

"Very well," the Professor sighed, "please continue."

"Thank you, Professor," the General replied. "Now, we're here for two reasons: firstly, we're going to explain to the Shadar why he was brought here. Secondly, we must review our continuing efforts to locate two former members of this council. Julius Santorean and Fergus Crouse betrayed us; they murdered three of our brothers in cold blood and must be brought to justice—whatever the cost!"

Godfrey lowered his head with a deep sigh. Jack could only imagine how their betrayal was affecting him. Stroking his long white beard, the old elf turned his attention to Jack. "We welcome you to this high

143

council, once again, Shadar. My name is Professor Halinard Hobblestone. I'm an ex-seer, alchemist, physician, and philosopher. And I believe that I speak for everyone when I say we're very grateful for your quick thinking, your heroism, and for saving the lives of many people."

With a low murmuring the council nodded their heads in agreement. "Furthermore," he continued, "we gave you three months to see if you could coexist. And after everything that's happened, not only did you save the villagers of the silver bridge, but you almost lost your own life in the process. For this, we are grateful beyond words. You've more than earned our trust; you've become a valuable and welcome ally. It's also been made clear that our General's own children consider you to be family. And so, we are ready to reveal our secrets, including a hidden history of your own world. But first, we must tell you the prophecy," he stated. "I leave it to you now, General."

Godfrey rose from his chair with a purpose, looking directly at Jack. "When the last Shadar comes forth, and the blue star falls. The veil will be lifted, and peace will be no more. Under a black sun he rises, devouring man and beast alike. The wicked become his servants, for none withstand his might. With an army at his back, he wields a sword of iron. The world of men shall burn at the siege of Mt Zion. War and famine plague the earth, as none could have imagined. Few shall escape the talons of the great Red Dragon."

Each word burned into Jack's soul. *When the blue star falls? I saw a blue star with Albion, after my first day of training,* he remembered.

"The prophecy was foretold by the High King, long ago," Godfrey continued. "Now that you've come forth, the blue star's going to fall. Our worlds must suffer many tribulations before he returns. He sent you to make a difficult decision; one that will affect the people of our world, and yours. And though I'm sure there are those who would like to sway you, this decision is yours alone..."

"It's time, Shadar," said Mugglegruffe, removing his pipe. "*You* will decide if Elorians are to re-enter Midland and help the humans find their way. This decision cannot be made with haste, but the wrong decision may harbour dire consequences for us all."

Jack scratched the back of his head. "This's insane!" he blurted out. "Do you honestly think humans will just welcome you with open arms? What humans don't understand, they fear, and what they fear, they kill! And they'll do it with powerful weapons, like guns and nuclear bombs! You'd all be captured and dissected, or exterminated!"

"What does *dissected* mean?" asked Marshall, with a look of horror.

Mugglegruffe shook his head. "I don't think you understand, Shadar. We know of the dangerous technology your people possess, but they're in need of our help. Humanity's being led astray. For hundreds of years they've been guided from the shadows by a coven of sorcerers, and recent technology has only hastened their evil advance. Don't you see? They're in league with the Red Dragon!"

"I don't think he's ready to hear this," Professor Hobblestone interrupted.

"No! He must!" said the wizard. "They control every aspect of your world, and humans continue to remain oblivious while the very fabric of your planet's being utterly destroyed. If the human race doesn't wake up and accept this truth, acknowledging that their entire history's been a lie—they will lose their immortal souls! The Dragon's the father of lies. His deception's coming; he will unite the world under a false sense of peace. Humanity will be blindly led astray, like a moth to the flame! Did you not hear the prophecy? The blue star could fall any day now. Your people aren't prepared for what's coming—the beast is on its way!"

"Look, I'm sorry, but unlike you I can't perform miracles," said Jack. "My people would rather watch television or play video games; they have no interest in this stuff. And everything they believe now, is all back-to-front. There's no reasoning with them. It's like talking to a bunch of lunatics. Everything that used to be good is now considered bad. All they wanna do is keep pushin' boundaries till there's nothin' left. They can't even take care of themselves, so how are they s'posed to look after their own planet?"

"Don't you see, Shadar? The sorcerers in your world have failed to unleash the Red Dragon, because he can't take physical form. His time is short. He's going to take possession of a man, and his power will be

145

sevenfold! Those who refuse to accept his mark will be hunted down and killed. He will unite your world with false miracles, and conquer what's left through acts of war. When the blue star falls, the veil between our worlds will begin to lift. The hidden doors shall again be re-opened. The Red Dragon will try to claim not just our worlds, but all! He needs an army to burn down the gates of Araboth and claim the throne of God. We're in this fight together!"

"Huh?" said Jack. "You mean the worlds that General Starborne talked about? My world became seven after the great flood, right?"

Mugglegruffe glanced at Godfrey, who gave him a slight nod. "Yes, there are infinite worlds in the universe, but only nine which contain the King of the Law's creations. Midland's the original creation, created five thousand, seven-hundred, and seventy-nine years ago. But after the Red Dragon and his followers were made formless, two hundred Arabothians fell and tried to create their own perverse kingdom. They corrupted creation and Midland became an abomination."

"An abomination?" he interrupted.

"They taught humans dark magic and warfare. They also took human wives, mixing their Arabothian blood with humanity, creating the giants, and dozens of other tribes. Yes, your world was splintered into seven when the great flood cleansed the earth. But what you haven't really been told is that every being in Eloria came from the Arabothian bloodline. The elves, dwarves; orcs, trolls, and many others, are all abominations. In the eyes of the King of the Law... none of us were supposed to exist. Most tribes are similar in form, yet distinctly different. Some inherited their nature from the Abyssians, like the giants, orcs, ogres, and trolls. Others, like the elves and dwarves, inherited their nature from the human bloodline."

"Wait..." Jack paused, "you're all human-angel hybrids?"

"That's right," Mugglegruffe confirmed. "Tribes like the faeries and elves inherited a human, but more spiritual form, a form which the Red Dragon and his followers possessed, before they fell from Araboth. The elves of Eloria lost their ability to take ethereal form, long ago. But the descendants of the hidden folk continue to remain unseen. They still occupy certain lands in your world. The dragons, spriggans, dryads, nymphs, and other creatures, also came from the Arabothian bloodline, but many were quarantined throughout the seven worlds during the great flood. But the giants were the most troublesome. Like their Arabothian fathers, they inherited the spark of creation in their blood, giving them the ability to corrupt a whole manner of different species with innumerable results. After corrupting mankind, the giants corrupted the animal life; they even sinned against the beasts of the sea, creating a multitude of deadly abominations."

"How?" asked Jack, struggling to believe.

"The details of such corruptions are too sickening to be spoken of, but it was a process that continued for centuries. Not all abominations were considered worthy, in which case, they were destroyed. You see, despite our differences to the other tribes, we still share the same origin. Only humans are the King of the Law's perfect creation, but when the Red Dragon persuaded them to sin, they, too, were corrupted, and lost their immortality as a result. Most tribes pledged their allegiance to the Dragon, because they felt they owed him their existence. Only a handful chose to serve the King of the Law, and we've been at war with the others ever since. For thousands of years we've fought the orcs and trolls, with no end in sight, until now. By entering your world, we risk exposing our own. But sooner or later the blue star will fall, and whether we like it or not, the seven worlds will become one."

The wizard paused and looked sternly into Jack's eyes. "The die is cast! We cannot change prophecy, nor should we ever try to."

"How do you get to the other worlds? And why do you say King of the Law, then at other times, say High King?" Jack demanded to know.

"We've told you that at the height of its abomination, the King of the Law sent a great flood to cleanse the earth. In fact, almost every culture in your world has recorded this event. The flood was so destructive that the earth splintered into seven worlds, divided, but linked through hidden gateways, some of which can only be opened by a seer. There are nine worlds in total, including The Dark Abyss, which will be a prison for the Red Dragon and his followers. And, of course, the High King's dwelling place of Araboth, where all believers shall find eternal joy."

"Believers?" he asked.

"Anyone who acknowledges their sin, and believes in the High King, who gave up his life for the sins of all, will surely find themselves in Araboth, inheriting eternal life."

"Even a murderer?" Jack scoffed.

"Whether it be murder, or any other infraction—the wages of sin is death. There's no room for such things in Araboth; only by the High King's blood may we enter paradise."

"I think I know where you're goin' with this…"

"Then stay your sarcasms and listen to the rest of the story!"

"Okay, okay," said Jack.

"As you've already been told, those of us, who remained loyal to the King of the Law, survived the great flood by retreating underground. Some of the evil tribes did as well, but by the dreams and visions of a powerful seer, we were led to a new world. The world was Eloria; it was a wild place, but soon tamed by the magic of iron. As for the differences between the two kings, you must rely on faith to find the answer. Though it seems you've already made up your mind," the wizard sighed, before striking a match to relight his pipe.

Jack was overwhelmed. The two kings were obviously deities, but Jack's faith was lost long ago. Yet, he felt a deep longing when Mugglegruffe mentioned the High King's atonement. When he was a small boy, Jack prayed to several gods, begging each of them to stop the violence he was suffering, but none of them answered his prayers. His world was evil, and Jack deemed it unworthy of receiving mercy from any god, especially the High King of Eloria. *If God exists, he must've given-up on us a long time ago. If not, then humanity's failed to create a just world. Either way, humanity's at fault…* he thought.

Yet, he couldn't help but think of what Elorians could offer his world. They had crystal technology, and a system of governing that was for the benefit of all, not just a few. They had fixed objective morality and ancient wisdom. Despite all this, Jack was still concerned.

148

Throughout his security career he had witnessed the dark side of humanity. He didn't have faith in the justice system or political leaders, and believed them to be incapable of change. But as he looked at each member of the High Council he saw a striking contrast. Unlike human leaders, they were full of grace, wisdom, and dignity; and he shuddered to think how the high council would function if politicians from the human world were thrust into the mix.

"Are you alright, young man?" the Professor asked.

Jack had been silent for several minutes without knowing it. "Look, I can't make a decision like this without weighing-up the risks and benefits. I need more time, at least gimme a few days to think about it?"

General Starborne looked around the table. "Those in favour of giving the Shadar more time, please place your medallion white side up," he instructed, before flipping his own.

All five members of the council flipped their medallions in agreement. Jack wiped the sweat from his forehead and breathed a sigh of relief. "This council has spoken, Shadar. We shall reconvene in three days to hear your final decision," Godfrey decreed. "Use this time you've been given, wisely."

"I'll do my best," Jack replied.

"Thank you, Shadar," said Mugglegruffe. "Now, please remove yourself from these chambers, and leave the matter of the traitors to us."

With a solemn nod, Jack removed himself from the council chambers. Entering his quarters, he headed straight for the kitchen. His kitchen table was covered with gifts from the people of the city. He grabbed a bottle of wine with a get well note attached to the neck, and when he realised it was from Sarina, Jack was brought to tears. *I can't imagine what humans would do to someone as innocent, loving, and compassionate as her...* he thought.

Sarina was probably waiting for him in the hall of the great tree, but Jack needed peace and solitude. His mind was full of dark thoughts. He opened the bottle and took a few gulps. Heading into the lounge room,

Jack sat in one of the lounge chairs. Half an hour later, there was a knock at the door. "Come in," he grunted.

Without speaking a word, Albion and Sarina entered his quarters and took a seat in the lounge across from him. Their body language was telling. "You knew about my task this whole time, didn't you?" said Jack.

They gave each other a quick glance. "Yes," Sarina confirmed. "We're sorry for not telling you, but it wasn't our place to say."

"How old are you, Sarina?"

"W-what do you mean?" she said, defensively.

"The day we met, you said you'd been watching me my entire life. So I'll ask again, how old are you?"

Sarina was reluctant to speak. Finally, she took a deep breath. "I'm one thousand, nine hundred, and eighty-six years old. And Albion's one thousand, nine hundred and eighty-nine. I'm sorry for not telling you."

Jack sat back in shock. "What about Mugglegruffe? How old's he?"

"Five-thousand and two," Sarina revealed.

"No wonder he called me *boy* the day we met! You're immortal, aren't you?"

"Only in the sense that once we reach maturity, we don't continue to age for a long time. When elves age it's for one of three reasons: one —we age with wisdom; two—ageing can be brought on by a trauma of the spirit; and three—it's a gift from the High King. But you've already seen that we can be killed in battle. It's not just us; every tribe in Eloria from the Arabothian bloodline was cursed with longevity," she replied.

Jack looked at them with sorrow. "Do you have any idea what humans'll do when they find out you don't age? They will catch you and dissect you a piece at a time... till there's nothing left!"

They knew he was suffering but were moved by his love and concern for their well-being. As they sat in silence Jack struggled to process Sarina's words. *I can't believe it*, he thought. *I'm in love with a two-thousand year old elf!*

"Do you want us to leave?" Albion asked.

"Yes," said Jack, "I need to be alone. I'll see you in the morning."

They weren't about to argue as they left his quarters. When the door closed behind them, tears began to well-up in Jack's eyes. "How could you've spoken to them like that?" he said to himself, feeling disgusted.

Jack loved his friends but his heart was conflicted. "Why do I feel more like an elf than a man?" he whispered to himself. "If I say no, am I betraying humanity? Will I be robbing them of a great discovery? I could never be one of them. I'll be dead in forty years—if I'm lucky. I wish I could forsake my own world and stay here forever."

With his task a great burden, Jack spent the rest of the afternoon consuming his wine, until he passed out.

Chapter 19

WISDOM OF THE FAERIE QUEEN

That night, Jack dreamt about the faerie queen. She was alone, standing in a dark forest. She was worried about something and was calling him to her. When he awoke, Jack found he was still in the lounge chair with an empty bottle in his hand.

He got up and stumbled into the bedroom. According to the clock on the wall, it was almost 5am. Queen Eleanor's voice was still fresh in his mind. *What if the dream was real?* he thought. *My dream about Barbatus turned out to be real. Maybe I had too much wine?*

Whether it was real or not, Jack knew his decision would affect every Elorian, so it only seemed fair to let the faeries have their say. "I've only got three days," he said to himself. "Does that include yesterday?"

It was difficult to think through his drunken haze. Since he was still dressed, Jack decided to leave straight away. He stumbled back into the lounge room, struggling to keep his balance as he swayed to and fro. After leaving his quarters, Jack started to wobble down the big staircase. He soon bumped into a lawkeeper, who stared at him, looking somewhat perplexed. "What's your problem? Is my hair stickin' up?" Jack mumbled, as the lawkeeper continued on his way.

After trudging down the hall of shields, Jack left the tower and made his way through the city streets, struggling not to trip over his own feet. Looking towards the south, he saw that the red sun, Orjares, was barely peeking his head above the horizon, burning with red and pink hues across the clouds. Some of the elves were setting up their stalls; they watched in confusion as he stumbled by.

He was heading for the imperial stables located beside the armoury. When Jack arrived, he began searching for his horse. It was difficult to see in the dark. Most of them were brown or white, but Jack's horse was black. There weren't many of those, so he concentrated on them. "Midknight, where are you?"

Peering down a row of stables, he caught sight of a black horse sticking its head over the wooden fence in a curious manner. Jack hurried over and found his saddle sitting on a wooden stand opposite the stable. "Midknight?" he whispered. "Is that you, boy?"

As if his words were understood, the beast jerked its head. Jack opened the gate and grabbed his saddle. Some of the horses looked tired, and their backs were marked by the sweaty stains of a long ride, which meant several knights had recently returned from patrol. *I hope I don't get caught,* Jack thought. *They might stop me from leaving.*

Jack knew how to saddle a horse, but his drunken memory was foggy, so he took his time to make sure he got it right. Once Midknight was saddled and bridled correctly, Jack mounted-up and rode out of the stables. "I shouldn't be riding under the influence. I wonder if they have a law against that?" he chuckled.

He still had to get past the guards at the entrance gate, but Julius had murdered the previous ones; Jack was morbidly hoping the new guards would allow him to pass as he rode to the southern end of the city. Approaching the gate he soon caught their attention. Riding with a confident swagger, Jack straightened his back and puffed out his chest. He then brought his horse to a halt and let out a deep sigh, before slouching in his saddle. One of the guards looked at his comrade, shrugged his shoulders, then placed his hands on the crossbeam. The other guard was hesitant but decided to aid his colleague. Once the doors were opened, Jack gave them a nod as he passed beneath the archway, leaving the Sapphire City.

He then rode across the silver bridge, and, upon reaching the village, Jack was getting flashbacks as he came upon the burnt rubble and dry blood. He feared the orcs and trolls, but it was the menacing Lieutenant of the Red Dragon, Barbatus, whom he feared the most. The demon was trapped in the human world, but the image of his blinding red light was still burned into Jack's mind.

Making his way through the village, Jack was sad to see it empty. The once bustling town was now silent as the grave. It was still in ruins from the battle. Most of the houses had been torched by orcs or smashed by trolls. He could still hear the screaming of the villagers and the clashing of steel against iron, as the battle continued to play on his mind. "This place's givin' me the creeps," his teeth chattered.

Jack quickened Midknight's pace, passing through the rest of the village with haste. When he arrived at the sea of grass, he started to make his way across the rolling hills, refusing to look back. The images of the dead were haunting him, especially those of the elven children, whose lives were so unfairly cut short. If it were in Jack's power to trade his life for any one of them, he would gladly do so. His eyes welled with tears, but the rolling hills were peaceful as they calmed his troubled mind.

He detected the scent of flowers on the cool morning breeze as he rode towards the towering trees. To his left, was the blood-stained grass of the battle; and, to his right, Jack noticed a big circle of ash in the distance, where the elves had burned the corpses of their enemies. *Where've our dead been laid to rest?* Jack thought. Then he remembered the place General Starborne had spoken of. *The hall of the dead, that's where the statue of Balinor Santorean's s'posed to be...*

Jack paused when he reached the edge of the forest. He had forgotten how dark the path was, and since Orjares had not fully risen, it looked even darker. A moment later, he shook away his fear, riding onto the path with the oak trees looming above. The forest was peaceful and inviting, yet dark and foreboding. And it wasn't long until he felt something was watching him. "I'm not alone..." he whispered, as his breath turned to ice.

The faerie queen had given him the gift of faerie sight. Therefore, if any faeries were using their glamour, Jack would be able to see them. But for some reason, he was feeling vulnerable, then he realised what was missing. "My sword! Julius and Fergus! If I run into 'em—I'm a dead man! Wait, I lost my sword in the battle. Shit! I didn't think this through," said Jack, shaking his head. "I shouldn't have drunk so much —you'd think I'd have learnt my lesson by now."

Just when he was thinking about turning back he heard a voice inside his head say, "Don't be afraid. You're well-protected in my magical forest. A faerie queen's oath can never be broken. My kin shall be with you as swiftly as a dragon defending its young."

Queen Eleanor! Jack thought. *I knew she could read my mind! Her voice is so soft and sweet...*

"Why, thank you, chosen one," her voice replied.

Oops! Sorry, I didn't know you were still there.

Having never spoken telepathically before, Jack made a conscious effort to void his mind of evil thoughts. Her words were reassuring. Despite not having a sword, he was sure the faeries would protect him. Taking this trip was a bit of a gamble, but Jack needed as much information as possible to complete his task.

"It's time for you to leave the path. Do not fear, turn to your right. My kin will be waiting by the sacred grove."

Okay, he replied in thought.

Jack followed her instructions and rode into the grove of towering oaks, which seemed to go on forever. Every now and then, he caught sight of a faerie in the distance. The faerie would point in the direction he was to follow, never uttering a word. After staying his course for several hours, he noticed some figures emerging from the foliage up ahead. It was a group of faeries! He counted four of them; they were all covered in dirt, leaves, vines, and green moss. He brought Midknight to a halt as one of them stepped forward. "You must go by foot from here. Our queen knows why you've come. She's anxiously expecting your arrival. Follow us, chosen one; the faerie queen awaits your presence," she said, bowing her head.

Jack quickly dismounted. "What about my horse?"

"Our sister, Ebony, will watch over him," she replied.

A young faerie stepped forward and took the reins. "It's alright. He'll be safe with me."

Jack remained close as they led him deeper into the forest. Looking up, he saw an oak tree of immense proportions. At first, he thought it was a trick of the light. But it seemed to be their destination as the faeries headed towards it. When they were less than twenty feet away, the tree's gigantic size became apparent. It was so immense that it made ordinary oaks look like shrubs. The base of it was about the size of an Olympic stadium, with branches so high they blocked out the sun! *Those leaves are the size of my car!* Jack thought, before suddenly feeling an odd sensation. *It's the tree! It's humming and vibrating as if it's alive…*

Standing at the base of the tree, the faeries stepped to either side of what appeared to be carvings of runes etched into the surface of the bark. Unexpectedly, they began to glow! Jack watched as the green illuminations became brighter, revealing a stone archway. It was beautiful! The arch was made of brown stone with glowing rune symbols on the sides, plus another symbol above, on the central stone, which was larger. For some reason, it reminded Jack of his clubbing days.

While marvelling at its beauty, Jack noticed the bark within the arch suddenly fade to black, like the opening of a door into a basement. The dark void sparkled with different coloured lights; Jack was standing in front of a magic gateway! As he stepped towards the doorway, one of the faeries began to recite a rhyme. "Appearing as stone it will be, yet once was burned and etched to tree. Brightly lit with burning power; do not enter if your soul be sour. When it glows, faeries be near. Your heart must be strong, so do not fear. A world of magic, tree root, and lust, but stay too long and you'll soon be dust. If you give in to the dark seducer, forever you'll be trapped inside Arathusa."

Jack was concerned about the lyrics, but looking into the doorway, he saw a figure approaching from the other side. A moment later, out of the tree stepped Queen Eleanor! She was wearing her beautifully carved wooden crown, with white flowers spread throughout her hair. She was indeed a beautiful sight. Her bright green eyes and shimmering body almost hypnotised him. "Don't be afraid," she said, taking a hold of his hand.

Walking backwards, she slowly pulled him towards the door of sparkling light. *What if it's a trick? What if I never return?* Jack thought.

"If I wanted to kill you, I wouldn't have gone to so much trouble," she said.

Jack's heart sank with guilt when he realised she had read his mind. As she was pulling him closer, Jack remembered the day she had blessed him. He was reminded that her blessing had saved him from the Shadow Man. Her eyes were glowing with power, and as she vanished into the portal of light, she gripped his hand tightly. Giving her his trust, Jack followed her into the void with his eyes closed.

A few seconds later she released her grip. Opening his eyes, Jack was completely astonished. He was now in a different world! The black sky was filled with colourful stars of bright green. He glanced back to see the gateway close and vanish from sight. It had opened in the middle of a stone circle, with a spiral of pebbles ending in the centre, where Jack could see what appeared to be a patch of dry blood. Beyond it was an endless forest of trees with tiny houses perched up high. The tree houses weren't artificial, but were made from the twisted branches of trees, almost resembling bird nests, which were covered in leaves of green and brown. Glowing from the gaps between the branches, Jack could see lights of fluorescent green emanating throughout the forest in a spectacular display. *This's incredible...* he thought.

"Be mindful of your thoughts," Queen Eleanor warned. "I'm not the only one gifted with such abilities in this realm."

"Can you read anyone's mind, or just mine?" Jack curiously asked.

"Faeries with my ability can read the minds of humans. Sometimes, we can read the thoughts of weak-minded elves, but not dwarves. If you ask me, dwarves have nothing in them. Mugglegruffe, of course, is the only exception."

"Oh, okay. By the way, I'm sorry for what I was thinking earlier."

"No need to apologise. If you had my knowledge, I'd be nervous too."

Before he could ask her to clarify, a ball of light came whizzing through the trees, missing Jack's head by centimetres! Hundreds of strange lights were now flying throughout the forest, but no two were the same. They were all different sizes and a mix of different colours.

Most were blue or white, and others were green, red, or yellow. Yet, they all seemed to have an internal illumination. "What the—"

Jack was distracted by laughter and could hear the sound of flute-playing as the faeries emerged. Hundreds were coming out of their dark hollows, laughing and dancing as they gathered around. He saw one of them dancing in a circle as toadstools burst from the ground beneath her feet! Some of the faeries were rising out of the leaf-litter, covered in dirt and grass. Shockingly, most of them were naked, and weren't the least bit shy about it! Jack was in a wild and untamed world. "Welcome to Arathusa," Queen Eleanor declared. "In your world, they call it the Land of Faerie."

Jack didn't know what to say. Only in Eloria had he seen such beauty, but Arathusa was quite a contrast. The glowing lights dazzled and enticed him, warming his very blood. "I-I don't understand," he stammered. "I feel like a fish out of water..."

Stepping closer, she placed her mouth next to his ear and took a hold of his hand once more. "You have nothing to fear, chosen one. Time will remain still in Eloria, as you bear witness to the reality of Arathusa, the world of dreams and fantasies. The elves will not like you being here. Promise to keep it a secret?"

"I promise," said Jack.

Holding his hand, she led him through the forest. A few minutes later, Jack was totally surrounded by faeries. They were smiling and giggling as he was taken to a large bonfire. He was half-expecting them to start dancing again. But as they gathered around the flames, the faeries became silent. Jack noticed a couple of wooden chairs, covered in green vines; each one featured a cushion made from a bed of flowers. "Please be seated," said the faerie queen. "I've summoned you here to receive my counsel."

Taking a seat, Jack couldn't help but stare into the flames of the bonfire. It was glowing with a neon-green colour, and even though it was several metres away, he was beginning to sweat. As he looked around, Jack noticed that most of the faeries were female. There were only seven males he could see. They were each of a tall, slim build and also weren't shy about hiding their particulars. But unlike the females, they had short, bright-yellow hair, and dark, sinister-looking eyes.

He was about to inquire, then a beautiful faerie with red hair approached. She was carrying a wooden plate covered in purple fruit. Queen Eleanor leaned forward and glared at her, causing the faerie to stop. Then, much to the dismay of the faerie queen, she smiled at Jack with a wild and lustful look in her eyes.

"No, Munamye!" Queen Eleanor scolded, as the faerie suddenly backed away, before re-joining the others, who were curiously observing the interaction.

It was customary in Jack's world to offer a guest food and drink. His Elorian friends, including Mugglegruffe, were familiar with this custom. *Maybe their food's bad for me, and the faerie didn't know?* Jack thought.

He turned to the faerie queen, who was looking at him with much curiosity, as if reading his mind again. Despite being amazed by this new world, Jack couldn't help but sense he had broken a law. "Your mind's burdened with sadness and turmoil, chosen one. A decision has been tasked to you. A decision, which may hold devastating consequences for my kin..."

"That's why I had to see you," said Jack. "How can this decision be mine, alone?"

She sighed, leaning back in her chair. "It's troubling for us, too. If the wicked men from your world enter Eloria, then sooner or later they'll invade Arathusa."

Jack now understood why she had summoned him. Just like the elves and dwarves, the faeries also feared the outcome of his decision. "How can one man decide the fate of so many? I'm no leader—I'm nothing special—I'm just a security guard."

Biting her lower lip, she appeared to be deep in thought. "The High King of Creation has chosen *you* to make this decision. It's a heavy burden, one you must bear for the sake of us all," she replied. "If you weren't the chosen one, then how could you have turned the tides of war and saved so many elves?"

"You know of the battle?"

"Of course," she smiled. "You defeated one of the most powerful sorcerers to ever plague the seven worlds. He was once a beautiful being of light. But when he followed the Red Dragon's path of sin, his heart became black. Hundreds have fallen before him, and now he's been defeated by you—a human, who'd only been wielding a sword for three months. In the human world, he can no longer harm any of my kin, whom he once sought to defile."

"You're forgetting something," said Jack. "If it weren't for your blessing of protection and the help of a wizard, I, too, would've fallen."

"Perhaps," she replied. "The world of Arathusa is very precious to my kin, but Eloria's our second home. What happens there, can also affect us. There're many servants of the Red Dragon who may try to enter this world, by way of Eloria—some are far more powerful than Barbatus."

"I know you're afraid of what might happen if my answer's yes," said Jack. "So if you have any advice, tell me now, before it's too late."

"All I can tell you is to be mindful of prophecy. When you return to the Sapphire City, ask Godfrey Starborne to take you to the hall of the dead. Within the confines of that sacred place, you may just find the answers you seek."

"Okay, but why'd you make me promise not to speak of this place? Aren't the elves and dwarves your allies? Would they be angry if they knew I was here? If that's the case, they must have their reasons?"

A tiny smile formed in the corners of her mouth. "You're wiser than you give yourself credit for. The elves have been our allies for almost two thousand years. But there was once a time when we were loyal to the Red Dragon, and fought against the elves in the Great War. We also entered your world on sacred nights, when the veil was at its thinnest; and if a wandering mortal entered the forbidden forest, we would capture him to increase our ranks. Terror would be his first feeling, but after eating our food, he'd be drowning in happiness and sinful pleasures. Of course, the moment wouldn't last—his life would waste away in minutes."

"Why do you say *he?*" said Jack, nervously.

"Your thoughts have betrayed you, chosen one. I know you were curious about our male kin," Queen Eleanor revealed. "Unfortunately, ninety-nine out of a hundred faerie births are female. You can imagine how this would cause problems. Our men don't mind; they can pick and choose, but it's harder for our women."

"What about women and children? Did you capture them?"

"Our men would have their way with human women. But they take too long to give birth, and would be sacrificed; the children would be sacrificed too."

"You sacrificed children?" said Jack, gritting his teeth.

"Yes, I'm afraid so. We've done terrible things, but no worse than humans have done. Did humans not sacrifice their newborns on the altars of Moloch? Did they not watch their newborns cook to death upon his brazen arms? Do they not still do so? Everything we've done, humans did first..."

"My people don't sacrifice children!"

"Are you sure about that?" she questioned.

Jack thought about it for a moment. "Well, not exactly... I guess the sins of the past have taken different forms. I still don't know how to feel about this. I can't believe what you did. I can't believe you did the bidding of the Red Dragon."

"Yes, it's true, we did horrible things. But we haven't stolen a human since our great punishment, nor shall we ever again," she explained. "The souls of those we took are still trapped here; only when Arathusa's destroyed, can they enter Araboth. Spirit-lights don't feel anything. They sleep until they're called, but remind us of our sinful past."

"What is the nature of faeries?" asked Jack.

"We were created when the world was full of evil and injustice. Our hearts were wild. We thought only of sinful pleasures, forbidden desires. Despite our alliance with the elves, they'll never trust us. The same can be said for the dwarves, but we've made them no promises. Mugglegruffe, the wise and powerful wizard of the woods, cares not for the spirits of trees, nor the flowers and plants as we do. Dwarves have always sought the gems and metals of the earth. Crystals and gold —that's all they care about. They condemn us for our past, but will you condemn us, too?"

Her admissions were horrifying, but the faeries hadn't committed such acts in almost two-thousand years. *Hang on, one of the faeries just tried to drug me with their food!* Jack thought. *Queen Eleanor stopped her, but maybe some of her kin still long for a return to the old ways? If I condemn them for their past, it's gonna be difficult gettin' outta here. I wouldn't make it out alive! I'd also be giving them the perfect excuse to go back to their old habits...*

"Well?" said Queen Eleanor.

"What you and your kin have done in the past doesn't matter. All that matters is what you do now. You've been kind and generous to me, and if it weren't for your magic I would've been killed. In my world, many people believe in a God of peace and forgiveness. I'll not judge you, or your kin. As long as your alliance with the elves continues, you'll have me as a friend and ally."

The faerie queen was moved by his words. "Thank you for granting us mercy, chosen one. By the way, I was reading your mind. And yes, it's true, some of my kin long for a return to the old ways, but that will never happen while I'm still Queen. You have my word."

"I'm sorry if my thoughts offended you," said Jack.

"Never mind, there's nothing to forgive. I, too, will always be your friend and ally. But before you leave Arathusa, I must give you a message to take back to the elves."

"Huh?"

She leaned closer with a stern look on her face. "My kin have seen one of the elven traitors, the one they call Julius Santorean."

"Julius!"

"Yes, chosen one. He was looking for shelter in Greenwood Forest. They secretly followed him using their glamour. He stole a horse near the village of Peniven, and when last they saw him, he was entering the forbidden lands." Queen Eleanor paused for a moment. She glanced at her kin, then leaned even closer. "He was last seen going into the trees of death... Darkwood Forest," she whispered.

The faeries gasped with fright. It wasn't the first time Jack had seen the mention of the place cause such a stir. "Albion Starborne was patrolling the border of the forest because the orcs were allegedly using it to cross into elf lands," Jack revealed. "Sarina was pretty upset about it. Why's everyone so afraid of that place?"

"No one knows for sure what evil dwells there. Long ago, some of my kin entered the forest and never returned. They say it's been cursed. No faerie's ever come out alive; it's been the same result for the elves. To enter the labyrinth of black trees means certain death. Only a handful of wildwood rangers have crossed the border. Most were never seen again, some have returned unscathed, and others came back with madness. The black trees are evil; they will devour anything that crosses their path. If orcs went into the forest I doubt they survived. It's said that even trolls have fallen prey to the darkness within."

"Why would Julius risk going in there? Wait—if I tell the elves about him, I'll have to tell them who told me. They'll ask about you, and I don't wanna lie to them."

Queen Eleanor ran her fingers through her emerald-green hair. "Well, since Julius is now an enemy of us all, you can tell them you've entered Arathusa, but only if they ask you directly. Still, I feel I should warn you, the elves will be suspicious if they discover you've been here. Don't be surprised if they question your loyalty."

"I understand," Jack nodded. "I have to tell them as soon as possible. They've been searching for Julius and Fergus since they betrayed us."

He arose from his chair as the faerie queen stood with a most curious look on her face. "You used the word *us,* which means your love for the elves is strong, as if you yourself were one of them..."

Stepping closer, she looked into his eyes, as if reading his mind again. "I know she loves you, too," said Queen Eleanor, as Jack's eyes widened in disbelief. "Do not fear—your secret's safe with me. I didn't have to read your mind; I knew she loved you from the moment I saw you together at the wizard's cabin. She'd have you believe that her willingness to save you was nothing more than a sense of duty. But I think you and I know better..."

"I've never met anyone like her," Jack struggled to whisper.

"I know what you mean. Sarina Starborne isn't like other elves; she has the most beautiful heart I've ever encountered. She's been good to us, but would slay a thousand faeries to protect you. That's how strong her love is. She is both fire and ice—far above rubies."

Jack wanted to ask if he and Sarina could be together, but was afraid of what the answer might be. "It's time for you to leave," said the faerie queen. "Remember my words; I know you'll discern the best outcome for us all."

With her kin following behind, she led him back to the stone circle. Standing before the centre, she raised her hands in the air with one palm flat against the other. Then, in a swift action, she separated them, causing the gateway to open! Jack headed towards the light, but stopped momentarily. "Goodbye, Queen Eleanor," he said, "thank you for your wisdom."

Instead of replying, she gave him a simple nod. With his eyes wide open, Jack stepped through the gateway. All he could see was green light. When it finally dissipated, he found himself back in Eloria. He watched as the magic door closed behind him. The fairies guarding the archway were gone, so he ran back through the forest until he reached the clearing, where he had left his horse. Up ahead, Jack's horse was still being guarded by the same young faerie, who was stroking the beast's neck, and Midknight was lapping up her affection.

"How was it?" she asked, handing him the reins.

"Um... interesting," said Jack, mounting his horse.

"What did you think of Arathusa?"

"I thought it was beautiful, but a bit dark for my taste."

"Arathusa's been dark since the death of our sun."

"Really? I just thought it was night-time. How'd your sun die?"

"We're not supposed to talk about it," said the faerie, glancing around. "It was the price my kin were forced to pay for their sinful ways. Some say he didn't actually die, that he was told by the High King to never give his light, even to the end of days."

"If you have no sun, then how do your trees survive?"

"Faeries are the handmaidens of nature. We can assist with propagation, but we also pray for abundance. Only a third of the forest is still alive. If you were looking down from above, like a bird, you would've seen this."

"I see," said Jack. "Thanks for watching my horse."

"That's okay. He was well-behaved. Oh, my Queen wanted me to tell you something before you left," she remembered. "If you get into any trouble, you can always seek refuge in the Forest of the Faerie Queen."

"Thanks, Ebony," said Jack. "That's your name, right?"

"Yes," she replied.

"Well, hopefully I won't have to seek refuge here, but it's nice to know I can if something ever happens. Anyway, I've gotta go. Take care!" said Jack, before turning his horse and riding away.

He didn't mean to be rude, but Jack couldn't get into another lengthy conversation, not when he had such valuable information for the elves, so he rode through the forest as fast as he could. When he reached the sea of grass, Jack rode all the way back to the Sapphire City, refusing to slow down until he made it to the silver bridge.

166

Chapter 20

The Hall of the Dead

Jack made his way across the bridge and into the Sapphire City. He rode towards the imperial stables, and realised it was mid-afternoon; the journey had taken longer than expected. He then rode into the stables, dismounted his horse, and removed the saddle and bridle. As he was placing the saddle onto its stand he heard a loud voice behind him. "Hey! You'd better get back to the tower of the high council! Sarina Starborne's gone mad looking for you!"

Jack spun around—it was the Elorian knight, Sir Tyrus! He was standing there, with his arms folded, looking rather annoyed. "Sorry, but I had to see the faerie queen," said Jack. "She told me that her kin saw Julius Santorean going into Darkwood Forest."

"What? Darkwood Forest? You sure they weren't mistaken? Faeries can't exactly be trusted, you know."

"Queen Eleanor was sure about it. Anyway, I s'pose I better go see Sarina," said Jack, before proceeding to leave.

"Hey! Make sure you tell the General when you see him!" Tyrus yelled, as Jack stepped into the city streets and headed towards the tower.

Arriving at the city square, Jack was amazed by how busy it was. There were elves bartering and trading goods, children playing and laughing, he even saw a few dwarves haggling with an elven merchant. Despite the recent attack on the village, he was glad to see the city was operating like normal.

After making his way back, Jack raced into the tower of the high council. He made his way down the hall of shields, past the big staircase, and arrived at the hall of the great tree. He was completely out of breath and could barely stand. Several elves were strolling about the room, chatting amongst themselves. Many of them were rich landowners, who resided in the tower for protection and business purposes. After catching his breath, Jack walked over to a green lounge and sat down. He was hoping for a moment's rest, but suddenly heard a loud cry, "Jack! Where have you been?!"

He looked up and saw Sarina running towards him as the elves were wondering why she had raised her voice in a sacred room. Kneeling down, she grabbed a hold of his hands. "I've been worried sick about you! You didn't tell us where you'd gone! The guards at the gate said you left when it was still dark! Don't you know orcs can see in the dark?! When you hadn't come back by midday, I thought you'd been killed!"

"Sarina, listen carefully," said Jack, "Julius was seen going into Darkwood Forest."

With terror in her eyes, she stood up and began slapping at him. "Jack! What in the High King's name were you thinking?! It's not your job to be looking for him! If he had caught you—he would've killed you! Where's your sword? You left the city, unarmed?!"

"Whoa, wait a minute!" Jack grabbed a hold of her arms. "I wasn't looking for him! I said he was *seen* going into Darkwood Forest—not by me! Queen Eleanor told me!"

They stood there staring at each other; this was their first argument. Sarina was breathing heavily, and Jack finally understood how foolish he had been. "Look, I need to tell your father about Julius. Queen Eleanor spoke to me in a dream, so I went looking for advice. I'm sorry for leaving. I should've told you, and I never should've left without you. I promise I'll never do it again, okay?"

"I'm sorry, too, Jack. I guess I overreacted. Darkwood Forest is at least three days ride from here. You've been gone for less than one. I don't know what I was thinking. Anyway, I forgive you," she smiled. "But if you ever leave without telling me again, I'll slap you back to your own world, got it?"

"Okay," he said, with a tiny smirk. "I'll never do it again, you have my word. But I have another confession to make."

"What?"

"I think you're terribly cute when you're angry." Again she smiled, wrapping her arms around him. "No one's ever been worried about me before. You're like a precious gemstone, hidden deep within a sea of shattered glass," said Jack, as they continued to embrace.

When they noticed the elves observing their interaction they quickly separated. Jack didn't think it was any of their business and glared at them until they looked away. Their first argument had been quite public, but now there was something else on his mind. "Hey, where exactly is my sword? I haven't seen it since that troll hit me from behind."

Sarina glanced down at the floor. "Oh, I completely forgot! Your armour and sword are with Marshall Tucker, the Master Blacksmith. Your armour was banged-up, and your sword needed to be cleaned and sharpened. That troll did a lot of damage, but the armour surpassed Marshall's expectations; it's just going to take some time to fix."

"That's alright," said Jack. "After you tell your father about Julius, can you take me to the hall of the dead? Queen Eleanor said I might find something there, something that'll help me make my decision."

"The hall of the dead? Only two people have a key to that place; one of them's my father. I've never been inside. The door's concealed at the back of the staircase. I know where he is, but you'll have to stay here, while I go look for him, okay?"

"No worries," Jack replied. "Take your time."

Sarina started to walk away, then suddenly turned around. "You'd better still be here when I get back," she warned.

"I won't move from this spot," said Jack, sitting back down.

Jack realised the day was almost gone, and if he only had two more days to make his decision, then his time in Eloria was almost over. Sarina returned a few minutes later with her father and brother in tow. *They look pissed!* Jack thought, standing up.

"You had the whole damn city worried about you, Shadar!" said Godfrey. "You should never leave without telling someone! Anything could've happened; there are more dangerous things than orcs and trolls wandering the wilds of Eloria."

"I know, Sir," said Jack, "and I'm very sorry."

With a deep sigh, Godfrey folded his arms and rubbed his chin. "I don't know why you sought the advice of the faeries, but I'm glad you did. Now we know exactly where to look for those cowards."

"But Queen Eleanor said Julius was seen, that he stole a horse near the village of Peniven before entering Darkwood Forest. She didn't say anything about Fergus—"

"Oh, I'm certain they'll be together. They've only got each other now," the General smiled, as if the traitors were already within his grasp.

Jack noticed a look of disappointment on Albion's face. He wanted to apologise to him, but was concerned about General Starborne, who appeared to be deep in thought. Godfrey looked at him suspiciously. "The faeries," he said, "you didn't eat or drink any of their food?"

"No," he replied. "Queen Eleanor spoke to me in a dream, so I went looking for advice about my decision, that's all."

"I see," said Godfrey, glancing at Sarina. "My daughter tells me you wish to visit the hall of the dead? Why is this so?"

"Well, Queen Eleanor said there's something I should see, something that might help me make my decision. But she didn't say what..."

"Pft! That's fairies for you!" Godfrey scoffed. "Very well, if that's where you need to go," he said, before removing a key from his pocket and handing it to Albion. "My son's been promoted during your absence. He still holds the rank of Captain but has been granted a seat on the high council. He's our new keeper of the dead. He led my army into battle at the silver bridge, despite my predicament, proving himself worthy of such an honour."

"Congratulations, Captain Starborne!" said Jack, bowing his head in respect.

"My son will take you to the hallowed hall. I can't join you, because I have some traitors to deal with," said Godfrey, before leaving the room.

"Come on, Shadar. I'll take you there now," said Albion.

"Go on," Sarina smiled, "I'll be waiting for you."

He gave her a nod, then followed the captain out of the room as they headed towards the big staircase. Albion led him around the side, but all Jack could see was a wall of green, where the staircase ended. He then watched in amazement as the elf pushed a small button, causing a panel to slide away and reveal a hollow interior. Jack peered over his shoulder and noticed a hidden door inside! Albion inserted the key into the keyhole, and slowly turned it until they both heard a loud *click*.

As the door opened Jack saw a dark passageway. Albion pushed a greenstone button on the side of the wall, lighting-up the darkness. The passageway was glowing with white crystal lights, the same technology used throughout the city. They shined along both sides of the stone steps, revealing the way down. "After you," said the captain.

Walking down the steps, they soon reached the bottom before heading along a straight path. Albion was very quiet. Jack was concerned that he may have betrayed his trust by leaving the city without him. Eventually, the long passageway opened-up into a silver room with massive stone columns. There didn't seem to be any more lights; it was dark and musty. Then Jack noticed a circle of marble with a giant crystal atop of it. The gemstone was at least twelve feet tall and formed like a cylindrical octagon.

Albion approached the object and pressed his finger onto a small button. Suddenly, in a burst of white light, the crystal lit-up the room to reveal statues of elven warriors. They ranged in size, and some had plaques on their bases engraved with symbols and words. Jack noticed that the silver walls were also painted with murals, displaying scenes of battles and fearsome creatures. "Welcome to the hall of the dead," said Albion, turning to him.

Jack reluctantly stepped forward. "Look, I know you're upset with me. And I'm sorry for leaving the city without telling anyone. I promised Sarina I'd never do it again, and I intend to keep that promise."

The captain looked at him in confusion. "My sister told me how sorry you were. What you did was stupid; I know you won't do it again. I'm not angry with you, Shadar."

"Oh, okay," said Jack. "Then what's wrong?"

Albion stared at the floor. "It's about my promotion. The only reason I've been given a seat on the council is because one of them was empty. I now must sit where a traitor once sat! An elf, who used to be my friend; it was you who inspired the army and won the battle for us, not me. I don't deserve a seat on the high council."

Jack slowly shook his head. "Of all the warriors in the city, they chose you. I've never seen your father so proud! It was you, Captain Starborne, who saved my life and led your father's army to victory. It was you who kept the orcs and trolls at bay when the villagers were locked out of the city. You're not just my mentor, you're my brother. And no one deserves a promotion more than you."

"Thanks for telling me what I needed to hear," Albion replied.

"All you needed to hear was the truth."

They smiled at each other with a deep sense of respect. "Well, you'd better start looking around. I'll stay here but give me a shout if you need anything," said the elf.

"Okay," Jack replied. The room was enormous; the vaulted ceilings were at least twenty feet high. Inspecting each mural, Jack's eyes were drawn to a large statue of the Red Dragon! It wasn't the whole Dragon, just its head and part of its neck.

Admiring the statue, he noticed an armoured warrior inside its mouth. There was also a mural above, depicting an army of soldiers being killed by Dragon's fire! The statue and mural depicted the last stand of Balinor Santorean, the former General, who died fighting the Red Dragon. At the base of the statue was an engraving: *In memory of General Balinor Santorean, who led his army into battle against the great Red Dragon. His bravery and tenacity against such a formidable opponent shall never be forgotten.*

Jack remembered when Godfrey told him the story of Balinor's demise. *I wish Queen Eleanor could've been more specific,* he thought. *I don't even know what to look for...*

He didn't want to keep Albion waiting. Jack looked at each statue around the room; they mostly depicted elven warriors. Then he noticed the names on the walls behind the statues. There were thousands of them; they were the names of fallen warriors too vast to be counted. He then came across something different, which appeared to be a statue of a king, seated upon a golden throne. From the look and shape of the figure, Jack knew it was no elven king—it was a human one!

"Albion," said Jack, "come 'ere a sec!"

"What is it?"

"Who's this king?" he asked, as Albion approached. "There's no plaque or engraving. He doesn't look like an elf. I think he's a man."

Albion looked at the statue and smiled. "That's the High King of Creation!" he chuckled. "He's a god—not a man!"

"Really?" said Jack. "Does he have a name?"

"I'm not sure. Mugglegruffe would know. All I remember about him are stories. I was only three years old when he came to Eloria to spread his message of peace."

"What kind of stories?"

Albion rubbed his forehead. "Well, my father said he came here the day Sarina was born, almost two thousand years ago. He spread a message of peace. He also punished the faeries and convinced them to repent of their wicked ways."

The die is cast, you cannot change prophecy, Jack thought, remembering the wizard's words from the last council meeting.

"What's wrong?" said Albion.

"Oh, it's probably nothing. I think we should leave."

"Okay," he replied, before heading towards the crystal light. Stomping his boot in frustration, Jack scanned his eyes across the walls, then caught sight of something else. "Wait!" he cried, as Albion was about to turn off the light.

Jack went to the other side of the room to look at another mural of the Red Dragon; only this time, the Dragon was being cast into a realm of darkness. "What's this one?"

Once again, the captain approached. "That's a painting of the Red Dragon's fate," he revealed. "It was prophesied that a king would rain lightning down from the heavens. It's said that he'll defeat the Red Dragon and cast him into the Dark Abyss for all eternity."

"That's what they call Hell in my world, right? Your father said if I had've killed Barbatus, that's where he'd be, imprisoned forever."

"Yes, but I don't think the Dragon will be defeated by any of us. Your arrival was the first sign to look for. Who knows, maybe one day the prophecy will come true..."

"Could the High King be the king of the prophecy?"

"He certainly is," Albion replied, "at least according to Mugglegruffe."

Further along, Jack discovered another three murals; they were painted together in a circular pattern. The central painting contained three figures. Jack recognised the High King, who was seated at the right hand of the central figure; and in the High King's left hand, was a book with the tree of life on the cover. The central figure was larger than the other two, and Jack could see that like the High King, he was seated upon a golden throne. On the base of his throne, was an inscription that read: *King of the Law*. Lastly, the figure standing to the left of the King of the Law was wearing a white robe and appeared to be ethereal, like a ghost. The inscription beneath him read: *Spirit of the King*.

The second painting in the circle of three was the tree of life, the sacred symbol of the elves. Jack was surprised to learn that each branch represented a different law. "These must be the laws of the elves..." he whispered to himself.

The seven laws on each branch were inscribed as followed:

1. Do not consort with the wicked.
2. Defend those who cannot defend themselves.
3. Be charitable to those in need.
4. Do not condemn your brethren, for I am the Judge.
5. Obey my Father's commands, but ye are saved by grace alone.
6. Whosoever takes the sword shall live and die by the sword.
7. Vengeance is mine; I will repay.

Jack never paid much attention to the religious texts in his own world, but something was familiar. It was like putting the pieces of a puzzle together. There was a strong connection between the two worlds. There was something universal about the beliefs of humans and elves. Long ago Jack convinced himself that God was just another fairy-tale, but that never stopped him from wanting to believe. Like others, he wanted to believe in a loving and compassionate God. And he was now starting to believe that if he couldn't find God in his own world, perhaps he could find him in Eloria...

He gazed up at the third painting, which again was the tree of life. Instead of revealing the seven laws, it revealed the nine worlds. There were seven worlds, caused by the great flood, but there were also another two worlds: The Dark Abyss, and the High King's dwelling place of Araboth. "Wait a sec, the tree of life isn't just a symbol of laws. It's like the world tree of Norse mythology," Jack realised.

According to this new rendition, the seven branches represented the seven worlds, six of which were cast into separate realms during the great flood. And the seven leaves on each branch represented the seven laws of Eloria, which applied to the rest of the worlds; excluding the realms of Araboth and The Dark Abyss. *Wait—what happened to the rest of the names?* Jack thought, stepping closer. The names of six worlds had been scratched off.

Upon closer inspection, Jack noticed an older layer beneath the paint. According to the older layer, the seven branches were the seven worlds, and the seven leaves on each branch were the seven spirits of God, which governed them. The three roots of the tree, of course, represented the trinity of God: The King of the Law, The High King of Creation, and The Spirit of the King.

"The tree of life's a universal symbol. It has different layers and meanings," said Jack, aloud. "I still can't see the other names—bugger it! Why've these names been removed?"

Albion stepped closer to survey the damage. "I don't know, Shadar. Only the keeper of the dead has a key to this place."

"Who was the keeper before you?"

The captain paused for a moment. "Julius! That rotten piece of troll dung! My father took the key from his quarters this morning."

"Don't worry about it for now," said Jack. "Let's just get out of here."

"Okay," the captain sighed, before switching off the crystal light.

Chapter 21

THE FINAL COUNCIL MEETING

Leaving the hall of the dead, Albion pressed a small button, closing the wall behind them. Jack stood by as the captain checked to make sure the wall was flush. "I thought it was gonna be some kind of burial chamber."

Albion shook his head. "No, little brother, we bury our dead in the earth, beneath the hallowed hills of the sea of grass. The hall of the dead's where the names and deeds of our fallen kin are recorded, so they'll be remembered. Those who forget the past will be doomed to repeat it. We must never fail to preserve the future."

Jack wasn't sure what he meant but decided not to question him further. The hall of the dead was a sacred place that should only be entered on days of remembrance. Walking around the staircase, they returned to the hall of the great tree. Sarina, who was patiently seated, stood up to greet them. "Did you find what you were looking for?"

"I'm not sure," said Jack. "I need to talk to Mugglegruffe. Did he go back to his cabin last night, or is he still here in the city?"

Sarina turned to her brother. "Have you seen him?"

"Oh, I'm sure he's still here. He wouldn't leave the city without telling anyone, unlike some people," said Albion, smirking at Jack. "He's been busy since the battle. But if something's afoot, he'll stay close to the tower of the high council."

"Looking for a dwarf?" said a familiar voice.

Turning around, they saw Mugglegruffe standing behind them. "How do you do that?" Sarina laughed. "You're always in the right place at the right time."

"As a servant of the High King; he places me where I'm needed most. But in this case, I happen to be seeking you, Captain Starborne, for we need to discuss your recent promotion."

"I think Jack needs to speak with you more urgently, my wise friend."

"I've just spoken to your father, who informed me that you had taken our Shadar to the hall of the dead. If that's the case, there's nothing more to be said—no more advice to be given."

"Please!" Jack begged. "I have to know more about the three kings, especially the High King. Is he the king of the prophecy, the one who'll defeat the Red Dragon?"

The wizard sighed. "Listen, Shadar, you know of the prophecy, and you know of Eloria's past. Your decision can't be swayed by further knowledge. And though you won't admit it, you know exactly who the High King is. So from this point on, you'll just have to listen to your heart."

"Listen to my heart?" Jack scoffed.

"Listen to your heart, listen to logic, or better yet—listen to both! Contrary to Midlandian belief, they can both be right, you know."

What is it with this guy? Why can't he just gimme a straight answer? My decision could affect billions of lives, and no one seems to care, he thought. But Jack knew better than to pester the dwarf, who had only ever told him what he needed to know, and nothing more.

"Now, Captain Starborne, if you'd please follow me. We have much business to discuss," said the wizard, tapping his boot.

"Bye for now," said Albion.

As they walked away, Jack thought about Mugglegruffe's words. *Listen to my heart, or listen to logic? My heart's just a muscle that pumps blood to vital organs. How's that s'posed to help?* He then looked at Sarina in despair. "What am I gonna do?"

"I don't know what to say," she replied. "I guess it's up to you now. Like he said, there's no more advice to be given."

Jack gave her a nod, then spent the rest of the day within the confines of his quarters, pondering every possible scenario that may affect his decision. By nightfall, he finally gave-up and retired for the night.

The next morning, Jack awoke with a single thought on his mind. All he could think about was the giant green sapphire on the rooftop. Since first arriving in Eloria, the idea of seeing a gemstone the size of a house seemed ridiculous. Despite not wanting to climb so many stairs, he couldn't leave without at least doing it once. He quickly bathed, got dressed, and made himself a cheese sandwich for breakfast. After breakfast, he went next door to Sarina's and knocked, but the door remained shut. *I thought rangers had super-hearing?* he thought, before knocking again. A few seconds later, she opened the door in her bed robe.

"Jack? What's going on? Is everything alright?" she worried. "You're not leaving the city again, are you?"

"Sorry for waking you, I didn't realise how early it was. I need someone to take me to the rooftop, so I can see that giant sapphire," he smiled.

"Aaargh! Is that it?!" she scowled. "Sometimes you drive me insane!" she said, grabbing him by the shirt and pulling him inside. Sarina then pointed towards the lounge room. "Wait there! I'll be out when I'm ready."

Jack watched as she returned to her bedroom and closed the door. Waiting in the lounge room, he noticed four portraits hanging on the wall, above the fireplace. Stepping closer, he saw that each painting had a golden plaque attached to the bottom of the frame. He recognised the portraits of Albion and Godfrey, but the others, were of two, beautiful she-elves. Both had blonde hair and blue eyes, but only one was wearing armour. The plaque beneath her portrait read: *Evelyn Starborne.*

"Maybe that's Sarina's mother?" Jack whispered to himself.

Turning his attention to the last portrait, the she-elf was wearing a white dress. She was very beautiful, and despite having blonde hair and blue eyes like the other she-elf, her face was distinctly different. The name attached to the frame read: *Suara Starborne.*

"Hmm, I guess either one could be her mother," he surmised. After waiting almost ten minutes, Sarina finally re-emerged. She was wearing a lovely yellow dress decorated in blue flowers. She also had sandals on her feet, the ones she had been wearing the day they had met. "Well, come on!" she said, with an adventurous smile.

As they stepped into the hallway, Jack watched as she closed the door of her quarters without locking it. The elves had a lot of trust in each other. The only doors they actually seemed to lock had nothing worth stealing in them. Over the last three months, he had found them to be sentimental beings, who valued morals, whilst leaving precious gemstones paving their streets. Everything in the city had become so natural to him, yet very illogical, and somewhat back-to-front, compared to the standards of his own world.

"You look divine in that dress," said Jack, as they scaled the big staircase. "I think yellow suits you."

"If that's your way of an apology for making me walk up twenty-six flights of stairs, then apology not accepted," she said, with a hint of sarcasm.

Sticking his head over the bannister, Jack gazed up towards the towering ceiling. "Did you say twenty-six flights?"

"Yes. And by the time we reach the top, we'll both want to go back to bed."

"If we live on the seventh floor, the whole tower must be thirty-three, right?"

"Yes, Jack, but please don't talk—I'm trying to count!"

By the time they reached the thirty-third floor, they were both exhausted. He continued to follow as she approached a tall ladder, covered by a manhole. "After you," Jack coughed, struggling to catch his breath.

Sarina looked at him slyly. "Why? So you can see up my dress?"

"Whoa! No! I wasn't tryin to—I was just being courteous!" he stammered.

"I'm just teasing you!" she giggled. "But I'm still not going up first."

Jack rolled his eyes and began to climb the ladder with Sarina following behind. Reaching the manhole, he pushed it aside and climbed onto the roof. Standing up he found himself in front of the giant sapphire. It was light-green in colour and was nestled in an iron frame of immense proportions. The gemstone was shaped and

180

polished, and despite being the size of a house, it was like peering through a piece of glass. Jack felt something pulling his leg. He glanced down to see Sarina reaching up, and took her by the hand.

"Oh, you're such a gentleman!" she smiled, making it to her feet. "It's amazing, isn't it? It was a gift from the dwarves, they've been excellent allies."

A gust of wind suddenly blew, and Jack realised there was no safety railing. "Be careful," Sarina warned, as he stepped towards the edge.

Jack was in awe of the vast expanding view. The city was beautiful! There were thousands of people below, and more. There were hundreds of houses and various buildings. He could see the jousting arena, which looked like a Roman Colosseum, only better! Looking outside the city, he could see the village of the silver bridge, and could just make out some of the people, who appeared to be trying to salvage what was left in the aftermath of the battle. Further southward, he saw the Forest of the Faerie Queen, just beyond the sea of grass.

He walked around the edge of the rooftop, making his way to the other side of the sapphire. Jack saw an endless forest. He was hoping to see the snow-capped mountains, where the dwarves lived, but they were too far away; so he looked north-west, towards the forbidden lands, but all he could see were more trees.

A dark thought entered his mind. He went back around the sapphire and looked down at the city again, trying to imagine what it would be like with human habitation. He could see black smoke rising up to the clear, blue sky. Rubbish in the gutters, and humans stealing the precious gemstones that paved the city streets. He could see politicians using bribery and blackmail to influence and control the high council. Lastly, Jack could see the clashing of human and elf culture, which would inevitably lead to conflict and war. "I can't take this anymore!" he gasped.

"What's wrong?" said Sarina, gently taking hold of his arm.

Jack looked into her rainbow coloured eyes. His heart was filled with fear. He wanted to tell her what he had seen, but a question came to mind. "Sarina, of all the elves in the city, why're you the only one with rainbow coloured eyes?"

She suddenly turned pale. "They're what you would call a birth defect," she replied, with sadness in her voice. "When I was an elfling, the other kids teased me about them. I can't recall how many days I cried. It's a rare condition. It happens sometimes, when a northerner marries a southerner. But my eyes can zoom-in on a target! And I can see just as well as the wildwood rangers—no bowman in the city can out-shoot me."

"Your eyes aren't a birth defect, Sarina," said Jack, touching the side of her face. "They're the most beautiful eyes I've ever seen."

She moved closer, then shied away, stepping towards the manhole. Jack approached from behind and wrapped his arms around her, resting his chin on her shoulder in a loving display, and whispered in her ear. "Of all the women, in all the worlds... you're the only one I want. Now... and forever."

Unexpectedly, Sarina broke free and ran to the manhole, before swiftly descending the ladder. At that precise moment Jack knew what had to be done. He couldn't procrastinate any longer because he had made up his mind. Replacing the manhole cover, he descended into the tower and proceeded to make his way downstairs. He kept an eye out for Sarina, but she was nowhere to be found. *I hope she's not angry...* he worried.

Arriving at the seventh floor, Jack paused for a moment. He looked down the hallway towards her quarters. He desperately wanted to see her but thought it best to give her some space. He then went to the third floor, where the council chambers resided.

When the guards opened the doors, Jack walked inside to find it almost empty. Only General Starborne was present; the elf glanced up at him. He seemed to have been studying some old maps. Godfrey could tell by the look on Jack's face that he wasn't visiting the chambers for recreational purposes. "Everything alright?" he asked.

"I've made my decision—" Jack tried to say, before the elf interrupted.

"You've still got another day. You should be using all the time you have."

Jack took a deep breath, wiping the sweat from his brow. "I've made my decision, General. I will inform the council tomorrow morning. I trust you'll let them know?"

Godfrey looked at him with much curiosity. "And if I refuse to alter the time of the meeting for your benefit?"

"This isn't for my benefit, General," said Jack, with a fiery tone. "It's for the benefit of every citizen in the Sapphire City. And if you refuse, well, I'd hate to be a prick, but I guess I'll be leaving without giving you my answer."

Jack hadn't spoken to an elf in such a manner; the General looked like someone had just hit him in the face with a wet mop. It was the same look on Jim's face, the day Jack had given him a piece of his mind. But unlike Jim, he greatly respected the General, and looked up to him the way a son looks up to a father. Judging by Jack's demeanour, the elf knew he was serious. Godfrey was used to getting his own way, but he couldn't risk prophecy by allowing him to leave without completing his task.

"Very well, Shadar. You've left me no choice. I'll reschedule the meeting. I just hope you know what you're doing."

"Thank you, Sir," said Jack, before leaving the chambers.

Jack returned to his quarters. He was half-expecting Sarina to be waiting outside, but she was nowhere to be seen. Jack was disappointed that she had left so abruptly. Unable to think of anything else, he remained in his quarters for the rest of the day.

The next morning, Jack got dressed and went to the council chambers. As he entered the room, everyone was seated and waiting for him to speak, including Albion, the council's newest member. Sir Griffin and Marshall were whispering to each other, possibly conspiring, but that didn't faze him in the slightest. Sitting atop his stool, Mugglegruffe motioned for Jack to sit beside him. "Morning, Shadar," said the wizard. "You must be the first in history to make Godfrey reschedule a meeting. I hope you make the right decision."

"Regardless of what you or anyone else thinks about the outcome, I'm glad to be sitting beside you once more," Jack replied.

The wizard smiled, then banged his staff on the floor three times. Ceasing their whispers, they focused their attention on Mugglegruffe. "This council's now in session!"

Professor Hobblestone stood up. "My friends and fellow councilmen, we've gathered here today, so that we may hear what the Shadar has to say. All I ask is that when he speaks you listen carefully to his words, and you allow him to finish speaking without interruption. He's unaware of how divided we are in regards to his difficult decision, so it's only fair that we allow him to reveal his answer without ridicule." The elf paused and looked at General Starborne. "Anything further to add?"

Godfrey shook his head in silence. Jack anxiously looked at the faces staring back at him as the Professor sat down. Resting his hands on the round table he rose from his chair. "I'm not much of a public speaker, so you'll have to bear with me," he started to say.

"It's alright, young man, just take your time," the Professor advised.

Jack took a deep breath. "I've been living in your city for three months. I've made a lot of new friends, and almost died protecting them and your way of life. This world's not without its dangers; I've seen the carnage that orcs and trolls can inflict. I've seen betrayal, in the forms of Julius Santorean and Fergus Crouse. But Julius was right about one thing, it's true that humans can't be trusted. I consider myself to be a trustworthy guy. But in general, humans are dishonest, disloyal, and full of greed."

Struggling with his conscience, Jack paused for a moment. "I wish I could say otherwise, but I can't. Allowing humans into Eloria, or vice versa, on a massive scale, would be downright stupid. Sooner or later, there'd be disastrous consequences for your people, and your way of life. It almost brings tears to my eyes when I think about how perfect this city is compared to the cities of my own world. But the people of the Sapphire City would soon be corrupted by the wicked ways of humanity if you allowed them to enter this world. All they'd contribute to your society is their own ideas of right and wrong; they'd bring nothing but immorality, decay, destruction, and death to your people."

Jack wiped the moisture from his eyes. "I wish I could tell you they're all like me, but I'm far from perfect myself. Maybe the High King sent me here because I've never found a place in my own world? If that's the case, then I s'pose you could say there was a method to his madness. I wish I could tell you of our great qualities, like respect, honour, trust, and a fine moral compass. But to be perfectly honest, they'd care more about the gemstones paving your streets than the lives of those who put them there. Humans have replaced the old ideals of morality and belief, with selfishness and materialism. They've become hedonistic, caring not for love, empathy, or matters of the heart. They marry for compatibility and social status. They take without asking and give nothing in return. Most of all, they're incapable of being content. If you don't give them what's yours, they'll take it by force. And if they fail to take it from you, they'll just take it from someone else, like the dwarves."

"May I interject?" Sir Griffin asked.

"No!" Jack snapped. "If one of you entered my world, they'd capture you and dissect you a piece at a time. They'd never stop cutting you up till they discovered the secrets of your longevity. That's the measure of human morality! And as far as your prophecies are concerned, if the veil's lifted and humans enter this world, so be it. But for me, that'll be a sad day, because it'll mean the end of you all."

There was a deafening silence. Despite Sir Griffin's brief interruption, the council had listened intently, so Jack continued. "You see, I love Eloria and its people so much, that if it's within my power to make this world last a bit longer, even for a moment, then that's what I'll do. I won't make a decision that condemns this world to ruin. I wish humans were capable of change, but for thousands of years we've been given that opportunity, and squandered it. We could've made heaven on earth, but instead—we built the devil's playground. Humans must reap what they've sown. They no longer build with the future in mind, all they do is destroy. My answer's no," he concluded.

Jack took his seat and looked at the faces around the room. Some appeared to be relieved, which was a comforting sign. Godfrey rose from his chair. "The last Shadar has spoken," he declared. "As General of the imperial army and Steward of the Sapphire City, and of Eloria, I hereby decree that none shall enter the human world without permission from this council. That's all I have to say for now," he stated, before sitting back down.

Jack had completed his task. His time in Eloria was over, but he couldn't leave without saying goodbye to Sarina. "I know my task is done," he said, standing again, "and if I could choose to stay here, I would. But as my good friend Mugglegruffe said to me at the last council meeting: the die is cast—you cannot change prophecy. I don't know if God exists in my world, but I'm startin' to believe he might exist here. And with your permission, I'd like to stay until tomorrow morning. Then I'll make the journey home at first light."

"Of course," Godfrey nodded.

"Um, I'll head back to my quarters now, but before I do, I just wanna say thank you. Thank you for your kindness, understanding, and of course, for your generous hospitality," said Jack, with a gracious bow.

They smiled at hearing his words. Over the last three months they had been surprised by his humility and patience. They were older and wiser than he and saw him as child-like. Jack didn't know how closely they had watched him. Many observed when he first entered the Sapphire City, looking upon its grandeur with the eyes of a child. His eyes were filled with wonder and awe. Struggling to find his place in a world of enchantment, his journey had been one of adventure.

The elves had grown fond of him over the last few months, and Jack had no idea how much his presence would be missed. He was disheartened by the looks of sadness on some of their faces, especially Albion's. As he was about to leave, however, the captain stood up and gave him an elven salute. It was a salute he had seen several times, one of many things he was going to miss about Eloria. Jack balled-up his fist, and saluted his elven brother in return as tears welled-up in his eyes. Then he left the council chambers, hardening his heart, to stem the flow of his sorrows...

Chapter 22

A KNIGHTING CEREMONY

Jack returned to his quarters to find that his sword and armour had been returned. It was all placed on the table in the lounge room, where he usually kept it. "If Marshall was at the council meeting, who brought it up here?" he said aloud.

The armour was clean and shiny and the dents had been repaired. Picking up his sword he drew it from the scabbard. There were no marks or stains on the blade, and the folded-steel pattern was as beautiful as ever, having been oiled and polished. The sapphire-blue eyes of the wolf seemed alive. "Boy did I miss you, my beautiful friend!"

He remembered his battle with Barbatus and how the blue flames engulfed the demon like a raging inferno. *It was like being inside the eye of a storm,* he thought. And just like that, Jack came up with a name for his sword. "I'm gonna call you, Blue Storm!" he declared.

Jack thought about his training sessions; Albion had been so patient with him. He was going to miss his friends, and was feeling a sense of loss and grief, knowing that he may never return. He was also thinking about Sarina, who had been his first Elorian friend. Jack was going to miss her most of all. *I'll never forget the day I saw her wearing that white dress, with flowers in her hair,* he thought. *She was so captivating, like something out of a fairy-tale.*

He slid his sword into the scabbard and stood quietly, continuing to reminisce. He was then distracted by the sound of someone knocking. Thinking it was Sarina, Jack hurried over and opened the door, but it was only Albion. Despite being disappointed, he smiled and invited the captain to enter. When Albion stepped inside, he noticed the armour as he walked over and stood in front of the table. "I see you got your gear back," he said, checking for dents.

"Yeah, Marshall did one hell of a job. He's quite the Master Blacksmith!" Jack exclaimed. "By the way, I've chosen a name for my sword."

188

"Really?" said the elf.

Jack drew his sword once more. "Say hello to Blue Storm!"

Carefully handing it to him, Albion proceeded to examine it. "Blue Storm, that's a good name for a sword," he smiled, before handing it back.

"What's yours called?" said Jack, placing his down on the table.

Albion drew his sword and held it up for him to see. It was silver coloured, with an engraving of a four-pointed star in the centre of a leaf-shaped blade. It also had a green, leather-wrapped handle, with a sequence of rubies decorating the cross-guard, and a larger ruby set inside the pommel. "This is Stargaze, sword of my Grandfather, Silvanis Starborne," Albion boasted. "Well, technically just part of the pommel. My grandfather didn't carry a sword; he carried a staff with a ruby set upon its tip."

"That's quite an heirloom!" Jack remarked.

"My grandfather was a very powerful seer."

"What happened to him?" asked Jack, as Albion sheathed his sword.

He was shot by the poison arrow of a dark elf before he could enter our promised land. Shot in the back by a coward, according to my father. He was the first of the seven seers, and led the elves and dwarves to the northern gate of Eloria."

"Was he the one your father told me about? The seer, whose dreams and visions led his people here, after the great flood?" Jack inquired.

"That's right," Albion confirmed. "The poison was strong. He barely had time to close the northern gate before he died. His staff and body turned to salt, leaving nothing behind but fragments of the ruby, which my father used in the making of this sword. My father also collected the salt. He buried it later, on a large green hill outside the city. Miraculously, the hill was covered in snapdragons the next morning—that's why we call it Snapdragon Hill."

"I'm sorry you never got to meet your grandfather," said Jack. "What about the dark elf who shot him? Was he ever seen again?"

"Yes, but we don't have time to talk about that. I came here for a reason."

Stepping closer, Albion softly rubbed his chin. Whatever was on his mind, Jack knew it was of great importance. "I never cared much for humans until I met you," he started to say. "But right now, I need you to come with me, by order of my father."

"I'm not in trouble, am I?"

"No, Shadar, quite the opposite," he smiled, heading towards the door. "Come on, little brother. Trust me, if you miss this opportunity, you'll regret it forever."

With a quick nod, Jack left his quarters and Albion led him up the big staircase until they reached the ninth floor. "Right, from this point on, there must be absolute silence. Only speak when spoken to and do exactly what my father says. You're about to receive an honour that no human's been given."

"Okay," he said, as they proceeded down a long hallway.

Jack noticed murals on the walls. They were quite detailed and showed knights battling orcs, dragons, and other creatures. At the end of the hallway, there were two knights guarding the large double door, as opposed to lawkeepers. The green doors were carved with a beautiful rendition of the tree of life, with Celtic knot work around the frame. As the doors were opened, Albion led him to a dark space. "Stay close," he whispered.

Jack peered into the darkness. There appeared to be knights standing about the room, like statues. They soon became clearer though, as they lit torches in their hands, continuing to remain silent. In the centre of the room, Godfrey was quietly waiting; and standing either side of him, were two knights, each holding a single torch. "Stand here, Shadar," said Albion, positioning him in front of the General.

"Before I begin," said Godfrey, "understand that this oath you're about to take, should you choose to accept it, is forever binding and sacred. And wherever you may reside, it will remain with you, until the end of your days. Are you willing to proceed?"

"Yes, General," Jack replied.

"Then, take a knee."

With his pulse racing Jack knelt as instructed. Godfrey drew his sword, resting the tip of the blade on the floor, with his hand at the end of the pommel. "Do you, Jack Campbell, swear to always be truthful, to always be humble, to protect the meek and defenceless; to rise up and defend the Sapphire City when needed, to obey the seven laws, and orders of your superiors, thereby upholding your duties as a knight of Eloria?"

"Yes, I swear it," said Jack, shaking like a leaf.

Raising his sword, Godfrey tapped the tip of his blade onto each of Jack's shoulders. "Arise, Sir Jack Campbell—Knight of Eloria."

As Jack stood, Godfrey waved for one of the knights to come forward. As the knight approached, Jack saw a green pillow in his hands with a gold ring in the centre. He looked at Godfrey, who gave him a solemn nod. Taking the ring, Jack glanced at the knight; it was Sir Tyrus. Then, placing the ring onto his pinkie finger, Jack noticed the blue sapphire, featuring the head of a wolf, engraved into the oval-shaped gemstone. Sir Tyrus placed his left hand on Jack's shoulder. "Well done, brother."

Before he could respond, Tyrus left the room as the other knights followed suit. One by one, they touched his shoulder before leaving the room, with each knight whispering the same words. Jack assumed it was either a sign of respect or a closing part of the ceremony. After the knights had left, only the Starbornes remained. Finally, Godfrey stepped forward and placed his hand on Jack's shoulder. "Well done, Shadar," he smiled, before quietly leaving.

And last, but not least, it was Albion's turn. "Well done, little brother," he whispered. Now, let's go have a drink!"

Jack followed him out of the room and back towards the big staircase. *I don't believe it,* he thought, *I'm a real knight...*

"You're one of us now," said Albion, holding up his hand.

"Nice!" said Jack, admiring the captain's ring. It was gold, with an oval-shaped ruby, and was engraved with a four-pointed star, like the one featured on the elf's blade.

"I don't think I've earned this," said Jack, as they headed downstairs. "I've only had three months' training—I don't even know how to joust."

"Nonsense," Albion replied. "You're a battle-hardened warrior. You just lack confidence. Next time, I'll teach you how to joust, like a real knight!"

"What if there isn't gonna be a next time?" asked Jack, sadly.

"What does your heart tell you? Are you coming back someday?"

Jack tried to make sense of what he was feeling. "Yes. I think I'll be back someday. Thanks for everything. I'd like to thank your father as well. Do you think I'll see him tomorrow before I leave?"

"I don't think so. My father's never liked goodbyes, not since my mother died."

Jack wanted to inquire, but was afraid of upsetting the captain, so he decided to change the subject. "Most of the knights had silver rings, instead of gold. Do they all have different engravings on their gemstones?"

"Silver rings have a green sapphire engraved with the tree of life. Most knights don't come from the nobility lines of great Houses; they use the emblem of the city instead. But always remember, that doesn't make them any less of a knight."

"Okay, but what's a House emblem?"

"When I say *House,* I'm referring to a family emblem. Only if a knight comes from the bloodline of a Baron, can he use the emblem of his House. They're not given any special privileges in the Sapphire City though. Only the Stewardship of my father's House is the recognised authority in the capital," said Albion, holding up his ring again. "This is the emblem of House Starborne. My father gave it to me when I obtained the rank of Captain. When the high council made him General of the imperial army, he took his position very seriously. And since he was representing the capital as Steward of Eloria, he thought it best to wear the city's emblem instead. So when he stopped wearing his old ring, he presented it to me as a gift—I had to earn it of course. I'll never forget that day. For the first time in my life, he was truly proud of me."

"What about the banners they carry on their spears?"

"Well, even though some of the knights have chosen to wear the city's emblem, they still fly their House colours with pride. Those who don't wear a House ring, but carry a House banner, are usually a cousin to one of the land Barons. They take pride in their lineage, but will never inherit any lands, which are passed down from father to son. You're not an Elorian, so we had to make some colours for you. That's another reason why Marshall asked you those questions that day," he smirked. "Believe it or not, your lineage comes from a great House, a true clan of warriors. But the old codes of chivalry are all but dead in the world of Midland."

"What? That doesn't make sense. I'm not a Baron or a wealthy land owner," Jack admitted. "How could I 'ave come from a great House?"

"According to Mugglegruffe, your lineage comes from one of the biggest Houses in the north of your world," he revealed. "In Eloria, you represent the human race. That means if humans ever enter our world, you must be their leader."

Reaching his quarters, they proceeded inside for a small celebration. "It must've been hard for your father to part with such a precious heirloom?"

"Yes," Albion replied, "but that's how things are done in our culture. Heirlooms are passed down from father to son."

"Have you seen Sarina? She kinda ran off on me earlier. I'd hate to leave without saying goodbye," said Jack, heading for the kitchen.

"She's gone, Shadar. She'll meet you at Mugglegruffe's cabin tomorrow morning."

As Jack went to open the cupboard, Albion suddenly stepped in front of him, blocking his path. "I don't know what's going on between the two of you," said the elf. "And though I have great respect for you, if you hurt my sister, I'll have no choice but to throw down my gauntlet. Understand?"

There was silence for a moment, then Jack nodded his head. "Believe me, Albion; the last thing I'd ever want is for Sarina to get hurt."

"Good," he smiled. "Well, this's your last night in Eloria, so we'd better start drinking. Here, come and sit down," he said, pulling out a chair.

Jack sat at the table as the elf grabbed a bottle of wine and two chalices from the cupboard. "You okay? I didn't mean to snap at you, but Sarina's my sister and I have to look out for her," said Albion, pouring them a drink.

"It's okay. I'd probably feel the same way if I was in your position. What's your father gonna do about the knights who betrayed us? I saw him looking at some old maps," said Jack, as Albion handed him one of the wine-filled chalices.

"Forget those traitors! And you needn't refer to them as knights anymore; they've been stripped of their knighthoods. My father and I will hunt them down and bring them to justice, no matter how long it takes."

"Then let's drink to justice," said Jack, holding up his chalice.

"To justice indeed!" Albion declared.

They bumped chalices and took a big drink, savouring the moment. After several hours of drinking and talking, Albion said, "Well, little brother, I'd love to stay and keep knocking them back, but duty calls, you know."

"Of course," said Jack, rising from his chair.

Albion placed his chalice on the table and followed him to the door. Jack had plenty of acquaintances back home, but he didn't have many friends; he was going to miss the captain's honesty, bravery, kindness, patience, and loyalty to family. As he opened the door, the elf stepped into the hallway. "Well, Shadar… I guess this is it."

Jack was lost for words. Albion had trained him, fought beside him, and even saved his life. "I'll never be able to thank you enough, but I'd follow you to the gates of hell."

"As would I!" said Albion, giving him a hug.

In Jack's world, it was often seen as taboo to be hugging another man, but Albion wasn't a man; he was an elf. And he wasn't just a friend, he was a brother in arms, and Jack would always think of him as family.

"Farewell," said the elf, "and always remember: nothing out of time."

"See you next time," Jack replied, as Albion walked down the hallway. The captain stopped for a moment and looked back. "I'll meet you at the silver bridge with Midknight," he smirked, before vanishing into the staircase.

Despite the captain's last words, as Jack closed his door, he had the strangest feeling he would never see Albion again. But the one person he couldn't stop thinking about was Sarina. *I can't believe she left the city. I can't keep suppressing my feelings like this. I know she feels the same way; I'm certain of it,* Jack thought, as he looked around his quarters. "I can't believe I'm going home," he said aloud. "I'm sure gonna miss this place. I'll even miss the clothing. Bugger—I forgot about my clothes!"

Taking elvish clothes back to the human world wouldn't be right, they belonged in Eloria. Jack went into his bedroom, opened the wardrobe, and carefully removed his human attire. He held up his jacket and heard a jingling sound in one of the pockets. Sticking his hand inside, he pulled out his house keys. "I almost forgot about them…"

He then grabbed his cargo pants and removed a square-shaped object. "My phone!"

Jack tried to switch it on, but the screen wouldn't light-up. "This happened before," he remembered. "Eloria doesn't have cell-phone towers, but that still doesn't explain it."

He shoved the phone back into his pants' pocket. "I wish I could throw these damn things away and stay here forever."

With his old clothes ready to put on, Jack went to the kitchen and grabbed the bottle of wine they hadn't finished. He drank from the bottle, while making his way to the lounge room. The rest of his last day was quite lonely. "I just wanna see Sarina again," he sighed, "even if it is for the very last time."

Trying to get her out of his mind, Jack focused on the friends he had made, the foes he had vanquished, and the day he had come so close to death. But thoughts of Sarina were still creeping in. All Jack could do was wonder how he was going to leave her, but he couldn't say goodbye, not without expressing how much she meant to him.

As the hour grew late, Jack returned to his bedroom, where he would sleep his final night in Eloria…

Chapter 23

SAYING GOODBYE

The next morning, Jack got out of bed and removed the elvish clothes he had slept in. He was sentimental about his elvish attire and wanted to dress like an Elorian for as long as possible. After putting on his human clothes, Jack placed his elvish ones in the wardrobe. Before leaving his quarters, he placed the golden key onto the lounge room table next to his sword and armour. There was no Elorian breakfast to be had, but that didn't bother him; all he could think about was Sarina.

He raced down the big staircase. A lawkeeper tried to salute him as he flew past like the wind, and before he knew it, Jack was leaving the tower of the high council. Slowing his pace, he wiped the sweat from his forehead, making his way through the city. Jack glanced towards the market district and saw a few of the elves waving goodbye. He gave them a wave back, wishing he had taken the time to see the heart of the city's trading area.

When he arrived at the entrance gate, the lawkeepers opened the large double door, giving him a salute as he passed beneath the archway. Leaving the city, Jack began to cross the silver bridge. Upon reaching the halfway mark he saw someone waiting on the other side. As he got closer, he realised it was Albion, and the captain was holding Midknight by the reins.

"Now, surely you didn't think we'd let you walk all the way to Mugglegruffe's cabin," he said, with a big smirk.

"Thanks!" Jack replied.

"No need to thank me. Sarina will bring him home when she returns. Mugglegruffe's expecting you," said the elf, as Jack mounted his horse and took the reins.

"Thanks again," said Jack, shaking his hand.

"Take care of yourself, Shadar."

"You too," he replied.

"Go on! Get out of here," said Albion. "Go see my sister."

With Albion heading back across the silver bridge, Jack took one last look at the Sapphire City. He was going to miss his elven home, but didn't have time to linger—Sarina was waiting. "Come on, Midknight!" he cried, before turning his horse and riding into the village. To Jack's surprise, the village of the silver bridge was under heavy construction. It warmed his heart to know it would once again be thriving.

When he arrived at the sea of grass, Jack slowed Midknight's pace. It felt alien to be wearing his old clothes again. He wished he was wearing his armour, with his trusty sword dangling from his hip. As he crossed the sea of grass, Jack breathed deeply through his nose, savouring the sweetness of the air. The cool breeze caressed his cheeks, bringing with it the faded scent of bluebells.

Before long, he was riding through the Forest of the Faerie Queen. The dirt road would take him to the narrow path, which would lead to Mugglegruffe's cabin. Jack kept an eye out for faeries, half expecting Queen Eleanor to stick her head out from behind a tree. When he reached the path, he cautiously followed it; Sarina could be minutes away, but he didn't want to risk injuring his horse by riding too fast. As the cabin came into view, butterflies were dancing in his stomach. Trotting up to the front yard, Jack quietly dismounted and led his horse around the side, before hanging the reins over the post of the side gate. Then he stepped onto the porch and knocked on the front door.

He expected the wizard to start shouting something about phoney trinkets. But he heard nothing of the sort; just the sound of footsteps, followed by the turning of a handle. And when the door opened, there stood Mugglegruffe, puffing away on his pipe. "Ah, come in, Shadar. I'll put the kettle on."

"No!" Jack blurted out. "Please! No tea!"

"Didn't you like it the first time?"

"Sorry," he cringed, "but no."

"Very well," said the wizard. "Come in."

Jack lowered his head, entering the cabin as his eyes darted around, but he couldn't see Sarina anywhere. "I know who you're looking for, but she's not here," said Mugglegruffe, closing the cabin door. "She'll meet you at the border of the southern gate. She said you'd know where?"

Jack sighed in disappointment. "Yeah, I know where..."

"She can be quite a rascal!" Mugglegruffe chuckled. "I've known Sarina since she was a child, and I've never seen her fuss over anything the way she fusses over you. In fact, she was awake most of the night telling me how much she wanted to see you."

"She can't wait to see me, eh?"

"Sarina may be a Starborne, but she's nothing like her father."

Jack was anxiously looking towards the door; Mugglegruffe could sense that he wanted to leave. "Alright, Shadar, I think it's time we had a chat," said the wizard. "Take a seat—I'll try not keep you long, but there's something you must know. So pay attention."

"Okay," he said, reluctantly approaching the small table. He was about to sit, but changed his mind and sat on the floor.

Walking around the table, Mugglegruffe sat on the other side. "I know what you desire, but it can never happen."

"Huh?"

"Come now, Shadar, I'm not the only one who's noticed the strong connection between you two. Despite how much you love each other, it's a forbidden love. And if it's ever exposed, Sarina could be exiled from the Sapphire City. She would pay a heavy price indeed for breaking the law," he explained.

"But why is it the law?" Jack begged to know.

"Long ago, the King of the Law handed down ten laws. They were recorded on three pieces of stone, and the consequences were harsh for any infraction," said Mugglegruffe. "And law eight clearly states that no human can intermarry with a descendant of Araboth."

"Are you talkin' about the ten commandments?"

"No, Shadar. These laws are older—they're pre-flood."

"I don't understand. I've never heard of the ten laws. When I went to the hall of the dead, there were only seven, one law for each of the seven branches on the tree of life."

Using a small piece of brass shaped like the tree of life, Mugglegruffe tamped the ash onto the unburnt tobacco in his pipe and took a few puffs, filling the room with a deep, fruity aroma. With smoke bellowing from his mouth, the wizard said, "The seven laws are barely two-thousand years old. I'm talking about ancient law. The ancient laws were given to us almost five and a half thousand years ago. They weren't perfect, but were the foundation of what was yet to come."

"Okay," said Jack, "let's say for argument's sake, you're right. Shouldn't the seven laws replace the old ones?"

"In a strange way, you're thinking is correct," said Mugglegruffe, blowing a couple of smoke rings. "But the ancient laws are still the foundation. They're like a guide, or set of rules, which every being should adhere to. Of course, adhering to a set of rules isn't easy, that's why the High King gave us a new covenant."

"I don't get these laws," Jack sighed. "It's not fair…"

"It's not your fault—it's not hers, either. When the Arabothians took human wives, they declared war on the King of the Law's creation. Everything was perfect before the fall. Evil has been waging a war with good since the very beginning. Evil cannot create anything new; it can only corrupt that which is good, and that which it cannot corrupt—it will destroy. Despite your fallen condition, no Elorian's a perfect creation like you. You've been told this history, but let me make it clearer: if you were to marry Sarina and have a child together, there's no telling what could be produced. It could turn out to be a giant or something worse. Or, by a stroke of luck, it could end up as perfect as you—but you mustn't take that risk."

Jack lowered his head in despair. "I guess the things we want most… we can never have. It's just that I've never felt this way about anyone before. I love her with all my heart. Did humans and elves ever intermarry?"

"Yes, they did. The Arabothian bloodline is an infection that remains in some humans to this day. The first elves were the colour of translucent gold, but as soon as they fell into sin, or mingled with humans, they lost their supernatural abilities. Some remained ethereal and pure. But most became more human, which accounts for the variations in skin-tone, eye colour, hair, and other abnormalities. If humans stopped separating themselves into tribes, and realised they were all of one blood, a lot of problems would be solved. After all, we're all one in the High King."

"That doesn't leave much hope for me and Sarina," said Jack.

"Hope is not lost..."

"What?"

"The blue star's going to fall—I can feel it! When the High King returns to Eloria, I'm sure he'll make a way for you to be together. Just be patient; slow and steady doesn't always win the race, but a little patience will take you far indeed."

"You could've said that in the first place!" Jack sighed in frustration.

Mugglegruffe placed his pipe onto a wooden rest on the table. "Yes, I could've given you the easy answer, but it wouldn't have been right. Only by knowing the whole story, can you comprehend the repercussions of what might happen if you choose to ignore my warning. The action of a moment can cause a lifetime of regret."

"I s'pose you're right," said Jack, nodding his head. "I do understand. And if I have to wait for the High King to return, so be it."

"I'm glad you've seen sense."

"So, how long til this prophecy gets fulfilled?" said Jack, twiddling his thumbs.

Mugglegruffe rolled his eyes. "I may have a lot of knowledge when it comes to the mystical, but prophecy moves in its own time. You may never return to Eloria; it's up to the High King. As for myself, I know I'll miss you."

"I'll miss you, too," Jack smiled. "And thanks again for saving my life. I couldn't have defeated Barbatus without you."

Mugglegruffe's eyes widened. "That's what I forgot to mention! You may've defeated one of the Red Dragon's Lieutenants, but he still has agents of darkness in the human world—wicked and evil men, who may try to harm you. Always be on your guard! Even a friendly stranger may end up stabbing you in the back."

"That'll make me paranoid," said Jack. "How're they gonna know who I am?"

"They communicate with the fallen Arabothians. They've sold their souls for money and power, but it comes with the price of servitude."

"What a bunch of lunatics. How'd my world get so evil?"

"Your world may be fallen, but you were right about one thing: it's humanity that's chosen to be blind. It's humanity that's chosen to go its own way, forsaking the ancient paths. If the Red Dragon wants to corrupt a people, he doesn't just walk up and knock their house down. No, he doesn't do that. He takes a chisel and chips away at the foundations, piece by piece, until it collapses on itself. That's how the nations of your world have fallen. By taking his time, your people have remained ignorant to his ploys. Always be aware."

"That makes sense," said Jack, "but what about Barbatus? Godfrey said he still lives. Is it true? Could he still return?"

"Yes, but highly unlikely. Besides, Barbatus wasn't as powerful as some of the Red Dragon's other Lieutenants; we should consider ourselves fortunate that such enemies haven't crossed our path, not that it matters what happens to our physical shells. Vengeance belongs to the High King, and his vengeance will make the great flood look like a sun shower."

Jack remembered the strange drawing Mugglegruffe had snatched away from him the day they met. He was about to inquire, when the wizard stood up and walked over to his desk, beside the bookshelf. Opening the top drawer, he removed a scroll of parchment and brought it to him. As Jack took the parchment, Mugglegruffe noticed the gold ring on his pinkie finger. "Is that what I think it is?"

"Oh, I forgot! I'm officially a knight of Eloria," Jack smiled. "I didn't realise I was still wearing it. Do you think they'd let me take it home?"

"Congratulations!" said the wizard. "And since you're an Elorian Knight, I must insist you take it with you. After almost giving your life to save the people, it seems only fair that you get to take home at least one keepsake."

"Thanks," he replied. "But what's the deal with this scroll?"

"Remember the prophecy!" said Mugglegruffe, as Jack unravelled it. "Memorize every word. When the signs come to pass, you'll be prepared for what happens next."

Jack read the words of the prophecy: *When the last Shadar comes forth, and the blue star falls. The veil will be lifted, and peace will be no more. Under a black sun he rises, devouring man and beast alike. The wicked become his servants, for none withstand his might. With an army at his back, he wields a sword of iron. The world of men shall burn at the siege of Mt Zion. War and famine plague the earth, as none could have imagined. Few shall escape the talons of the great Red Dragon.*

He rolled it back up and placed it inside his jacket. "Thank you, my friend. I promise to keep it safe."

"Alright, Shadar, as much as you like visiting me, I know there's a certain maiden who happens to be waiting for you. But regarding what we've discussed, I can only tell you our laws; and if you choose to ignore them, make sure the love between you always remains secret. However, I strongly advise that you exercise some self-control, because the ancient laws were created for a reason. And even if those reasons are beyond our understanding, it's still our duty to solemnly obey."

Jack smiled at him. "I'm sure gonna miss your wisdom. You've been very good to me, and I won't forget it. I've never met a being of such small stature, who displays so much confidence and courage. I wish there were more people like you in my world, people who weren't afraid to stand up for what's right."

"Alright, Shadar, I know you're going to miss me, but I have a lot of work to do, and you've got a rendezvous with an elf," he said, opening the front door.

Jack headed for the doorway but stopped in front of the wizard. Raising his hand, Mugglegruffe pointed at him. "Don't try to hug me!" he smiled. "We dwarves are not huggers! It took Sarina three years to get a hug from me—shaking hands is better."

"Okay," Jack laughed, before shaking his tiny hand.

"Farewell, Shadar. I hope you and Sarina make the right decision. And I hope your time in Eloria remains close to your heart."

After retrieving Midknight Jack trotted up to the porch. "I may be going home, but my heart will remain here, with the good people of Eloria," he stated, before riding away.

The wizard watched him disappear into the forest. As soon as Jack was clear of the cabin, he made his way back to the main road and continued along the trail. Many kilometres later, he came upon a clearing of blue flowers, situated by a body of water.

He then saw a figure in the distance. It was a beautiful maiden, wearing a white dress, holding a brown picnic basket. "Sarina!" he cried, riding towards her. Sarina's horse was nearby, so he dismounted and said farewell to his trusty steed. His hands were sweating as he approached. He stopped a few feet away and could see tears of happiness in her eyes. "Hello, my Jack," she softly said. "I'm glad you found me."

With such love and longing in his heart, Jack didn't know what to say. He just wanted to grab hold of her and never let go. He wrapped his arms around her as she dropped her picnic basket, which made a clanging sound. Still embracing, they rested their foreheads against each other's; Sarina touched her nose against his, playfully begging for intimacy. Jack looked into her rainbow coloured eyes. "I love you, Sarina Starborne. I love you so much I can hardly bear it," he whispered, as tears streamed down her face.

"I love you, too!" she cried. "I want to be with you, but it's against the law."

Holding her close, Jack passionately kissed her as they were hit with the powerful sensations of love, having finally shared their first intimate kiss. A moment later, they embraced again as she put her mouth to his ear. "The High King will return soon, and the seven worlds will become one. In time, there will be a new heaven and a new earth. Then we can be together, forever."

Finally separating, Jack took a hold of Sarina's hands and held them for what seemed like an eternity. "Listen, before I go, there's something I have to know."

"What is it?"

"What do you keep in that picnic basket?"

They laughed as Sarina picked it up. She then held it up close, so Jack could open the lid and see for himself. "You saved my life with those," he smiled, upon seeing her daggers.

"Yes, but you were worth saving."

She placed her basket down, and Jack took a hold of her hands once more, feeling their warmth. "You're the only one I want," he said, "and I'll wait till the High King returns, even if it takes years. But if fate should decide that I can never come back to this world, I'll be waiting for you in the next."

"Bye, Jack," she struggled to reply.

"Goodbye, Sarina."

Letting go, he turned and walked towards the forest. Jack desperately wanted to look back, but the pain of leaving her was unbearable. Each step was a struggle as he headed deeper into the trees, where he would pass through the southern gate. He kept his focus on the sound of the stream. Then, without warning, the oak trees were gone and he was surrounded by Australian gums. Having realised his journey was over, Jack let out a cry of pain as he fell to his knees. "I don't wanna be here!" he wept.

Finding the will to stand, he trudged along the game trail until he came to the railway tracks. Carefully crossing, Jack had to be extra vigilant of moving objects. There weren't any orcs or trolls, but after spending three months in Eloria, he had to remind himself of the dangers. Making it to his front door, Jack glanced back in the hope that Sarina had followed. She was nowhere to be seen. He took his keys out of his pocket, and when he finally stepped inside the house, Jack slammed the door behind him. *Ten years I've been paying off this stupid house,* he thought. *It doesn't feel like home, it feels like a prison!* He went to the lounge room and threw himself onto the couch. All he wanted was to stay in Eloria forever.

Chapter 24

BACK TO WORK

After sitting for several hours, Jack realised his circumstances hadn't changed. He still had to find a new job, but he couldn't stop thinking about Sarina. *Seeing something as captivating as a beautiful maiden sitting by a stream in a field of blue flowers, seems impossible,* he thought. Also, having seen the evil committed by orcs and trolls, security work now seemed like something below his talents, yet he was still dreading it. There was nothing confusing about vanquishing evil in Eloria, but in the human world *evil* had rights.

His world was all but void of anything innocent and pure. It was void of enchantment; it was a place where greed and corruption reigned supreme. Before discovering Eloria, Jack didn't believe such a world could exist without the evils of his own. He used to wish that if God did exist, he would triumphantly return and save the meek from the wicked. But in Jack's eyes—Midland was beyond saving.

When he first started security work, Jack believed he could make a difference; he believed he could change the world a piece at a time. He also believed, somewhat naively, that the corporation he was working for stood for justice. But after experiencing the evil politics, Jack knew he was nothing but a number, a spoke on a wheel. "There's nothin' worth fighting for in this world. There's no meaning or justice to be found. Right and wrong, good and evil, there are no good guys or bad guys. All we have left is the game," he said to himself.

Despite its own dangers, Jack believed that innocence, morality, and justice, only existed in Eloria. He used to blame God for the evil in his world, but now he understood that humanity was responsible. God had given humans a choice, but they chose greed and power over peace and love. There was even a time when Jack wished he was evil, because evil-doers seemed to get exactly what they wanted. Despite giving it a good try, however, it wasn't in his nature to hurt others. Jack's nature was to defend the righteous, but in a dog eat dog world he didn't think there were any righteous people left to defend.

With depressing and evil thoughts clouding his mind, Jack begrudgingly took out his phone and tried to switch it on. He was hoping his journey to Eloria hadn't broken the device; when the bright screen came on he breathed a sigh of relief. He glanced down at his Elorian keepsake on his pinkie finger. The engraving of his House emblem reminded him of his knightly oath. He was also reminded of the tree of life, and what the seven laws stood for. But the Elorian ways of justice and honour had no meaning in the human world. *This ring could be priceless,* he thought. *But I wouldn't trade it for anything...*

Unexpectedly, his phone made several beeping sounds, alerting him to some incoming text messages. Jack remembered that before leaving home, his phone had displayed several missed calls. Inspecting the texts, he realised they were from the centre manager of the shopping mall. The last message read: *The security manager position has become available again. Are you still interested?*

Jack's heart sank. He'd been gone for three months. Then he remembered that while in Eloria, one month was equal to one day. "That means I've only been gone for three days!"

He could hardly believe his luck. Jack searched through his list of contacts until he found Nathan's number. He pressed *call* and put the phone to his ear, expecting to hear his voice at any moment. "Hello?"

"Nathan, it's Jack, I had some missed calls from you, and I just got some texts from the centre manager. What's goin' on?"

"Jack! Oh, man, I've been tryin' to reach you! I was startin' to think you got kidnapped by aliens or something. Jim quit after you left—he's gone! The centre manager wants you to take the job. He said if I could reach you over the next few days, it was yours. You can start your probation tomorrow."

"Wait, Jim was the centre manager's brother," said Jack. "Why would he hire a guy, who made his own flesh and blood look like a fool?"

"From what I've heard around the office they don't even like each other. He gave Jim the position because he owed him a favour or something. Apparently, he was glad someone had the guts to put him in his place!" Nathan laughed.

"Okay. Tell the centre manager I'll be there in the morning. But first, I want you to contact Frank and Zoran, and tell 'em they've got their jobs back. As for Jim's guards, they can go back to wherever the hell they came from."

"Alright, Jack! See you tomorrow! I can't wait to tell everyone. And don't worry about those invaders—they're history! They left with Jim."

"Okay, Nath. I've gotta go. See you tomorrow."

"See ya, boss!"

After ten years of sacrifice his goal had been achieved. *I don't believe it! It's finally mine...* he thought, struggling to make sense of what he was feeling.

Awaking at 6:30am to the sound of his alarm clock, Jack got dressed and ate breakfast. Instead of his old security uniform, he was now wearing a grey suit, with a white shirt and blue paisley tie. He was no longer a supervisor; Jack was the new security manager. He felt a bit sorry for Jim, who may have been a fool with no security experience. But Jack had never embarrassed someone to the point where they had quit their job on the first day. Nevertheless, it was Jack who had spent the last decade earning the job, and it was rightfully his!

Arriving at the mall, he parked his car and entered through the staff entry. When he arrived at the office, Jack was greeted with smiles and looks of admiration. "It's great to see you back here, Frank," he said, shaking the guard's hand.

"It's nice to *be back* thanks to you, mate! But there's something different about you..."

Jack turned to Nathan, who was also staring at him. "What happened? You look like you've lost ten kilos in three days and gained it back in muscle!"

"What happened to your head, mate?" Frank asked. "Did you get hurt?"

After spending three months in Eloria, Jack remembered that his physical appearance had changed. He was also sporting a couple of scars from the troll's attack. "Oh, I… ah… took up boxing!" he blurted out. "Yeah, that's it! I just spent the last three days boxing non-stop. Talk about a gruelling workout, eh!"

"Damn, mate, you sure worked your ass off!" Frank chuckled.

"Well, I had to let go of some rage, especially after that argument with Jim. There's nothin' better than hitting a punchin' bag when you're pissed off."

Before they could inquire further, Jack hurried over to his new desk, which was Jim's for a day, and Roy's for nearly a decade. Roy was Jack's favourite security manager; filling his shoes wasn't going to be easy.

"I'm gonna go unlock now, boss," said Frank.

"Okay, Franky, I'll catch up with you later," said Jack, sitting down. He glanced at Nathan, who was monitoring the cameras. "Hey, Nath, any major incidents while I was gone?"

Nathan turned in his swivel chair. "Nah, it's been pretty quiet. A couple of slip and falls, but nothing major—your fight with Jim's been the only topic as of late."

"I bet," said Jack, with a smirk.

After sitting there for a few minutes, Jack was starting to feel like an empty cup. Despite accomplishing his dream, it now seemed insignificant. All he could think about was being back in Eloria, he wanted to see Sarina. He wanted to look into her beautiful rainbow-coloured eyes and kiss her soft, sweet lips. *I miss them so much,* he thought. *At least I had a purpose in Eloria. I wasn't a spoke on a wheel—I was essential—I mattered!*

His passion for security work had been swept away by the Elorian tide, and Jack realised that what he'd said to Mugglegruffe was true: he had indeed left his heart in Eloria.

Whether he liked it or not, Jack was back in the human world and had to get on with things. After meeting with the centre manager and signing a contract, he delved into paperwork for the rest of the day. It was mostly basic administration, like approving tenancy requests for after-hour's security, and approving contractor works in restricted areas. It was very boring, and he struggled to keep his eyes open.

By late afternoon, Jack couldn't fathom doing his dream job for any longer, but like everyone else, he had to make ends meet. So he said goodbye to his colleagues, feeling guilty that his new position allowed him to leave earlier. When he arrived home, Jack changed into a t-shirt and shorts. He missed his elvish clothes. They were probably still in his quarters, waiting for his unlikely return. *I hope they catch the traitors*, he thought. *I wish I could be there to see Julius face the council and answer for what he's done.*

Jack thought about Mugglegruffe's words. The dwarf's warning about the wicked men in his world was playing on his mind. Despite having access to modern weapons, Jack wanted his sword. He felt naked without Blue Storm. *I've accomplished my dream, and now I'm depressed again*, he thought. *The other guards would love to be in my position. Why does it feel so meaningless?* Jack could only hope that in time, he would forget about Eloria and accept his mundane existence. But if Eloria was in his blood, there may be no turning back.

He went downstairs and switched on the television. He began flicking through channels, and as he went past the news channel, something caught his eye. Flicking back, he was shocked to see something ominous. Jack turned up the volume. A large, blue light had been filmed in the night sky, before crashing into the ocean.

According to the story, the light's appearance had coincided with the largest plague of locusts to ever sweep the middle-east. The light was eerily similar to the blue star of the prophecy. Jack still hadn't memorised the words. He raced upstairs and removed the scroll from the drawer of his bedside table. He could feel a sense of urgency as he unravelled the parchment. *When the last Shadar comes forth, and the blue star falls. The veil will be lifted, and peace will be no more. Under a black sun he rises, devouring man and beast alike. The wicked become his servants, for none withstand his might. With an army at his back, he wields a sword of iron. The world of men shall burn at the siege of Mt Zion. War and famine plague the earth, as none could have imagined. Few shall escape the talons of the great Red Dragon.*

A cold chill ran down his spine! Jack took a few deep breaths. Calming down, he was about to scoff at himself, then his eyes were drawn to something else. He reached in his drawer, removed the gold ring, and placed it on his pinkie finger. It was as if the ring had willed him to put it on, but Jack didn't dare hope he was about to return to Eloria.

"Hmm… when the last Shadar comes forth, and the blue star falls. The veil will be lifted, and peace will be no more," he said, reading aloud. "I know I'm the last Shadar, but how could that light've been a star? The star in Eloria was bigger. Maybe it broke-up in outer space, and what crashed in the ocean was a fragment?"

As he struggled to understand the electricity went out. "Damn! Not another blackout!"

Jack searched for a flashlight. A strike of lightning suddenly lit-up the room, followed by a loud clap of thunder. "Now, that's a thunderstorm!"

He could hear the sound of rain pounding against the roof. Failing to find a flashlight, Jack made his way back downstairs to the couch. The television screen was pitch-black. "This sucks!" he growled. "I wanted to see the rest of that but I'm stuck in the bloody dark!"

Jack was so frustrated he couldn't even be bothered looking for candles and matches. Every few seconds, however, the lightning would strike, allowing him to briefly see. A few minutes later, Jack heard a banging noise; he brushed it off as being nothing but thunder in the distance. Then he heard it a second time, only it was much louder! Jack stood up, listening intently. "Bang! Bang! Bang!" There it was again. "Where's that comin' from?"

Someone was knocking on the door! Leaving the lounge room, Jack navigated his way through the dark house. He reached the front door, cautiously opened it, but all he could see was a dark silhouette. *What if it's one of the wicked men?* he thought.

But when the lightning struck again, he was shocked to see Sarina! "Jack!" she cried, throwing herself into his arms.

Sarina was weeping uncontrollably. She wasn't crying tears of happiness, but grief. "Oh, my God!" said Jack. "What're you doing here?! What's happened?!"

Sarina had never been to the human world, and Jack was horrified by what might happen if humans discovered that she possessed the gift of eternal youth. "Please help us!" she cried, burying her head in his chest.

"What's happened?!" he repeated.

"It-it's my father and brother! They were helping with repairs at the village and were attacked by orcs—they were captured! Today, we received a note from Julius, saying that unless you enter Darkwood Forest and meet him face-to-face, they'll be executed!"

"It's alright, we're gonna get them back! I promise!" said Jack. "I've only been home for a day. How long's it been in Eloria?"

"It's been a month! They were taken eight days ago. Everything was supposed to return to normal, but now something's happened!" she gasped. "The blue star has fallen! The veil between the worlds is lifting! Time is becoming one."

Jack now understood the prophecy was true. His time in the human world was over, but his duty to Eloria had only just begun…

Ingram Content Group Australia Pty Ltd
Printed in Australia
AUHW010603240723
381232AU00006B/6